I0598578

The Omega's Alphas

CLAIMED BY THE ALPHAS

JAYCE CARTER

Claimed by the Alphas
ISBN # 978-1-83943-910-0
©Copyright Jayce Carter 2020
Cover Art by Erin Dameron-Hill ©Copyright August 2020
Interior text design by Claire Siemaszkiewicz
Totally Bound Publishing

CLAIMED BY
THE ALPHAS

Dedication

To the men who have said what I write is
unrealistic:

Step up your game!

Chapter One

Ashley frowned as she realized she was completely lost.

Why did she have no sense of direction? Other people could find their way no matter what, but she got lost crossing a street if she were distracted.

Add to it that she'd just moved in, and it hadn't taken much for Ashley to find herself entirely turned around with no idea which direction her apartment lay.

It had been her first shift working late at the seedy bar, the only place she could get a job, and she hadn't thought about how different the city would look at night.

It turned out that three a.m. looked nothing like five in the evening.

I'm sick of starting over. She'd repeated that to herself while she'd gone through the motions at her job, trying to learn yet another trade.

How many was that? How many dead-end jobs had she picked up because they paid in cash and didn't require paperwork?

Too many to count.

And here she was again. New neighborhood. New apartment. New job.

She thought back to her empty apartment, to the bags she hadn't even been able to bring herself to unpack. Not that she had anywhere to put the stuff, since she had no furniture to her name.

The night had been brutal, and her feet ached. Nine hours of running orders had exhausted her, but the tips had been worth it. At least she wouldn't have to worry about starving.

Ashley pulled at the strap of her purse and peered around, searching for some sign she recognized, something that would lead her in the right direction.

Her prepaid cell phone let her make calls, but without data on it, she couldn't use it to find her way.

Every step reminded her of just how tired her feet were. The bus had dropped her off at the right stop — at least, she thought so — but after that? *No clue.*

She had walked herself right into an unsavory area, though. Or a more unsavory area than usual. Her apartment wasn't great, and she slept with a can of pepper spray clutched in her hand, but at least the street lights outside her apartment worked.

The flickering of these said she should hightail it out of there as fast as possible.

If only she knew where *out of there* was…

A rhythmic sound caught her attention, and no matter how much she tried to ignore it, it wouldn't stop.

Footsteps.

Ashley risked a glance over her shoulder to find a large male figure following her.

Stop being paranoid.

She turned one corner, then another, but she couldn't shake him. The heavy smack of his shoes against the concrete grew louder as he got closer.

Worse, Ashley didn't see anyone else. It was too late for normal traffic and too early for people going off to work.

She quickened her steps, turning down another alleyway, rushing to put distance between them. She could take a few quick turns, lose the man behind her then somehow find her apartment.

At least, that was the plan before she twisted around the last corner and ran into a very large body.

The impact bounced her back a few steps, but she kept her balance, ready to apologize, when she met the gaze of the man she'd run into.

A chilling grin was spread across his cracked lips, one that made her stomach drop. Worse? He lifted his gaze past her, and the man who had been following her, the one who had dogged her steps for blocks, stood there.

They exchanged a knowing look.

Should have just taken a cab.

* * * *

Torrin shook his head as he looked down at the corpse before him. *What a waste.*

Not the man himself. He doubted the now-dead beta had ever done anything in his life worth mourning over, and Torrin felt no real guilt over them ending it.

Instead, it was the lost opportunities, the information, the possible influence now gone.

People were, in general, useless when dead, and the slice across his throat showed this man to be very dead indeed.

"Do you think he was telling the truth?" Liam asked, his gaze on the body.

Torrin shrugged. "Perhaps. We'll know soon enough."

Erik had wiped the blade that had made that slice clean on the beta's shirt, like a little ritual he could never quite let go of. Then again, Erik was a man of ritual. "I would bet the information is good. He thought he could sell out to you and keep living the high life."

They always thought that. Every lowlife in this city assumed they could manipulate Torrin, that they could manipulate anyone and never pay for their crimes.

Not that Torrin was some avenging spirit setting right wrongs. His cheek twitched at the thought, at the absurdity of anyone thinking of *him* as the hero of any story.

No. Torrin was, at best, the anti-hero, and that was likely giving him too much credit. He'd gotten where he was in life by being vicious, by putting down anyone who opposed him, anyone who caused him trouble. That last part had brought them here to deal with the beta, a man who had stolen from Torrin and thought he could disappear into the shadows of the city.

"Should we dispose of the body?" Liam tucked his hands into his jacket.

Erik sheathed his knife at his hip. "No reason to. In this area, it'll be assumed to be another gang."

Torrin nodded. "Leave the body. Let's get back, because I'd prefer not to spend all night out *here*."

Liam huffed a soft laugh as they left the apartment, closing the door behind them. The building was silent at that time of night, and it was the sort of place where people minded their own business. It was one of the few good things about being in that area of town—no one got involved and no one ever saw anything.

It all made getting in and out undetected an easy matter.

It was three in the morning, and since he had a meeting at nine, it seemed he wouldn't be getting much sleep.

Not that that was all that unusual. Work consumed Torrin, both his happy place and his hell.

They went out through the back, because a camera sat at the front entrance, and while he doubted it actually worked, he tended toward caution.

A chill met them when they exited into the back alleyway, though it was the slightly sour stench of garbage that bothered him.

"Leave me alone." Soft, feminine words caught his attention. Not fearless, but rather uttered like a plea.

Erik and Liam both twisted their heads in the same direction, as if called by that voice, like a siren's song.

At the edge of the alleyway stood three figures. The two men Torrin wrote off immediately. Determining threat was a life skill for him, and he did it flawlessly. They were bottom-feeders, the sort who preyed on the weak and lived in the cracks, afraid of the light and anything bigger and tougher than they were—which was everything.

The third was the woman who had spoken. She was five-four or so, and curvy in a way that gave him far more ideas than were appropriate given the situation. Her hair was dark brown and in a messy ponytail, the ends curled as if she'd had it done nicely before putting it up. Fear skirted across her features, shining in her large dark eyes as she backed away from the two approaching men.

"Come on, honey," one of the men said in a voice that dripped perverted lust. "We ain't rough."

A growl came from Torrin, a surprising and rare reaction. He didn't show emotion. He rarely smiled, never laughed and surely didn't *growl*.

Yet when the woman's back hit the wall of the building behind her, when she had nowhere left to retreat and could only whisper that same plea again, Torrin *felt* that anger inside him.

He took a step forward, but the action forced his hand to tighten around his cane and his hip to protest, a reminder that he wasn't as quick as his cousins. Erik and Liam had mirrored his movement, as though they all felt the same draw. They didn't get involved as a rule, since they had enough of their own problems. Even he couldn't imagine walking away, though.

Dealing with the two would be an easy matter for them.

The woman never saw them, her attention on the men she thought were the threats. While Torrin and his kin didn't harm defenseless females, there was no doubt he was far more dangerous than the men who had thought to victimize her.

Erik's hand went to his knife before it paused, as if he'd thought better of it. *No need to leave another two bodies.*

Not that Torrin minded putting down the assholes. Which, again, was strange. He killed when needed, but otherwise?

It was that same rage that gripped him, the one that for some reason wanted *these* men to pay.

Was it the female?

Dangerous.

Liam set a hand over the side of one man's face and yanked, striking his head against the dumpster. He dropped to the ground, unmoving. It wouldn't kill him, most likely, but Torrin struggled to care if he recovered.

Erik, always the more subtle of the two, wrapped an arm around the other man's throat at the same time. The man struggled against the grip, but couldn't get leverage and quickly succumbed to the choke hold. As soon as he went lax, Erik eased his body down.

The woman flattened herself against the wall more, eyes wide enough for Torrin to realize that they weren't brown. Instead, they were a dark blue.

"Don't hurt me," she whispered, her soft voice sounding sweeter the nearer Torrin got to her.

He closed the distance until he stood just in front of her.

She smelled amazing—sweet and wild. His mouth watered as he took in every detail of her. She was younger, twenty-five at most, and wore a pair of shorts that showed off long, tan legs. She wasn't thin, but instead had the sort of body Torrin could lose himself in for hours, with curves and softness that would drive a man to his knees in praise.

He wanted to touch her, to grasp that ponytail and pull her into a kiss.

And the moment his hand moved as if to do so, Torrin froze.

What the fuck?

He backed away, his steps almost clumsy as he frowned at his reaction.

"Get her home," he said before turning around and walking toward the street.

He knew nothing about the girl beyond two very important facts.

He wanted her—*badly*—and she was far too dangerous to give in to.

Chapter Two

Liam stood there alone with the strange girl, Erik having chased off after Torrin.

Deciding who would deal with her had been an easy choice.

Torrin had all the emotional knowledge of a sheet of drywall and Erik frightened even Liam at times.

Neither of them should deal with a frightened woman whose bottom lip trembled.

And what a woman she is…

Liam had a strong love for the fairer sex, never hesitating to engage in a bit of fun. Something about women always drew him in. They were magical, really, special in a way men weren't. No matter who the woman was, each one had managed to surprise him, to charm him in their own way.

Though none of those had come close to that burst of want when he'd spotted *this* female.

"Just let me go," she said.

Liam slid on his most charming smile. "I'm not going to hurt you, sweet. You seemed like you needed a little help."

She took her red lip between her blunt teeth, those striking blue eyes of hers moving over the bodies as if they were the proof of why she shouldn't trust him.

"What are you doing out here so late? This isn't a safe area."

"I got off work and lost my way."

"Oh yeah? Where do you work?"

She opened her mouth to answer then snapped it shut, as if just remembering she had no reason to trust Liam. Telling strangers where they worked was the sort of thing smart women didn't do.

"Just making friendly conversation. Where do you live, at least? I'll walk you back."

"I just moved here," she said, lines showing up between her eyebrows. "I got off at the Harrison stop and…"

"And you got yourself lost? It's fine. I know most of this city pretty well. What street is your place on?"

"Carrington," she whispered.

Carrington? Liam didn't let his smile drop, despite the punch to his gut. There was nothing on Carrington he'd let any person he cared about live at. The street was trash, with pay-by-the-hour motels and the sort of apartments people paid weekly for, mostly because they might get killed before they needed to pay for another week.

He kept the growl from his voice. *She* wasn't his problem. "I know where that is. Come on. It isn't far."

She didn't move, her gaze suspicious.

"My name's Liam," he tried. "This isn't a great area, as you saw. I just want to get you home safe and sound, I promise. How about your name?"

She hesitated again before her gaze fell to the still bodies. Whether she answered out of fear of what he might do or she realized he hadn't hurt her yet, she answered, "Ashley."

"Pretty name. Now, come on, let's get you out of here."

She stepped past the bodies, pausing as if worried about leaving them.

Which was just too damned sweet.

And more than a little naive.

"Don't worry about them. They'll be fine." *Well, fine-ish.*

Again, she nodded and fell into step beside Liam as they exited the alleyway. Torrin and Erik had already left, which was probably a good thing.

If she was jumpy around Liam, he could only imagine how she'd act with them hovering as well.

And the growl Torrin had let out had been more than a little interesting. Nothing got his cousin that worked up.

"So, what is it you do for a living?"

Ashley stuck her hands into her pockets, darting her gaze around as though nervous. Of him? Just generally uncomfortable after the close call? "Waitress."

That explained the outfit. He'd bet she made good tips with shorts *that* short and her curvy ass.

In fact, he wouldn't mind cruising in some time and watching her run around in those shorts, tray in hand —

"Liam?"

He looked over at her, her expression saying she'd been talking and he'd missed it.

Great job being attentive.

"Sorry. What was that?"

Her lips curled the slightest amount, just in the corners, as if charmed by his distraction. Even that ghost of a smile was brilliant and showed she was a far sweeter girl than he'd realized.

Which was horrible, because he had a thing for sweetness.

"I asked who those other two were."

"Oh, right. The blond is Torrin, my cousin. The one who looks just like me? Erik."

"Is Erik your brother?"

"Twin, and before you ask, we *do* satisfy twin fantasies, but our charge is three hundred for the night."

The joke drew forth a pretty flush over her cheeks. *Shy?* Why the hell did that do it for him? Or maybe the better question was why everything seemed to do it for him when it came to her?

"Why did they leave?"

"Because I'm the most charming, and they were making you nervous."

She seemed as though she'd debate that fact before stopping herself. He suspected she wasn't a liar by nature, which made him wonder if she stumbled over the attempts. *What a pair that makes them, huh? Liam lies like he breathes.*

It was part of life if he wanted to *keep* breathing in his world.

"Well, thank you all for your help."

"You really shouldn't be walking around this time of night alone. This area of town isn't a good place."

"I've noticed." Before she could say more, she tipped her gaze up toward the building across the street. "You found it."

Liam groaned at the apartment complex she was looking at. Of all the shit-holes on the street—and there were quite a few of them—that was without a doubt the *worst*.

He held his tongue. She wasn't his. He had no right to tell her anything about where she should live or what she should do.

But, damn it, this wasn't the sort of place she should be.

"How long have you lived here?" Liam held open the door, making it clear he intended to walk her all the way to her apartment. Her building might be even more dangerous than that alley.

"A week." Her lips tipped down before she curled in further. "It's not that bad."

Liam tried to wipe the look off his face. No reason to make her feel like shit. "Sorry, I'm just a fan of more neutral wall colors."

Ashley huffed softly, as if she heard and appreciated the deflecting lie as they took the stairs up three flights. The fact that she was winded and took the last ones slower showed she hadn't gotten used to using them.

And she had worked all night on her feet already.

At a door down the hallway, she slid a key into the lock and turned it. As she opened the door, she reached up and pulled a toothpick from the frame.

He'd been around enough to know that cheap, easy trick. Stick something in the closing door to signal if the door had been opened while they were away.

Why would she know it? Just from living in places like this?

As if Ashley had heard the question, she responded. "The lock doesn't really work well. I talked to the super, but I don't think he'll be fixing it anytime soon."

Liam closed the door and focused his attention there. The frame showed cracks, implying it had been kicked in a time or two before and never replaced. There was no deadbolt, and sure enough, after a quick test of a bit of jiggling, the lock on the handle failed.

Fuck.

Liam pulled his phone out and sent out a quick message. Sure, they couldn't pursue anything, but that didn't mean they couldn't do the bare minimum of making sure Ashley didn't have people walking into her place with just a little handle shake.

Though when Liam turned around, it got *worse*.

"Where the fuck is your furniture?"

Her back went straight. "I told you, I just moved in."

"Yeah, but normally you take your stuff with you." Her place was empty. Not just under-furnished, but entirely bare. The small studio apartment had an open kitchen with a few bags on the counter, nothing in the living space and a few blankets on top of a plastic sheet in the corner where the bed would go.

At least she had the sense to cover that disgusting carpet before sleeping on it.

"I didn't have anything, okay?" She slid off her jacket and set it on the kitchen counter—not like there were other options. "I didn't ask you to come in, so maybe don't judge me? I'm doing the best I can."

Liam rubbed his hand over the top of his shaved head, trying to ease the tension in his body. Why the hell did he care?

Then it hit him. He met her gaze. "Omega?"

Her eyes widened for a moment before she nodded. "So stop feeling like you need to save me. I'm doing fine."

Like hell she was. He kept that thought to himself as he repeated that this *need* to help her was biology, nothing more. Alphas like Torrin, Erik and himself were driven to want and protect omegas, no matter if they knew or liked them.

He could ignore that because he was not in a place where he wanted an omega.

"So, thanks," she muttered in a way that implied she wanted him gone. Wounded pride didn't look good on her, and hell, it wasn't fair to judge her too harshly.

He didn't know shit about her, and any girl willing to live in a place like this on her own had to be tough.

Though, with how soft she seemed, he had to wonder about her history. She hadn't grown up around these sorts of places, because no girl who had done so would act as sweet or naïve as she did.

Liam shook his head. *Nope.* He could not keep going with that line of thought, because it was headed nowhere good.

"Sure," Liam said. "Try to stay off the streets at night. Take a cab."

By the looks of her apartment, that wasn't going to be happening. Cabs were an expense, and people who didn't have furniture didn't splurge on such things.

He walked out of the door, leaving her behind even when everything inside his screamed not to.

Good thing he'd become an expert at ignoring his instincts.

* * * *

Erik growled softly at the apartment. Liam had messaged him an hour before, and suddenly Erik wished *he'd* been the one to walk the little spit of a girl home.

Not just a girl, but an omega, according to Liam.

Liam, who stood beside Erik's truck with his gaze floating up the building as if he could see her through the bricks.

Liam always had been too easily swayed. It was the reason Erik had no intention of letting his brother back into that omega's apartment or anywhere near her.

Erik would have been content to walk away, but Liam wouldn't do that, not without fixing the girl's security situation.

Fine.

It was an easy fix. It wouldn't take more than an hour, tops, to upgrade the frame, replace the door and put in proper locks. Erik had even brought a few locks for windows, just in case.

When he finished that, Liam would be able to relax and hopefully put the near-miss out of their minds.

They had too many things on their plate to be dividing their attention, and he suspected the curvy little omega would prove one giant distraction.

"Maybe I should go back up," Liam said.

"Like hell. Get your ass back home before you dig us any deeper."

"You'll scare her."

"And? Maybe it'll do us all some good if I do."

Liam offered a glare toward Erik, paired with a soft growl. It wasn't that Liam didn't mean it, that he wouldn't attack Erik, but as brothers, they'd been fighting their entire lives.

What was another throw-down?

But he needed Liam gone, so Erik gave in. "I'm not going to scare her. I'll replace the door, fix the locks and do it all with a smile." At Liam's lifted eyebrow, Erik sighed. "I'll do it without snarling. How's that?"

Liam let out a long, slow breath, as if he needed to prepare himself for walking away, which said what Erik already knew. This was a clusterfuck waiting to happen.

"Okay," Liam said. "You're right. I'll go."

Erik didn't move until Liam got into a cab, until the car pulled away from the curb and disappeared down the street.

Finally.

He hauled the items up the stairs. It would have been easier with a partner, but again, he couldn't trust Liam to use good sense. The process took thirty minutes, but by the end, he'd brought everything he'd need up and rested it outside the door to Ashley's apartment.

He'd hardly looked at the omega earlier. He tended to not look at women. The times he succumbed to those baser needs of his typically happened in bars, when he and Liam would find a female who was only too happy to be sandwiched between them. Those times were quick, dirty releases. He'd never cared what the women looked like, never bothered with much else but getting off. Liam tended to focus more on the woman, but Erik?

He was scratching an itch, and that sort of single-minded focus must have done it for women, because they were never short on volunteers.

So while her scent had tantalized him in the alley, he'd tried very hard to not pay attention.

When he knocked, however, and when she answered, he didn't have that option.

"I thought you were leaving."

He got ready to explain he was Erik, not Liam, since he'd grown used everyone mixing them up. Growing up as twins had made that commonplace, with only their closest few able to tell the difference.

Except Ashley actually looked at him and took a step backward. "Erik."

It drew a frown from him. "Not many can tell us apart."

She didn't smile. "Your eyes are different. You also smell different."

Smell? It had never occurred to him that he and his twin might be able to be identified by scent.

22

Erik pushed aside the thought. "Liam asked me to repair your lock situation."

"You don't need to do that."

Erik nodded at the supplies just outside the door. "I've already brought everything I need. It shouldn't take me long."

"I can't afford that. I'm sorry."

Erik hesitated. He lived around people who took everything they could, who wouldn't turn down a favor for anything. He didn't know how to deal with someone different. "I'm not expecting any payment."

"So why do it?"

"Because Liam will not relax or forget about you until he knows you have the bare minimum in security."

She furrowed her brow, as though the words didn't quite make sense.

Erik went to work on the door as he spoke, wanting to finish the job and the conversation as quickly as possible. "You know he's an alpha. One of the rarely discussed but often hated parts is a drive to protect omegas, even those we don't know. You were in danger and we helped. It makes Liam feel responsible."

"But not you?"

"No, not me. I'm less easily swayed by a pretty face than Liam is." Erik was so used to lying that when the words left his lips, he couldn't tell if they were a lie or not.

Not about being less swayed—that was true. Liam was far more likely to be led around by his dick. Erik reacted with a cooler head and usually after thinking things through. However, whether he was affected by her? Well, that he wasn't sure about.

He'd fix her security so he could calm his brother down, then they'd forget all about the little brown-haired omega who had turned their night upside down. *If she causes this much trouble in a night, imagine if we spent longer together.*

"Good."

Erik glanced over his shoulder at her, the statement odd, as though she'd read his mind.

At his look of confusion, she spoke again. "I'm glad you don't fall for that. I didn't ask any of you to take care of me. Don't get me wrong, I appreciate your help with…" Her voice trailed off, something uncomfortable in her expression. It was fear, but not sharp.

Sharp fear had a sting to it, something quick, like stubbing one's toe. Instead, this was shadowed, the sign of disease that lingered with a person.

Erik understood that sort of fear all too well.

She recovered quickly. "Just, thank you. But don't make any mistake—I wasn't out there looking for alphas to take care of me. I'd just as well have you all out of my life as quickly as possible."

"At least we can agree on something." Erik turned and went back to work on the door while Ashley moved around behind him.

The work went without issue. Erik replaced the door and frame, then drilled the hole for the deadbolt.

Erik had done construction, back when he'd first been trying to make ends meet. Torrin had already been setting up a business, but their work as a trio had been slow-moving. Someone needed a consistent paycheck to keep them all afloat, and Erik had managed it.

While he didn't use the skills often anymore, they at least helped him in cases like this one.

Before long, Erik had finished the door. He tested the lock then rechecked his work. The last thing he needed was a chance of it failing, for Liam to worry or find some reason to return.

He set the old door in the hallway so he could take it with him before turning to find Ashley in the kitchen, with two cups on the counter.

Erik lifted an eyebrow at the mugs.

"Hot chocolate."

"What are you, five?"

Ashley pursed her full red lips. "I don't like coffee. Plus, I need to get some sleep after you leave."

The sun peeking through the window made Erik glance at his clock. Six-thirty in the morning. "Do you work this evening?"

Ashley shook her head before she picked up her cup and sipped. A speck of the dark chocolate sat on her full bottom lip, and Erik's gaze locked onto it.

He tore away and lifted his own cup. Not because he especially cared for hot chocolate, but rather because he hoped tasting the actual drink would strike away the temptation to take it from her lips.

It also gave him the chance to really look around. Liam hadn't been kidding.

There was almost nothing in the place.

Not my problem.

Erik went to the windows, cup still in his hand. He frowned. "Why are the windows nailed shut?"

Ashley walked over, though she kept space between them. "I did it. There weren't any locks, and the windows open to the fire escape."

"They open to the fire escape in the event of a fire," Erik said before setting his cup on the windowsill. "If you nail them shut, what happens if there is a fire?"

"What happens if someone tries to break in?" Her voice wavered at the question, and it took Erik by surprise.

Again, those shadows. She was afraid. Of life? Of living alone? He wondered what her life had been like, what had led her to living in a place like this.

Whatever she thought about said it wasn't a pleasant story, but he kept himself from asking.

If he asked, he'd know, and knowing would only make this harder. Whatever troubles in her life had happened, they were nothing compared to the trouble he would bring to her door.

"I'll add locks to them and remove the nails."

Again, Ashley disappeared into the background as Erik worked. He pulled the nails, then secured the new locks.

"No one will be able to get in?"

Erik turned after finishing the last latch and leaned against the windowsill. The question had been soft, and no matter how much he told himself to walk out, to not ask, he couldn't do it. "Is there someone you're worried about getting in?"

She shook her head, but the lie was loud and clear.

Shut up. Walk out. Don't ask.

"What's scaring you?" He cursed when he couldn't stop digging deeper. Clearly, he needed to get the hell away from her and do whatever it took to keep Torrin and Liam away, too.

After he dealt with this problem.

Ashley went to walk past him. "Nothing."

He stepped closer and set a hand on her arm. "I can help."

"You really can't."

Erik wanted to set her cup down beside his, to tug her closer, to grasp her ponytail and tilt her face up to his. Whatever problem she had was *nothing* compared to what he'd dealt with. It probably wouldn't take more than a few hours of his time to resolve it.

That was worth doing, to be able to walk away knowing shit was handled.

Not because he cared. *Nope.* It was basic self-interest.

"You want us out of your life? Then tell me what's going on."

Her shoulders drooped, and the breath that left her was slow and drawn-out, as though she'd been holding it for a very long time. "It's nothing you can help with," she finally said. "You'll only make it worse by being involved."

Erik wanted to deny it, but the set of her jaw spoke volumes. Whatever it was, she wanted him nowhere near it.

Which was a blessing, right?

He had enough on his plate without taking on anymore.

Erik stroked his thumb along the soft skin of her arm, dropping his gaze to watch the action. It was…almost soothing.

Which had him staring, a strange quiet as he touched the warm skin of her arm.

As quickly as it happened, he shook himself awake and released her.

It was just another example of all the reasons he needed to get the hell out of there.

He'd walk away and never see her again.

And not a moment too soon.

Chapter Three

Ashley sighed while she dragged herself through her day. After Erik had left that morning, she'd managed a few hours of fitful sleep.

The thought of those three alphas was something she couldn't shake. Liam had been sweet and charming. His eyes had flecks of green in them, and the brown seemed like warm honey. He'd been easy to talk to, as though she'd known him for years.

Erik had been easy to distinguish from his twin, despite them dressing alike and looking nearly identical. Rather than the green flecks, Erik's eyes had blue, an icy tone in the brown as cold as his personality. He'd been more demanding, more straight-to-the-point, but not unkind.

They both had shaved heads, strong jaws and sinful physiques. They had dressed in black suits which were perfectly tailored and likely to cost more than a year of rent for her tiny apartment. It seemed criminal to cover up bodies like those, even with such fine clothing.

And worse? She'd sort of enjoyed them worrying over her. It had been a long time since anyone had helped her, since she'd had anyone in her corner.

Erik's offer had been like a life raft, and even if she couldn't accept, it had made her feel less alone.

Which was a nice change.

She couldn't even remember the last occasion she'd spent time with anyone outside of work. A year?

The depressing thought had her glancing at her phone, so tempted to dial one of the numbers she knew by heart, one she'd memorized from her old life. Just one familiar conversation would be enough. She wanted to hear a voice she knew, to talk to someone who knew her in return.

But then her reality came back to her and, as always, she didn't go for her phone.

Just like when Erik had asked, she held it all in. Each time she'd reached out, it had only gotten worse, only made things harder.

That had taught Ashley a lesson she didn't enjoy but couldn't refute — it was better to stand on her own.

Though the locks and new door helped. Ever since moving in, she'd set a large, heavy free weight in front of the door at night. It wouldn't keep the door from opening, but it would give her a warning.

Between that, the windows and her little toothpick trick, she'd been able to sleep.

Not well, and not for long, but anything was better than nothing.

Each time she closed her eyes, though, she'd remember that horrible voice on the other end of the phone. He hadn't cursed, hadn't even yelled, and that was worse. Instead, he'd been sweet, soft and coaxing.

It drew a shudder from her and made her stomach clench. How long would she have here? How long before everything was ripped away again?

A knock on the door had her jumping to her feet, eyes wide.

No one knew where she lived other than the alphas, and they wouldn't show up again. They'd made their position clear — one she agreed with.

Another knock. "Furniture movers."

What the hell?

In the hallway stood an older, heavy-set beta, his eyes on a clipboard. "Ashley?"

"Yes."

"Got a full truck for you. Gonna take a few hours though, with all the stairs. Bed, couch, table — "

"I didn't order anything."

The man stopped and flipped over the paper on the clipboard. "It was ordered for you. Already paid for." He paused, then huffed a laugh. "And they left a damn good tip."

"Who ordered it? I don't know anything about this."

"Torrin Kansas did first thing this morning. Normally it would take a couple days to deliver but, well, like I said, he tipped well."

Torrin? And she had a last name, finally. She should have said no, but somehow the confusion about it, the surprise, had her stepping back to let the man in.

Memories of the man came back to her, the only of the three she hadn't seen again. She recalled his hair, so blond it bordered on white, and reaching to the collar of his shirt. His eyes had been dark brown, odd against the lightness of his hair. He'd been dressed impeccably, just as his cousins were, but he'd had a cane. Not something he'd held as an accessory, but something he'd leaned against as he'd walked forward.

Still, Ashley couldn't just accept it. Nothing came for free. "Can I have his number, please?"

The man frowned. "A man buys you a few grand in furniture and you don't even have his number?" He let out a laugh. "Guess you're memorable, huh? Sure, here." He set the open clipboard on the counter, then tapped the bottom, where a phone number sat. "I'm going to go down and set up with the boys so we can get this figured out. Do you care where anything is put?"

Ashley shook her head as she picked up her phone and dialed the number.

It rang as the mover left, and Ashley had no idea what she was going to say.

What was there to say? A man she hadn't spoken more than a few words to had just bought her a bunch of furniture. Why? What did he expect in payment?

The ringing stopped when a woman answered. "Hello?"

Does he have a mate? Why did that idea bother her? What if he thought she was going to be some sort of mistress?

Ashley found her voice. "Can I speak to Torrin?"

"Who is this?"

"Ashley." Would he even recognize the name?

A pause, a shuffle on the other side of the line, then a smooth male voice. "Hello?"

She froze, unsure what to say.

Another pause, the closing of a door, then he spoke again. "Ashley? Is that you?"

She licked her lips before she could answer. "Why are there movers here?"

"I was told you lacked furniture."

"So? That isn't your problem."

He spoke in an aristocratic tone, words slow and careful, and fancy enough that Ashley felt as though she didn't quite live up to him. "It was something I could remedy rather easily, so I did."

"I can't pay you back."

"I don't believe I asked you to."

Ashley scraped her foot on the old, dirty carpet of her apartment. "Then what are you expecting from me? Because I won't..." She couldn't bring herself to actually say it.

"Won't what?"

Ashley could almost *hear* a smile in his voice, which was strange, because he hadn't struck her as the sort to ever smile.

"Was that your mate?"

"Who? Oh, the woman who answered? No, that was my personal assistant."

"She didn't answer like a business number."

"Because it isn't. It's my personal phone, but she answers it for me during the day since I have meetings. And for the point you didn't finish making, no, I am not expecting you to sleep with me as payment."

Her cheeks heated at the statement. Even if she'd considered that, having Torrin say it out loud was different.

The words, in his smooth, deep voice, were so much more sinful than they should have been. It brought forth brief flashes in her head, thoughts she hadn't had much experience with and certainly no desire as of recently.

"Ashley?"

He must have been talking, and she missed it, distracted by his statements.

"I can't accept this. It's too much."

"Money is of little consequence, trust me. Accept it, because it can't be returned."

"And why? Why would you do it?"

A slight pause before he ignored her question. "Do take care of yourself, and since I doubt you slept enough last night, go to bed soon."

Ashley frowned at the authoritative tone, and worse, at the way she almost wanted to listen.

"Don't tell me what to do," she whispered instead.

"Do as you should, and I won't have to. Goodnight, Ashley." The line went dead, leaving her standing there, phone in hand and Torrin's smooth voice sliding through her body.

The goosebumps on her skin remained, even after the call ended, and knowing she'd never see any of the alphas again didn't stop the reaction at all.

She really wanted to see them again, no matter how unwise that was.

* * * *

"You sent her furniture?" Liam's grin was full of mockery, as though he was thoroughly amused by Torrin's actions.

Torrin slid his phone into his pocket and tried to remain impassive. "It seemed the best way to cut ties."

"And we have to cut ties?" Liam had his feet up on the edge of the desk despite knowing how much Torrin hated when he did that—maybe even because of it. Torrin's cousin did love to play the brat. "The fact we keep thinking about her says maybe that isn't the right choice."

Torrin leveled a look at Liam. "You already know the answer to that. Anyone we took as a mate would be at risk."

"We've survived everything thrown at us."

"Not all of us."

Liam's smile fell. "That was different. We've learned a lot since then. It wouldn't happen again."

Torrin shook his head, then dropped his gaze to his laptop screen. It was easy for Liam and Erik to dismiss Torrin's concerns. *They* hadn't suffered as he had. They hadn't lost what was most important to them, as he had. So of course Liam thought it would be different.

Torrin, however, couldn't be so sure.

"You can't just keep doing this." When Torrin didn't respond, Liam went on. "Eventually, you have to get past Gilly. What happened was horrible, but you can't keep cutting people out just because you don't want it to happen again."

The name brought forth a smiling face in his mind — the freckles, the blue eyes and, worse, how she had looked afterward. Beauty was so easy to strip away with enough violence.

"You don't understand."

Liam nodded, as if agreeing. "Maybe I don't know what it feels like to go through it, but I was right there with you afterward. I helped pick you up. I know what that looks like."

"And yet you're so quick to risk it anyway? You, who haven't, in all these years, risked yourself in such a way even once?"

Liam scowled, crossing his arms, looking almost petulant. "I'm not saying she needs to be forever, but damn it, do you really want to just end this before it even starts?"

"Yes. Sometimes you have to choose what you want most. We have made our decisions through the years, and to think we could have everything now would be foolish." Torrin didn't say the rest, the truth that their choices had consequences, and they would eventually pay the price for the things they'd most valued in their lives.

No one got anything for free, so it was good they'd cut ties with Ashley.

When the time came to settle the debts of the choices Torrin had made in his life, he alone would pay for them.

* * * *

Ashley held the beers on her tray, her feet sore in hour six of her shift.

The belt at her waist had her tips, and they made the entire thing worth it.

She stopped at a table, setting the drinks down in front of each customer before grabbing the folded bills between one of the men's fingers.

He caught her hand. Over the smells inside the bar, Ashley couldn't scent his designation. It all muddied together, something she hated because she felt as though she'd lost one of her senses.

"How about you join us? A few shots, sweetheart."

"Sorry, but I'm working."

"When are you off?" The man was young and cute, she supposed.

It felt hard to be sure anymore. She'd spent the last few years avoiding any sort of connection, so she didn't trust herself to know if someone was attractive.

Except the alphas from a few nights before. *They* had been attractive.

"Sorry, but I can't date customers." The rule was true, but she'd have said it even if it wasn't.

"Who said anything about dating?" The man grabbed her ass and pulled her closer.

Ashley pushed away from the man, and he let his hands slip free. "Let me know if you need anything else."

The man nodded, laughed and focused his attention back on the drink and his friends.

That was the thing. Drunks tended to come on strong, but they gave up fast, too.

She dropped the tray off at the bar and leaned against the counter, rising to the balls of her feet to stretch her calf muscles.

"Hey, Ashley." The bartender and manager, Carla, came over. "I think someone was calling for you earlier."

"What do you mean?" Dread started inside Ashley, but she didn't let it take hold, not yet.

"When I first got here, someone called. They asked if Ashley worked here, so I said I don't give out employee information. They said Ashley had brown hair, blue eyes. I figured it was some customer who was trying to score information."

Ashley's chest tightened. *He couldn't have found me already, could he?* "I need to take a ten," she said through a narrowing throat.

Carla responded, but Ashley didn't hear it. Instead, she kept moving, needing fresh air, to get control of her breathing.

The back door of the bar had a fenced-in staff-only area. A picnic table sat there, along with the dumpster and doors to the storage space.

Once outside, Ashley collapsed on the bench and leaned forward. She dropped her head down and tried to slow her breathing.

She could *hear* that voice in her head. It was too soon. She shouldn't have to pick up and leave yet. She'd just started to set up a life.

36

It isn't fair!

"I could break his hand."

The voice made her jerk up, smacking her back against the table.

In front of her stood Erik, his gaze unwavering. He didn't apologize for startling her, didn't rush to her side. No, not Erik. Already, she knew he wasn't the sort.

He just waited for her to catch her breath while he stood there in silence.

Ashley leaned forward again. She wasn't afraid of Erik, didn't need to watch him.

The bench creaked as he sat beside her. "The man inside. I'd be happy to break anything on him you want me to. He'd certainly offer an apology for his behavior then. Would that make you feel better?"

Ashley let out a soft laugh that wheezed through her tight throat, thankful for the joke. "I don't care about him."

"Then what's this about?"

Ashley stayed leaning forward but turned her head to peer up at Erik's face. "What are you doing here?"

"Business brought me. I didn't know you worked here, though I suppose it explains the outfit you were in the other night."

That made her heart speed, as if he were almost implying he *liked* the way she looked in the skimpy shorts she wore to work.

Instead of responding to that, though, Ashley remained on topic. "The only people who work in a place like this are ones who can't do it in legal places."

"I had a meeting with a business associate who is fond of places like this." Erik didn't offer more before changing the subject, though his tone said he wasn't a fan of the atmosphere. "Why are you out here, Ashley?"

"Even waitresses get breaks."

"Most don't hyperventilate during their breaks."

"I'm not like most people."

"So it seems."

Neither spoke for a while, but his presence helped Ashley regain her breath and her standing. Maybe it was because she felt…safe. It was odd, since she didn't know Erik.

The logic of it didn't change the reality, though, and she did feel calm. It was as if the issues couldn't touch her right then. Whether that was foolish or not didn't change that she wanted to enjoy it.

She rested her forearms on her knees and let herself think through it.

Maybe Carla was right, and the man was a customer. *Or maybe…*

"Did you call looking for me? Or maybe Liam or Torrin?"

Erik lifted an eyebrow. "No. We'd agreed none of us would come looking for you, and like I said, we didn't know you worked here. Is that what set you off? Did someone call for you?" He narrowed his eyes. "Are you running from someone? Is that why you nailed the windows closed?"

The answer rested on her lips, and she *wanted* to tell him. Not because she wanted him to fix it, but because she wanted to be able to tell someone. The weight of the truth, that she could never let anyone close or even explain what was wrong, had worn her down to nothing.

She opened her mouth, wanting to spill the ugly details, but she couldn't. It was too dangerous for all of them.

Instead, she shook her head. "Why did you all agree to leave me alone?"

Erik pressed his lips together, then looked away. "Because we aren't in a position to offer anything, and you seem to undo our good intentions. Normally, I could trust Torrin and Liam to enjoy you but not get attached, but with you? You are dangerous, so we agreed it would be best to all leave you be."

"And yet you followed me out here."

"As I said, you are detrimental to our self-control. It seems even I'm not immune."

Ashley shivered as a breeze skimmed over her skin and she realized how little she was wearing. She had hardly finished the tiny reaction to the chill before Erik moved, pulling off his coat and draping it over her shoulders. "You are a disaster," he scolded.

The heavy fabric around her shoulders held Erik's scent. She breathed it in and enjoyed the sense of security it gave her, the way it did something unusual to her.

When she'd never reacted to any man in a positive, normal way, she had thought herself broken. She'd assumed it was a reaction to everything that had happened, yet there she was, growing wet from Erik's masculine scent, from the way his button-up shirt showed off his impressive body.

Guess I'm not as broken as I'd thought.

Erik inhaled loudly, and even outside, she had no doubt he could smell exactly how much she wanted him.

What would he do? Kiss her? Pull her closer? *Do I want him to do that?*

Instead, Erik rose. "I should go."

Oh. Ashley got to her feet as well, sliding off the jacket. "Thanks," she said without meeting his gaze. "And good luck with your business."

She went to pass him, but Erik grasped her arm.

He caught her chin and lifted her face until she had to look him in his dark eyes. He said nothing until she did, until her gaze met his. "You will be careful, and you will call Torrin again if you are in danger."

"You said I was dangerous."

Erik stroked his finger along her jawline. "You are. However, knowing you'll call might help us relax." He frowned, then shook his head. "I keep saying that, but it doesn't seem to matter."

Ashley wrapped her fingers around his wrist, but she didn't pull away. If anything, she leaned toward him, drawn by a pull she didn't understand and could only feel.

Her gaze dropped from his dark and fathomless eyes to his lips. Full, a light pink and enough for her to start fantasizing about what they could be used for.

"To hell with it," Erik muttered with a groan before he pulled her forward with his grip on her jaw. His lips were firm against hers, taking a kiss that made her knees weak and her pussy clench.

Ashley wrapped her arms up and around him, and Erik did the same, grasping her and pulling her tight to him. Every hard inch of his body was unyielding against the softness of her curves.

The kiss was everything she could have imagined and more, especially with how assertive Erik was. He wasn't nervous, didn't kiss her as if unsure. Instead, he moved with complete confidence and purpose, even when he forced her head to tilt more, when he pressed his tongue to her lips in a demand—one she happily gave in to.

His cock, rigid against her, told her how much he wanted this as well. Funny, since he'd seemed unaffected by her so far.

His rigid shaft said differently.

He growled against her and bit down on her bottom lip hard enough to sting before he moved back, taking his jacket with him. "Just what I thought. Too damn dangerous."

With that, he pulled away and walked back in through the door.

Ashley was confused, her body alive in a terrifying way she'd never felt, but at least she wasn't thinking about the call anymore.

That's something, right?

Chapter Four

Erik stood beside Liam as they waited in the apartment that wasn't theirs.

"You kissed her?" Liam's face reminded Erik of when they'd been children and Erik had stolen the last cookie.

"It wasn't planned."

"You plan everything."

"My plan had been to meet a contact there. None of us expected her to work there."

"And you couldn't just ignore her? The way you've told Torrin and me to do?"

Erik gave Liam an exasperated look. "She was having a panic attack."

"That normally only bothers people who have a heart." Liam offered a grin before continuing. "She was jumpy that first night. She was almost assaulted, but even still, it seemed deeper than that."

Erik nodded, walking over to a desk and thumbing through the items on top. "She was grabbed by some asshole in the bar, but I don't think that set her off."

Liam's back straightened and, sure enough, a growl left the alpha.

Erik moved to scan the spines on the bookshelf. "I was very clear in a way that will keep the man from signing his name for a while about why touching her was a bad idea. However, she asked if we'd called her job."

Liam's anger drifted away, as if the question distracted him. "Do you think she's hiding from someone? It would explain her apartment and why she didn't want us around."

"It makes as much sense as anything else."

"We could—"

Erik shot his twin a hard look to stop that train of thought. "No. We are not going to dig into this any deeper. She has Torrin's number. *If* she calls, we can take it from there, but we are not going to go looking for trouble. Everyone has problems, and we are in no place to take on hers. In fact, she'd likely be in *more* danger if we did."

Erik managed to keep a straight face as he lectured Liam, even though Erik had asked Ashley the same thing, had been ready to take on any issue she had. Giving good advice and following it were two different things, though.

Liam moved his gaze around the apartment, as if taking in where they were, the reality of their life, before he sighed. "I guess you're right."

Erik's lips tipped down. He didn't enjoy telling Liam the truth. Somehow, breaking bad news had always been Erik's job. He had to be the realistic one, the one to temper his brother's enthusiasm. Liam wanted to believe the world was a very different place than it was, and perhaps Erik liked that, at times.

He did the things that needed to be done so Liam could still believe, at least some of the time, that the world was as he saw it.

It had stopped wearing on Erik when he'd accepted that as his place. Besides, at least one of them could be happy. That seemed better odds than most people got.

Then he thought back to that kiss...

Ashley's lips had been soft and giving and sweet, things that just didn't exist in his world. Would she be like that if they went further? If he stripped off her clothing, if he spread her out before him, would she still be that same girl?

"Really?" Liam's tone and nod at the effect of the thoughts on Erik's groin made Erik take a deep breath.

Yet another reason that Ashley was off the table for good. He couldn't get turned on every time he thought about her. The girl was already proving to be a problem, and that was after hardly spending any time around her.

The door creaked open, and Erik slipped his fingers around his knife while Liam palmed his gun. The man who lived there was trash, a person who the world wouldn't miss, who had never done a single good thing in his life.

Still, it had been a very specific mistake that had brought Erik and Liam there, when the man had decided to cross them by helping an enemy set up an ambush. Erik had lost three men that night, and this man would pay for that betrayal with his life.

Even if he deserved it, though, even if the man was the filth Erik saw him as, it was a perfectly clear example of the life they lived, the life Ashley needed to be nowhere around.

She didn't belong in their world.

* * * *

Ashley checked the lock on her door for the fifth time, her heart racing.

Her phone rang again, sitting on the table as though it might hurt her if she just touched it.

Restricted number.

Just like the other calls she'd ignored for the past fifteen minutes.

Even still, she *knew* who it was. It was who it always was when this happened, when she settled in and tried to build a life.

The same voice would drift over the line and steal it all away.

Stop being a coward. Maybe it's just a telemarketer.

Ashley didn't believe that. She couldn't. Life had proven to her time and time again that some people were meant for happy, calm lives and others were meant for shit.

Her place was obvious.

With trembling hands, she picked up the phone. She missed the answer button the first time, but she got it the second. "H-hello?"

"I missed you."

There it was. The voice that haunted her nightmares, the one that stalked her no matter where she hid. She'd run, moved states, fled from the east coast to the west, and still he'd found her every time. *Gregory.*

"Why are you doing this?"

"You know why." *Calm. Always calm.* Nothing ruffled the man who had stalked her for years. It never mattered what she did—he seemed, at best, mildly disappointed in her actions.

"Just leave me alone."

"I can't. I'm growing tired of this game, however. I'm not getting any younger, and each time we do this, you steal another day from me, another week, another month."

He'd stolen *years* from her, but she kept her mouth shut. No matter how angry she got, she never yelled at him, never fought him directly. What was the point of doing it? She *never* won.

"I'm not going to be with you," she said.

"You will. You've simply lacked proper motivation."

Motivation. The word chilled her to her core. He'd proven how far he would go enough times.

She gripped the phone in her hand and paced the short distance in her apartment while she tried to breathe through the terror. "What sort of motivation?"

"Stop."

The command came with such certainty, the snap in it stilling her feet, forcing her to freeze in place.

Glass shattered, and the dingy carpet inches from her feet seemed to explode. Ashley leapt backward, falling so her ass hit the ground, and she scooted away.

Someone shot through the window and hit the floor inches from where I was standing.

"Calm," he purred into the line, as if *he* weren't the cause of her panic. "That was a demonstration, dear. If only you would listen to me, only obey, I could keep you from such harm. Just as when I said stop, and you listened, you were saved. If you only would do that, I could give you a good life and keep you safe."

Ashley trembled as she sat there, as she stared at the hole in the floor, as he tore apart the tiny bit of peace she'd thought she'd made.

A sigh came through the phone. "I have business to attend, but I'll get into town in a few days. I hope you'll have had time to think by then, to make a good choice. I would hate to have to find you again."

When the line went dead, when Ashley was alone with only the terrifying calmness of his voice lingering in her head, she curled her knees to her chest. She wanted to break down, to cry, but nothing came. No tears, no racking sobs to help her deal with the situation.

Only the breeze from the shattered window, the reminder that her tiny sanctuary was no such thing.

I can't do this again.

* * * *

Torrin stared at his phone as it sat on his desk as if he could *force* it to ring.

Which, of course, he didn't want to happen.

They needed to put the omega far behind them. Her not calling or reaching out should have pleased him. It was what they wanted — what they *needed*.

Still, he'd kept his cell with him. That was the most pathetic part. Instead of leaving it with his assistant as was usual, he'd tucked the phone into his pocket and taken it with him everywhere.

"You're sulking," Liam said as he entered the large office.

Which was the exact reason Torrin preferred Erik's company. Erik was the quiet one, the one who faded into the background and didn't constantly question him. Liam preferred noise, even when that noise was simply hearing himself talk.

When Torrin lifted his gaze from his phone to the two men, a familiar tingle started in his chest.

So many things they'd lost over the years. Family, friends, lovers. It had always ended up being just the three of them from the very start, and, Torrin thought, *probably until the end.*

That gave him both a sense of comfort and an undeniable tension. He would forever carry the weight of watching out for his cousins, the weight of their safety and happiness.

Not that he'd done a great job with happiness.

Success? That he could manage. He could make them rich and powerful. He could work their contacts to keep them safe. Providing them with some semblance of happiness wasn't anything he understood, though.

What did he know about happiness?

After another moment, Liam spoke, his tone that of a man who had wanted to say something but had held off. "You know, if things settled down…"

The meaning was clear. Torrin had known Liam long enough to read him, even when he was trying to be subtle. "No."

"No? Just no? Like it isn't a group decision?"

"It isn't, at least not for us as a group. She is better off without any of us, and we are better off not being distracted."

Liam looked as though he wanted to argue, but instead went quiet. Torrin's truth was hard to argue with.

It didn't please him, as being right usually didn't. Too often, being right had more to do with accepting an ugly truth that others didn't wish to. It left him with a heavier weight on his shoulders than that of his cousins, as he held up the truths so they could ignore them.

Erik's phone vibrated, so he pulled it out and hit a button on the screen. "Hello? When? Is she hurt?" A hard set to his jaw said the conversation wasn't a good one, and there was only one *she* who Torrin had known to put such an expression on the stoic man's face.

It seemed they hadn't quite gotten Ashley out of their lives just yet.

* * * *

Boards on the window did nothing to raise Ashley's mood. They blocked out what little light the apartment had gotten, making it into even more of a cave. The police hadn't been all that helpful, and the best the super could do on such short notice was secure a piece of plywood to the open space.

He'd commented on the extra security but had only cared to say she needed to fix any holes if she took the locks with her when she left.

So when all the fanfare left, when she was again in the small apartment by herself, Ashley could only stare at the wood blocking her view.

Did I really think I could get away? That I could start over and have a real life?

Gregory had sworn she never would, that she was his, and right then, she felt that to her very core. It was as though he held a leash she could never slip, no matter how far she ran. She'd reach the end of it and he'd yank, sending her tumbling back.

Which meant packing up yet again. Starting over again. *What's the point?*

Exhaustion threatened to drag her under, to pull her so deep into apathy that she just waited there until he showed up.

She feared she had no strength to run anymore, to resist. A person only had so much they could take before they cracked.

A knock at her door would have had her jumping before, but she couldn't bring herself to worry. Gregory wouldn't arrive for a few days, and he never lied.

She unlocked the door and opened it to find Liam there, his smile already familiar.

Ashley held it together despite how much it helped to see him.

Or maybe it hurt? She wasn't sure. She only knew it made her feel *something*.

Then she noticed luggage set on the floor by his feet. "Are you moving in?"

He laughed softly. "No, but you're moving out."

"Excuse me?"

He picked up the luggage and slid past her, though it forced her to move backward so they didn't touch. "Heard about your little mishap." Liam nodded at the boarded window.

He set the suitcase on the coffee table that Torrin had bought, the furniture something Ashley still hadn't fully gotten used to.

"How did you hear about that?"

"Erik had an alert set up on your address. The police came, so he was notified."

"What, is he stalking me?" She meant it as a joke, but the word stuck in her throat. It seemed she wasn't quite ready to make jokes about such things.

Liam continued as though she hadn't tripped over her question. Maybe he'd heard it but ignored it or thought it was because she was worried about Erik. "You have to know there is some sort of pull for us. While we were happy to leave you be, that only worked if we knew you were safe." He cut another unhappy look around the apartment. "I knew this was a horrible place for you from the start."

"It's what I can afford." She *knew* it was a bad place to live, but she didn't care for his judgment. She was doing the best she could.

"Yeah, well, you aren't staying here anymore."

"Did you not hear me? I can't afford anything else. The super said they could fix the window in another week or two—" She paused as it hit her. She wouldn't be there in a week or two. How quickly she'd forgotten already.

Or maybe she just liked to forget. It was how she got through the day most of the time. Forget Gregory was always closing in, forget that she'd need to pick up and leave once he found her. How else was she supposed to get through her shifts at work? How else could she sit there beside other, normal people and not lose her mind over it all?

Liam stared at her as she worked through it in her head, a curious expression across his features. It was as though he were trying to read her but couldn't quite get a grasp on it.

He shook his head and pointed down at the luggage. They had nested bags, so that at the end, three bags sat open. "Fill these with everything you need for the immediate future. If you have more that doesn't fit, we'll have someone return to get the rest of it."

"What about the furniture?"

"It'll go into storage. Don't look at me like that—you won't have to pay anything."

"I can't just move."

Liam caught her chin, forcing her gaze to his. Funny that he had seemed so easygoing before, yet the strong grip of his fingers and the steel in his gaze said he might not be so easy to push around. "Your window was shot out, Ashley, and a bullet put in the floor inches from your feet. There is a good chance that the people who lived here before you were drug dealers or worse, who have enemies who might not realize — or care — that they've moved. You staying here is out of the question, and as you've said yourself that you can't afford anything else, we've arranged a solution. You will pack the things you want to bring with you and come with me."

"Or?" The question came out breathlessly.

He curled his lips into a half smile. "Or I'll toss your pretty ass over my shoulder and carry you out. If you don't have any clothes in the new place, I can't say I'll mind a bit."

Ashley couldn't breathe. It was the heat of his gaze, the smirk of his lips, the warm strength of his fingers. He looked so much like Erik and yet so different, and all of it stirred up the want inside her stoked by Erik's earlier kiss.

Would Liam kiss her the same way? Erik was dominant, skilled and confident. Liam was those things, but he had a playful edge that Erik lacked.

Liam inhaled noisily, a groan on his lips in response. "You can't expect me to stay professional when you do *that*." His last word came out with so much meaning, full of things she wanted that she'd never had, never tasted, never felt.

"That's what this is? Changing the locks on my place? Buying furniture I didn't ask for? Showing up and telling me I'm moving? That's all professional?"

Liam loosened his grip, yet she felt it just as strongly. He danced his fingers slowly over her jawline and throat in a feather-light stroke. "Pretty much."

"Then what would not professional look like?" Why did that sound like a dare? *Because I want to see how he'll react. I want to push him to do something, because this is torture.*

"Not professional would be bending you over the new, very nice couch and fucking you until we're both so worn out I might actually manage a full night's sleep without thinking about you." As he teased her with his words, he brushed his fingertips across her collarbone.

Goosebumps rose on her skin and a thin moan slipped from her.

He tilted his head, grin widening. "You like that idea, don't you? Oh, sweet, aren't you full of surprises?" He closed the distance between them and took a kiss. It was softer than Liam's but no less devastating. His lips coaxed hers to respond, teased her to meet him, to give him everything.

And she did. She wanted to. She needed to let go of everything but him.

Except when she leaned closer, when she yearned for the press of his body against hers, he backed off.

"Get your things," he said with a rough voice that made it clear that pulling away was the last thing he'd wanted.

"Why?" At his look, she clarified. "Why stop?"

He huffed a soft laugh, one dark and full of masculine humor. "Because while I needed a taste, and fair is fair, my brother and I don't take females separately."

"Not ever?" The question came out breathless.

Something crossed his handsome features, darkening that cheerful nature. He chased the shadows away with a smile that didn't quite reach his brown eyes. "Not anymore, no. So, if you're still interested in anything not so professional, it'll have to wait."

Ashley couldn't stop herself as the idea of those two washed over her like a searing blast of air. Liam's coaxing, playful touches and Erik's strong hands. Those two nearly identical faces, yet men so very different, at the same time?

Suddenly the fear of Gregory, the reality of having to uproot again, didn't seem so scary.

She doubted the world could reach her if she was pressed between Liam and Erik, and right then?

She couldn't think of any place she'd rather be.

It turned out Liam had the self-control of a fucking legend, if him resisting the siren-like scent of Ashley said anything. Hell, he'd better get nominated for sainthood after pulling away.

Then again, he'd sat her in the back of the town car and he'd sat up front with the driver.

Being alone with her was asking for trouble.

He carried her bags, waving the driver off. Something about taking care of her made him want to snarl at the offer of another male's help. *Mine.*

He sighed at the primal part of him, the stupid and outdated side that wanted to sink his teeth into her as he fucked her, that wanted to leave marks on her so others knew she was spoken for.

She had almost nothing to pack, as it turned out. He'd kept his mouth shut when she'd filled only the smallest of the bags he'd brought, though she'd acted as if it were normal.

The only possessions she had in her life could fit into a carry-on?

Again, a desperation to know more, to understand her, grew. Where was she from? How had she ended up like this?

He pressed open the door to the apartment they'd readied for her, and her gasp accompanied her stopping short.

Liam ignored the reaction and entered, the light from the setting sun pouring in through the large wall of windows on that side.

The apartment was nice, open, large. It had sat empty since Kara, their wily omega friend, had refused to use it. The two apartments were the only ones on that floor. Torrin had thought the distance would keep Kara close enough to watch but be far enough for privacy.

Leave it to the difficult woman to never do the smart thing, however. That habit had left her with mates, now, who Liam couldn't stand.

He shoved the annoyance away to turn and find Ashley still standing at the threshold. "Come on. Not like the room will bite."

"This is too much. I can't afford this." The words afford came out on a whisper, as though embarrassed.

She thought we'd charge her?

She clearly had no idea how little they cared about finances, or how much they cared about her safety.

"You can't afford free? Just how bad off are you?" He meant for the joke to break the tension, to make her laugh and maybe just relax.

Instead, she winced.

Great job. You're supposed to be the one who's good with women.

He gave it another shot. "We own the entire building. This place is always empty because that" — he pointed at the door across the hall — "is where our place is."

"You and Erik?"

"And Torrin. We aren't a fan of close neighbors, so this apartment sits empty. We wouldn't rent it to anyone, so no one is out anything. Other than you won't have to worry about getting your windows shot out."

Again, that darkness in her face. *Fear?* Probably just remembering the event. That would have shaken up anyone, especially someone as seemingly innocent as her.

"I can't accept this," she said despite the longing in her expression to do just that.

"Yes, you can. In case you haven't noticed, we aren't great at taking no for an answer. And if you think you're stubborn? Trust me — we're worse."

Ashley's shoulders dropped. Was it bad of him to enjoy winning so much? The best part was when she walked into the apartment, though. It might not be where he slept, but having her closer, having her in a space that was still his, was a claim he wanted on her.

She remained silent during the tour, though the tightening of her jaw said she wasn't happy with something. The place was pure luxury, so he doubted the problem was that it didn't live up to her expectations.

She nibbled on her bottom lip. *Lucky damned lip.*

"Talk to me," he said, softening his voice.

"I can't stay here. I don't even know you."

The less she knew about them, the better. Still, saying that would cause the flighty omega to run, and Liam just wasn't feeling cardio right then. At least, not the running kind. He wouldn't mind if he got his heart rate up another way.

Her expectant look made him realize he'd zoned out. He offered an unrepentant smile—no doubt she scented his lust—and shrugged. "What are you worried about?" When she didn't answer, he waved her toward the couch and took a seat beside her. "What if I make a list and you stop me when I hit the right one? Worried about the money? Well, don't be. Like I said, the place was sitting empty."

Her lips pressed together, the pink of them blanching.

Liam only smiled at her giving in, so he continued with his list, since all her fight hadn't left her.

"I'm not going to expect you to pay us back." When she didn't relax, he sighed in understanding. "You won't be asked to work it off, either."

The blush that sprang up on her cheeks drew a groan from him. Why did he like the innocent ones? Innocent ones didn't survive in his world, yet the sight of her actually blushing from such a vague suggestion had him hardening.

Which had him hesitating. "How old are you?" His reputation wasn't exactly squeaky clean, but he'd be damned if he went after a minor.

"Twenty-four."

He breathed in. *Thank fuck.* Sure, she was a lot younger than he would normally have considered, and twenty-four was pushing his comfort level, but at least she was legal.

Quick math in his head let him realize she was fifteen years younger than him. It made his upcoming big four-oh birthday hang heavily over him.

"When do you work next?"

"I don't." At his look, she continued. "I couldn't work my shift after the window, while I was waiting for the police, and they weren't very happy about it."

He wondered if they could get her employed somewhere else. If not at their company, then at one of the many they dealt with. Anything would be better than there, and Torrin would make sure she was well compensated.

That, however, was a conversation and plot for another day. He was pretty sure moving her into a place they owned was as far as they'd get with her.

Things took time when dealing with someone as flighty as her. She wasn't going to be a quick fling, someone he could work into bed in five minutes and shove from his life.

Ashley was a long game, and he was more than ready to play it.

* * * *

Ashley couldn't settle in the large apartment. She'd never had so much space to herself.

She thought back to before she'd had to pick everything up the first time, when she'd still lived at home. They'd had a large house – a necessity when housing four alphas together – but she'd been the child. Her bedroom hadn't been huge and it certainly hadn't been like *this*.

That had been the most difficult part of life over the past six years – the loneliness, the isolation. She'd gone from growing up in a home with five fathers, when there was always at least one or two home, to sleeping in tiny apartments by herself and eating meals on her own.

She'd lost her sense of security, too. In her old home, she'd slept well. It had never even occurred to her how dangerous life could be. It never was dangerous, not under the roof of her childhood home.

Then she'd met Gregory and realized how wrong she'd been.

Now she understood what lurked in the shadows. She'd seen what the world was really like and she hadn't had a good night's sleep since.

It was as if those monsters from her dreams, the ones her fathers had always kept at bay, had managed to claw their way from her nightmares to reality.

Ashley twisted to find the digital clock that hung on the wall. Two-twenty-six.

She got out of bed, tired of staring at the ceiling, tired of trying to fall asleep when it just wouldn't happen.

She wore a large shirt that hung just past her ass with a cartoon kitten on the front, and a pair of long socks that had racoons on them. The outfit was stupid, but it was comfortable and reminded her of home.

She pulled open the slider to the balcony, because she wouldn't dare try to leave the apartment. For all she knew, Erik and Liam had an alarm on the door.

She hadn't risked running into either of them again, not after seeing Liam and settling in.

The balcony was large and open, much like the rest of the apartment. It stretched to both sides along the building with metal railings standing between her and the city below.

The building wasn't that tall, with only five stories. It meant they were low enough to not make her nervous but high enough that it felt private, especially since they sat on the top floor.

There were different sections of seating across the long balcony, some together with couches and chairs and others with tables for dining. It faced east, meaning the sun would shine onto it in the morning.

Ashley lowered herself into one of the larger chairs with thick cushions, cuddling back into the comfort of it.

A scent caught her, something dark and smoky. It wasn't Liam or Erik, but it was familiar.

"You're up late."

Ashley jumped at the sound. She'd spent so long just waiting to hear the dreaded voice that had haunted her, spent so long in silence, that the unexpected words startled her enough to let out a very undignified yelp.

Except, when she twisted, it wasn't Gregory there. Torrin stood with two cups clutched in one hand, his cane in the other, and dressed down enough that Ashley almost didn't recognize him.

Not that she'd seen him much. The entire first night was hazy at best.

His blond hair was pushed back from his face and he wore a pair of pajama pants and a plain black T-shirt. His dark eyes stood out, especially compared to his hair. "I didn't mean to startle you." He set one of the cups on the small table beside her before backing off and lowering himself into a chair far enough away for her to feel comfortable.

When he'd come closer, though, she'd realized — the scent on the chair was *his*.

Does he sit out here a lot?

"The balcony stretches around the building and between the two apartments," he explained. "I assume Liam didn't mention it?"

"No, he didn't."

Torrin nodded, then took a sip of his drink. "Liam tends to leave out things when he wants to. I'm sorry for startling you, but when I saw you out here, I thought perhaps you would care for some tea."

Ashley shuddered as she tried to let go of the rest of her anxiety, the one that made her jumpy. After a moment, she picked up the cup Torrin had left, the scent of lavender and peppermint strong. A sip revealed a hint of sweetness along with it, just a whisper of honey.

She licked her lip to savor it. "Thank you." When his eyebrow lifted in question, she continued. "For letting me stay. I can't afford this place, but I want to pay something. I don't want a handout."

Torrin's face didn't shift. It was unnerving how difficult it was to read him, how little showed in his expression. "That isn't necessary."

"I want to feel like I'm pulling my weight." Especially because, for the first time, she felt an unfamiliar hope, like maybe she had a shot at settling down.

With her apartment empty and no name on the new place, maybe Gregory would assume she'd moved on.

"Liam told me you lost your job."

Ashley dropped her gaze from his, unable to take the weight of it. "It wasn't a great fit. I told them I won't be back. Don't worry, though. I can find a job and take care of myself."

Torrin said nothing at first. He tapped the outside of his cup, drawing her attention there. His fingers were long and aristocratic, with perfectly trimmed nails. Everything about him was perfect in a way that made her look down at her racoon-covered socks and cringe.

Finally, after another drink, he spoke. "I'll have my assistant contact you tomorrow morning. She'll match your skills with an appropriate job and help settle you into a new position."

The offer made her fidget. "You don't need to do that."

"I didn't ask."

"I don't have a lot of skills."

"I highly doubt that. Trust me, we'll find something that works well for you."

Ashley took another drink of the tea, letting it soak into her. She traced her thumb along the rim of the cup. "Why are you doing this for me?"

"You've asked both Liam and Erik that question. I'm sure they've answered."

"They seem...interested." She forced out the word, trying to sound in control and failing to not stumble over it. "And Liam said they take women together."

Torrin's gaze had the weight of a car, and he seemed to wield silence like a weapon. "They do."

"Well, that explains why they want to help me. I don't quite understand why you're being nice to me."

"Do I need a reason?"

"Everyone has a reason. No one does anything unless they get something out of it." Just saying that made her cringe. *I'm too young to be so jaded.* She risked meeting his gaze. "So what are you getting out of it?"

He took another sip as he studied her, then nodded. "I'll answer the question you aren't directly asking. I'm not looking for a relationship. I won't sleep with you. My cousins are the only family I have, and they're interested in you, and that brings you under my protection as well."

Ashley frowned at the statement, at how it didn't feel entirely true, especially with the way his gaze felt so full of something predatory. She reacted to it, too. Her nipples tightened beneath her shirt, and a heat in her core said she *liked* the way he watched her.

His nostrils flared and that look thickened. He breathed in deeply, then released it in a slow, controlled exhalation. "You should go to bed, Ashley."

"I can't fall asleep."

"Why not?"

Ashley opened her mouth, the commanding edge of Torrin's voice enough to nearly draw an answer from her. Except she stopped before she blurted it out. She couldn't tell him the reason, couldn't talk about Gregory, about her fears, about the mess of her life. Not only did she not want to risk it—Gregory could buy off or manipulate people—but she also didn't want to let that ugliness touch this odd security she'd found. It was as though if she opened that door, all the filth of her old life would infect this one.

Torrin reached behind him and pulled a throw blanket from the seat, then tucked it around her without touching her. "Stay out here as long as you'd like." He took a seat again.

"You'll just sit there?"

He took his phone from the pocket of his pajama bottoms. "I can keep myself busy, no worries."

Ashley watched him, the glow of his phone screen lighting up his features.

She opened her mouth to ask something, but he spoke first, silencing her.

"Close your eyes, Ashley."

It reminded her of his voice on the phone when he'd ordered her furniture, when he'd ordered her to get sleep. The demand warmed her, made her feel safe in a strange way.

She curled beneath the throw, her eyes fluttering closed, and to her amazement, she fell asleep.

Torrin let the screen of his phone go dark once Ashley's breathing evened out. She'd fallen asleep after a few minutes, the tension slipping from her.

It gave him the chance to finally look at her. When she was awake, his gaze unnerved her. He could tell by the way she would look at her feet or anywhere other than him. He couldn't help it, feeling as though, if he only looked a little deeper, a little harder, he'd understand her.

Her face was youthful, sweet. Her hair was soft and braided, and she appeared even more adorable with the absurd socks she wore. Her eyes, when open, were unfairly large with a blue that seemed to drift between brown and green depending on the light. All in all, she had the look of a doe, far too innocent and tempting.

And yet his words had been true. No matter how raw they made him feel, keeping her at a distance was his only option.

So even though he would never have her, never taste her, never let her know how much he wanted those things, he did the only thing he could.

He watched over her while she slept and tried to let go of the things he had to resist.

Chapter Five

Erik rolled his head, trying to loosen the tight muscles as he waited with Liam to speak to Linda, their receptionist.

She'd finished the interview process with Ashley — and interview was a funny name, given that she was guaranteed a job — and now it was time to discuss options.

"Think we could get her to be our personal assistant?" Liam asked, a grin across his lips. "Torrin has an assistant, and I think Ashley would be perfect. I could just keep dropping things she needs to pick up."

"We would get nothing done, and you'd be sued for sexual harassment."

"She wouldn't sue me. You kissed her. You know exactly how badly that girl wants it."

Erik couldn't argue *that* point. Ashley was drowning in lust.

How long had it been since she'd been properly fucked?

At twenty-four, she had to have gone through a few heats, and the idea of servicing her through one broke his normally still exterior when he groaned.

Liam curled his lips more. "Yeah, that's what I thought."

"It doesn't matter. She would distract us, and she needs space."

"Space is the last thing I want to give her."

"It isn't about you. She needs room to create a life of her own. The closer she is to us, the more likely she is to discover the less savory areas of our life. Do you really think she'd react well to that?"

At that reminder, Liam sobered.

A girl like Ashley would not ease into their life, into the uglier areas, into the truth. They would forever be keeping her in the dark about it, and the more their lives intertwined, the less likely they'd be to be able to do that.

A knock on the door had Liam calling whoever was there to enter.

Linda came in, the familiar woman as close to a friend as they got. She was a beta, making her a safe choice to have near. Not that Liam and Erik hadn't slept with her in the past. They'd done so a few times, when work had gone late, and Linda had been the one to pursue.

It was nothing serious, like all things with them. That seemed to be the way of life for them. *Nothing serious.*

Usually that meant random, convenient women for Erik and his brother. For Torrin, it meant one-night stands with women he would never see a second time.

"How'd it go?" Liam's question broke Erik's train of thought and brought him back to the topic at hand.

Linda sat at the table, a vision of competence and confidence. It wasn't her body that they'd hired her for. The beta was all teeth when it came to business, and she was loyal as they came. "We have a problem."

The words made Erik frown. "What sort of problem?"

"Ashley. She gave me a last name of someone who doesn't exist. No social security number, no work history. The bar she worked at paid her in cash under the table."

Liam leaned forward. "It's not unusual for omegas to go into hiding, especially if they've been officially documented."

Linda gave Liam a look that implied he was an idiot for letting a pretty face sway him. "If we ignore that legally employing her is impossible, she can work in a few areas. She's competent with the computer, good with filing. Any sort of receptionist or back office job would fit, but honestly? Her best attribute is her personality. If you can stick her somewhere to deal with people, she's going to do great. As long as you trust her, that is."

Erik had to agree. Putting Ashley in a back room to file would be wasting her, and Erik was never one to waste a good resource.

"Isn't Renee going on maternity leave?" Liam asked.

Linda nodded. "She wanted to go a week ago, but we haven't had anyone to cover for her. The last temp we tried lost us a client." She pursed her lips for a moment, her eyes locking on the window the way they always did when she was thinking. "You know, I think Ashley would do well there. It's pretty much all customer relations with the high-end clients. She'd set appointments, smooth over things when you all mess it up."

"Perfect. Talk to Renee, and we'll get training started tomorrow so hopefully she can start her leave by Friday."

Erik didn't acknowledge Linda leaving, choosing to glare at his twin instead.

"What?" Liam's tone was all innocence.

"I thought we agreed it would be best if she didn't work closely with us."

"You said it, but I didn't agree. Besides, she won't work directly with us."

"She'll be the go-between for us and the higher-end clients. How do you figure that isn't working directly with us?"

Liam waved off Erik's concerns, as he often did. He never took anything seriously enough. "You know, between her not using a real last name and nailing her windows shut, I've been thinking..."

Erik had thought the same more than once. "She doesn't seem the type to be in trouble with anyone. What's the worst she could have done?"

Liam nodded. "Yeah, I know. It's probably just being an omega. If she were documented by a hospital, maybe she had a pushy alpha following her or her parents were quick to mate her off. That could be it."

"Whatever it is, I doubt she'll be saying anything. I've dealt with interrogation subjects who are less tight-lipped than she is."

"Well, we've loosened a few lips before." Liam lifted an eyebrow along with the statement. "Even if it's nothing more than her being worried about being an omega, I'll rest easier knowing it."

"Torrin isn't going to be happy about her working so closely, or her having secrets."

"Torrin is never happy."

Erik couldn't argue with that. Though he thought back, because there *had* been a time—a very short one—when he'd been happy. Perhaps Torrin hadn't been laughing loudly or anything like Liam, but he'd been content. Then that had all changed and back they were, with little mattering to Torrin beyond taking care of the few he considered close.

"Do you ever think that if Torrin just—"

"Don't," Erik warned as he rose from his seat. "*What if* games are easy to play, but rarely useful."

Liam sighed, a low, sad sound. "I know. I just hate seeing him let the world pass him by."

"You can't change people who don't want to be changed."

"Like you being an insufferable bore?"

Erik offered the slightest of smiles in response to his brother's joke. "Exactly. Now, come on. Ashley won't be happy about accepting the job, and I suspect we'll do better working as a pair."

* * * *

While Ashley had thought her own apartment was amazing, she'd had no idea what was behind the door to the alphas' place.

Standing in their living room, she realized how out of her element she was.

She'd grown up modestly, but the huge windows, the expensive furnishings, the art—it all screamed money.

How can they afford all this?

She knew from her interview that they owned the company, which handled business consultations. She'd just never expected it to bring in the sort of money to have the life they lived.

Liam was in the kitchen, Torrin was working in his home office from what she'd heard — she'd yet to see him — and Erik just watched her.

Liam had stopped in at her place to ask her to join them for a conversation about her options.

Options. She hadn't had any of those in years.

She'd had to focus on nothing more than survival, yet here she was, with a nice place to live, the possibility of a job and three very handsome alphas who made her have filthy thoughts she'd never had before.

If Gregory would just leave her be, she'd have a good life. She'd get things settled, make a home...maybe even find love.

At that thought, Liam walked out of the kitchen, a wooden tray balanced on one hand and three bottles of water tucked beneath his other arm. He set the tray down on the coffee table.

Slices of meat and cheese sat in neat rows, the presentation surprisingly good. Her fathers' best attempts at presentation usually resembled school lunches.

"Don't look impressed." Liam handed her one of the water bottles as she sat on the couch. "I had the cook put it together before he left for the day."

"You have a cook?"

Liam took a seat beside her. "Erik and I can't cook and Torrin is always too busy."

Again, she felt out of her element.

Though it did give her a good path to questions she needed to ask. "What is it exactly you all do? I kind of understand from the interview, but I'm not sure of your roles."

Liam went still for a telling moment before he smiled wider. "Officially, Torrin is the CEO of Kansas Enterprises. It started out as a consultation company. Basically, businesses would contact us, and we'd come in and revamp their organization to get it running better. We'd look at marketing, at distribution, at personnel and change what needed to be changed. We still do that, but we also buy struggling companies, turn them around then sell them again once they're profitable."

"If Torrin is the CEO, what do you do?"

"Officially, security," Erik said as he sat in the chair beside the couch, placing him perpendicular to Ashley and Liam.

It was the first time she'd been around both of them, and suddenly Liam's words came back to her.

Together.

Heat licked at her cheeks when she considered what he'd said, because she couldn't think about it without picturing it. She had never felt like a small woman, yet being caught between their large and strong bodies made her feel downright tiny.

A thrumming sensation ran up her spine like a caress, her body reacting to the pictures splayed across her mind.

"It's rude to daydream." Liam's smirk accompanied the statement that shook loose her fantasies.

"I wasn't," she tried to deny, but who was she kidding? She'd never been a good liar.

Erik snorted out a derisive sound, something that called her out on the deceit before he continued to speak. *What were we talking about? Right, their jobs.*

"Unofficially, we're equal shareholders in the company. Torrin does the work on the front end while we deal with more sensitive matters. Not having our names on the building lets us handle issues a little more quietly."

"And you live together?"

Liam answered that one. "Yeah. We have since we were kids."

"But only you two..." Again, that damned warmth to her cheeks said she had turned bright red.

She drew in a breath, trying to clear her head, but instead that intoxicating scent of aroused alpha flooded in. It made it worse, whispering promises to her body that she was not at all sure she was ready for.

How could she be? She felt like an amateur skier who wanted to play around on the bunny hills and these two alphas were nothing short of the expert course.

Liam's warmth pressed against her side, him having moved closer to her on the couch. "Torrin isn't much for relationships, so yeah, it's usually just the two of us and a very lucky female. Have you been thinking about that?"

Ashley shook her head, but at least Liam didn't seem annoyed with her obvious lies.

He reached up and slid his thumb along her jawline, the touch innocent and yet full of what was to come – and she was sure it would happen, because she couldn't consider the possibility she'd miss out. "Yes, you have. Have you ever taken two alphas at once?"

Never even one.

Liam leaned in and brushed his lips over the path his thumb had traveled, and her skin went electric beneath his skillful touch. "Well, this will be fun, then.

We've done it enough, sweet, so you have nothing to worry about." He spoke in a whisper against her, his breath hot. He must have read the *no* on her face.

She should slow down. She should explain that she hadn't been with anyone before. Instead, the words wouldn't come. Would they stop? What if she had to explain *why* she hadn't, at her age? Would they decide they no longer wanted to deal with her?

The couch dipped on her other side, and a large, warm hand came to rest on her thigh. The touch made her jump, a reminder that there were now four hands to touch her, to pleasure her, to tease her.

It wasn't wrong, and she didn't have trouble with the idea of having more than one alpha—how could she when she'd been born into such a family dynamic?—but she struggled to keep up, to keep her footing.

"What's your name, Ashley?" Liam asked the question just before his lips toyed with her earlobe. He didn't just kiss it. Instead, he used his lips like the most sinful weapon, sucking her lobe then tugging softly with his teeth. Each touch sent a zap of sizzling energy through her, right to her already desperate clit.

His question confused her, which wasn't a hard thing to do, considering that her brain couldn't keep up with anything more complicated than simple math. "Ashley." The answer transformed into a moan when Erik chose that moment to nip her shoulder.

"Your real name, sweet. What you told Linda wasn't true."

Ashley closed her eyes, trying to focus on the conversation by cutting out her sight. Besides, each time she got a glimpse of either alpha, the lust washed her further away. "I didn't lie," she said.

Erik scraped his teeth across her pulse, then soothed the sting with his tongue. "You did. What are you hiding from, Ashley?"

Her hand flew out when Erik latched his lips to the spot he'd tormented, when he sucked hard there. She grasped Erik's forearm and Liam's shoulder, needing something to make her feel steady. "Nothing," she breathed out.

Erik slipped his hand up her side, over her ribcage, until he cupped her breast. The touch was intimate and new and more than a little welcome. It scrambled the rest of her thoughts, especially when he squeezed and let out a masculine groan against her neck. The spot he'd sucked ached—no doubt he'd left a mark—and each pulse from it mirrored the feeling in her cunt.

"Tell us the truth," Liam pressed when he moved his seeking fingers down to the waist of her pants, teasing along the edge. "I want to help you, but I need to know that it's nothing. Just talk to us, and you won't regret it."

Ashley opened her mouth, ready to say everything, to spill about Gregory, about the danger, about her fears. She'd do *anything* for them to keep going.

Except then she remembered. She recalled the last time she'd tried that, when she'd sat in a police station looking for help, for a lifeline, and found only people Gregory had already bought and paid for. She'd learned trust was too costly a mistake.

She couldn't risk it again.

All that lust shifted and transformed and became something ugly. *Fear.*

Ashley yanked away from the touch of the alphas, her legs shaky and her body in chaos. Her heart pounded so hard, it *hurt,* and worse yet? She struggled against wanting to take her spot between them once again. "I should go," she said in a voice that was far too weak.

Erik's gaze was steady, as always. "Just tell us. You don't want to leave. I can smell you, smell how much you want us. All you have to do is explain."

But she couldn't. The words wouldn't come, not when the price was so high.

Liam was up and off the couch a heartbeat later, crowding her with his large, muscular body. "Are you afraid of being registered? Just protecting yourself? We'd never turn you in. Hell, we can get you proper paperwork, so you don't have to work under the table anymore."

They could do that? She knew other omegas did that, got fake names, bought the identification they needed for a normal life. Ashley didn't know anyone capable of that, though, had no idea where to even start for such a thing. "You can?"

"Easily," Liam assured her.

Erik also rose, coming to stand beside Liam, again reminding her how similar the twins looked. Only their eyes gave them away. "With the paperwork, you could settle down. You wouldn't need to hide anymore."

I could be someone else, someone outside Gregory's grasp? It was so tempting to believe. Her body's reaction made it even easier, though. She wanted them, wanted the things they'd promised with their touches, and if it meant risking everything? She wasn't sure she cared.

A growl left Liam, dark and wanting. "Fuck it. We'll discuss it later, Ashley, if you'll just let us *have* you." It wasn't begging that came from Liam, and that was almost enough to make her laugh. It was a request, yet as close to a demand as one could be.

Except she remembered how out of control they made her feel, how powerless. They'd already proven they didn't mind using her wants to their advantage.

What if Liam asked again? What if he pressed for answers during? Could Ashley really deny them the truth? Could she hold strong?

Given the drenched state of her panties and her achingly hard nipples, the answer was big fat *no*.

So no matter how much she wanted them — and she did, badly — she took a step away from everything they promised and everything she had fantasized about.

Erik was the one to pursue. He pressed her against the wall to take a kiss, one she melted into. It was primal and simple, nothing but her body and his and the coursing waves of desire that passed between them.

But the fear that had swamped her hadn't quite left. Even Erik's domineering lips couldn't chase it away, and one shove to his shoulders had him backing off. His chest rose and fell quickly, his gaze predatory.

"I have to go," she said again in the most pathetic tone before slipping from their place and retreating to her own.

They promised her everything she'd ever wanted, and yet she was terrified that the price was too high.

* * * *

Torrin couldn't find the little omega. His cousins had told him what had happened, and he was not happy about them frightening her.

He trusted them with his own life—something he did not do lightly—but that didn't change that they'd been too aggressive.

Torrin wasn't thrilled with how Ashley had become so tightly entwined in their lives, but he was even less pleased with the idea of them scaring her off.

He suspected she was hiding in her apartment. The alarm on her door had shown she had entered and not left yet, but she hadn't shown up on the balcony, either.

Avoiding him as well?

It stung, but he couldn't blame her.

It wasn't as though Torrin had ever been the sort people trusted in, that they ran to for protection or comfort.

Not that he should be trusted by most. A few, though? So few he would run out of names before fingers if he counted them, but those that were included, he'd do anything for.

His cousins, of course. Kara, the omega who was almost a sister to him. And somehow Ashley had landed herself on that list. It seemed he didn't need a second hand to count them.

Worse? Liam and Erik, despite their prodding and scheming, hadn't truly learned a thing. She was off the grid, as many omegas were, but that didn't explain why she had reacted as she had.

Was she simply afraid of them? But then why stay there? A name put her in no worse danger than living next door would.

Torrin sat in the chair on the shared balcony, just as he had the night before. His phone hung heavy in his pocket, especially because he'd suddenly started carrying it with him at all times.

Suddenly? Don't lie to yourself. It was about Ashley. He didn't want Linda to answer the phone for him. He didn't want to risk Ashley calling and having him not answer.

And right then, the phone beckoned him to reach out. Her old phone had been turned off, but during her interview with Linda, they'd given her another one.

Before he could talk himself out of it, he hit the saved contact. *I am simply calling because Liam and Erik upset her. She is, after all, living beside us, and will soon begin working for us. This is business. Nothing more.*

Even Torrin winced at how untrue that was.

"Hello?" Fear wrapped around the single word that came from the other end of the line.

"It's Torrin."

A breath rattled across the phone, as though his name relieved her.

And why did that cause some strange warmth in his chest?

"Sorry," she said. "I wasn't expecting anyone to call. I should have figured you'd have my number."

"Do you want to come outside? I have tea." He cringed at the clumsy offer.

Silence came over the line, the denial loud and clear before she spoke. "No. That's probably not a good idea."

And just like that, Torrin decided his cousins deserved a far worse reaction than a stern lecture.

Still, Torrin settled into the chair and set his cane aside. Even if she didn't come out, that didn't end the conversation. "I'm sorry for the behavior of my cousins. They wouldn't want you to feel uncomfortable, or worse, unsafe." He tried to keep his voice soft and reassuring. "They would never force you, never do anything you didn't want them to — "

"I know." Her response was quick, as though to shut down the conversation. "I don't know what they said, but it wasn't like that."

"You're clearly uncomfortable now, which means they didn't act appropriately. I want you to feel safe here."

"I do." The response did not sound like a lie — and he'd found her to be a terrible liar — but it was still said with hesitation. He could hardly blame her for that. She knew little about them. How could she fully feel safe with males who were strangers?

"So why won't you come outside?" He paused, then frowned. "Is it me who makes you uneasy?"

Another pause, filled only with the soft breathing from her, as though she was sorting her thoughts out.

"I only want to help — "

"I'm a virgin."

His cock grew painfully hard immediately, before his mind had the chance to even fully understand the words.

She's a virgin? Why did that matter? Torrin had sworn off her already, yet the strange possessiveness swamped him as he thought about her being untouched by another.

A growl left him like some primal response.

Perhaps it was good she hadn't come out.

"That's why I left," she said softly. Whether she'd heard the growl, he had no idea. "I wasn't ready, and it was overwhelming. They weren't being pushy, but I didn't know how to explain that, either. They made me feel out of control."

He closed his eyes and tried to sound unaffected. "You're twenty-four years old. How are you still a virgin?"

"I had protective fathers, then it was never the right time. During my heats, I'd just take sedatives." Her words came out defensive.

"So you left because of that, not because you were afraid of Erik and Liam?"

"Are they mad?"

Her sullen question charmed him. "No, they aren't mad. Confused and feeling guilty, but not mad. They'll understand better once they're told. Might I give you some unasked-for advice?"

"Might as well. It isn't as if I'm doing a great job on my own."

"You are a horrible liar, so try to be honest, at least with us. You might be surprised how much simpler things become."

Her reactions made more sense as he thought back. Where they were worried about her being in danger, fear over her own reaction could account for much of the odd behavior. Over-protective parents, possibly pushing for an early mating—as was common with omegas—could easily be the reason for her fake name.

It all made sense.

"Do you want to come outside, now? The tea is still warm."

"You're easier to talk to on the phone." A rustle of fabric on the other side of the line spawned images in his head.

He pictured her in the far-too-tempting shirts she wore in the evenings. Her curvy legs, her large chest, her innocent eyes…they all made him hold in a groan. The fabric was possibly the blankets on the bed, and he could see her tucked in there, her brown hair fanned out around her. *Stop thinking about it.*

He drew his attention back to the conversation. "I'm not so bad in person, am I?"

"You're unnerving."

"I've been called worse." Usually he didn't mind it, but right then? He didn't care for the description.

"I just feel like I can't read you, but it always seems like you can read me. It's like you can see right through me. It's intense."

Intense. Was there a better word? One that held more sinful undertones while being innocent on the surface?

It brought forth all the intense things he'd love to show her, especially since she apparently didn't know them.

Instead, however, Torrin buried that down deep enough that he hoped she couldn't hear the want in his voice. "Well, I don't mean to unnerve you. I'm just not used to having nervous omegas around."

His attempt at the dry joke seemed to work when she chuckled softly. "Really? I mean, you have the perfect little set-up here to put up a convenient woman across the hallway. I can't believe you've never done that."

Torrin eased back further, surprised by how comfortable he felt speaking with her. He wasn't a man who spoke much, usually being more than happy to let others do the talking and to let his actions speak for themselves. However, Ashley's voice helped him relax. He even pretended for a useless moment that they were not so far apart, that rather than being on the phone, they were in a dark room, only inches of space between them while they lounged in bed.

"Believe it or not, you are the first. Not that Erik and Liam haven't shared females in the past, but it's been casual for a very long time."

"This is casual," she pointed out.

"You don't really believe that."

She released a soft breath before changing the subject. "And you? You keep talking about them, but you've never moved a woman in here either?"

Torrin thought back to the last woman he'd cared for, the last one he'd seen more than once, the one after which he'd made his rule of one-night stands. "My life is complicated, and romance isn't something I can afford."

Or any woman I care about can afford.

He remembered the blood the most. Funny that after so many years, he couldn't get *that* part out of his mind. He'd seen plenty of bodies, plenty of death in his life.

The first time, he couldn't have been more than six, and he'd walked into a room just in time to see his uncle shoot another man. That memory, like so many others, brought forth nothing. He wasn't sorry, wasn't angry, didn't feel cheated. It had been his life, had shaped him into the man he'd become.

But the blood that had spread out from Gilly's body — *that* threatened to break through his icy exterior.

At least it reminded him of the truth of his situation. It was too dangerous.

Ashley yawned, the sound enough to break loose his negative thoughts.

"You should probably get some sleep," he forced himself to say, despite how little he wanted to get off the phone.

"You're always trying to send me to bed."

I wish I was in that bed, too. He growled softly at his own unruly thoughts. Normally, he had better control of himself. "You strike me as the type who doesn't always take care of yourself. Lucky for you, I not only don't mind telling you what to do, but I excel at it."

She let out another soft laugh, and he could *feel* her smile through the phone line. "I've taken care of myself for a while now, but it is nice to talk, so maybe you'd give me a bit of an extension on the bedtime?"

Torrin didn't fight the full smile that tugged at his lips as he picked up his cup of tea. If she wanted to talk to him, he was pretty sure he'd talk all night.

Chapter Six

Ashley hung up the phone after having smoothed out a scheduling issue with an irate client. He'd started out fuming, but by the end, he'd changed his tune and been thanking her.

Working felt nice. Not just working under the table, not just trying to survive, but doing work she enjoyed. The alphas had picked something absolutely perfect for her. She felt useful, challenged, and even after just her first morning of work, she hadn't felt so content since before she'd first been driven from her home.

Maybe even before then.

She'd yet to see the alphas, and Renee had set her up, given her access to the scheduling apps, and by ten in the morning had taken off, complaining of sore feet.

Which had left Ashley alone for the past three hours, during which she'd done everything scheduled for the day and more.

Her stomach grumbled, and it reminded her that she'd yet to take lunch.

Though she also had another three weeks before she expected her first paycheck. She'd grown used to getting cash from working under the table, so she had no real idea how she'd feed herself.

There was food in the fridge of the apartment, so she could easily move to one meal a day to make it stretch.

The math she was doing in her head halted when the door opened and Liam walked in. He offered a sinful smirk, one that melted her.

He held up a bag. "You haven't taken lunch."

"Were you spying on me?"

Liam shut the door to the office behind him before placing the bag on the desk.

The office was like most other things she'd seen from them—impressive. A large window sat along the back wall, and the desk was huge.

Liam took boxes from the bag, spreading them across the desk. "Of course. I did tell you Erik and I handle security." Liam popped open the lids and the scent of food wafted out.

"How much do you think I eat? There's enough to feed six here."

"Didn't know what you like." He pointed at the different boxes—a salad in one, chili fries in another, hamburgers in yet another. Box after box revealed options of every sort.

"There's way too much," Ashley said.

Liam shrugged. "Torrin is like a mother hen sometimes."

Torrin did this? The thought stilled her. Gregory had attempted to help a few times, especially at the start, before she'd run away, but he'd always demanded appreciation for his actions. Once he'd bought her a car, making a huge show of bringing it over, of making sure she knew exactly how much he'd done. It had been one of a hundred red flags she should have seen sooner.

Torrin, however, had done this without even showing up, without mentioning it. He'd done the same with the furniture, content to take care of her without her even knowing.

Liam pulled out a chair of his own, then pointed at the food. "Hurry up and pick something, because I'm starving."

Ashley laughed before grabbing the hamburger.

Liam pulled the fries over to him and sat as well, making it clear he planned to eat there with her.

And she couldn't say she minded it.

Erik was exhausted by the time he reached Ashley's office. Liam had sent him a text message letting him know about lunch, but he couldn't get away from his meeting.

Some contacts were easy to handle — people who gave him what he needed without trouble, either because they wanted to stay on his good side or because they wanted something from him.

Then there were the others, ones who required far too much of his time. One such meeting had stolen hours of his morning.

It meant when he entered the office, his mood was far darker than normal and he had no doubt the food had grown cold.

A single look at Ashley, however, sparked something inside him. It was as though, with nothing more than a look, she could help him slide off that weight.

Her hair was pulled back from her face, showing off her blue eyes and her flushed cheeks.

Just what were they talking about to draw a blush like that?

Torrin's warning echoed in his ears. *She's a virgin?* He recalled how her skin had tasted, the sweetness that had clung to her when he'd scraped his teeth over her pulse. How she was still a virgin he didn't know, and he couldn't quite wrap his head around his own opinion of it.

While he'd be a fool to not admit he liked the idea, he also groaned at the reality. Being taken by Liam and him for the first time was not ideal.

Virgins should have their first time with someone they love. It should be awkward and sweet and memorable. It shouldn't be with killers who are lying to her about who they are.

Not that *should* had ever kept him from what he wanted.

Shoulds were for other people, for those who gave a damn about social niceties. That wasn't a world he'd ever lived in.

Which meant he had no doubt that the sweet little omega there wouldn't be a virgin all that much longer, especially with how she'd melted at their touch.

A loud gulp from Ashley made Erik realize he'd been standing in that doorway for far too long, all but eye-fucking her.

Instead of apologizing, Erik simply shut the door and took a seat at the large desk.

Liam pushed a box of food over to him. Heat radiated from it when Erik popped the top, and he frowned at it.

"Torrin ordered this one later."

Of course he did. Torrin always is one step ahead, isn't he? Inside the box sat lasagna—Erik's favorite—and he couldn't stop a small grin. Nothing ever got past Torrin, including that Erik would be late. He must have ordered it for later so it would stay warm.

"How has your first day been?" Erik took a fork and ate while he waited for Ashley to fill in the conversation.

"It's been okay."

"She's being modest," Liam offered. "She's already done more than a day's worth of work. She even made Hardwitch happy."

Erik lifted an eyebrow. "Hardwitch is never happy. Just how did you manage that one?"

Ashley dropped her gaze. *Embarrassed?* "He isn't that bad."

"He made a temp cry and quit the first day."

"Maybe they were just sensitive—"

"The temp's last job was in the army."

Ashley paused, as if trying to decide if he was being serious, before breaking into a soft laugh.

He *was* being serious, but he'd let her think it was a joke.

She smiled, her food already set away. "I can read people pretty well. He wants to be the smartest person in the room, but he wants other people to know it. It wasn't too hard to get him on board with the meeting change."

"Better keep an eye on her," Liam said, sitting back in his seat. "She's charming enough that if we aren't careful, she might just talk us right out of our pants."

Ashley's mouth fell open before she stuttered out something that didn't a make a lot of sense. After a moment, she tried again. "You can't just say that."

"Why not? I remember how you smelled last night, how you teased us. We were just trying to give you a job offer, and I've got say, I don't think your behavior was all that appropriate." Liam's grin was broad across his lips.

"That's not what happened!"

"That's how I remember it. Erik?"

While Erik didn't love games as much as Liam did, he had to admit, he enjoyed Ashley's reaction. "I'm afraid there might have to be a discussion with HR about it."

Ashley reached over and pushed Liam's shoulder in a playful shove, to which Liam captured her wrist. He tugged her until she sat in his lap, her back to his chest.

She wiggled, but his strong arm kept her in place.

"Relax," Liam all but purred. "Your chair just didn't seem very comfortable."

"And your lap is?"

"Yes, it is. Though if you keep wiggling, you'll find it isn't quite as soft."

Her gasp was scandalized, and Erik found his mouth dry and his appetite gone. He thought back to his last time indulging in a female.

Months?

Things had been so busy, he'd hardly had time to think, let alone have fun. The last 'fun' had been a redhead he and Liam found in one of the shadier bars in the city. She'd been fun, and her nails in his back had helped to stave off the loneliness.

However, he had a feeling it would be nothing compared to the woman who had gone still in Liam's lap.

Liam's lips played against her earlobe. "Are you really a virgin, sweet?"

A tiny shiver ran through her, her eyes closing as she nodded.

The way she lost herself to desire fascinated him. The tiniest touch and she no longer seemed capable of thinking straight. The all-encompassing reaction was maddening.

"Good girl," Liam praised as he slipped his hands along her waist and ribs. "So how far have you gone? We can play the bases game." He brushed the undercurve of her breast through her button-up shirt, rewarded with a gasping moan.

Erik pushed aside his food and flipped the lock before crossing the office, moving around the desk so he could position himself just in front of them. The movement of Liam's hands was like magic, skirting across her without touching anything too personal, as though each was nothing more than a promising tease.

"I haven't…" There went that red on her cheeks again. Why was her shyness so attractive?

Erik reached out and caught her chin, the action making her snap her eyes open. "Have you been fingered? Oral?"

Her head shook, and he hardened painfully with each denial, each thing she'd never done, each one he wanted to show her.

"Kissed?" That one got a nod, but he paused. "Besides us, I mean."

She blew out a soft moan when Liam's fingers teased up the side of her full breast. "Once."

The tone said it wasn't a memorable time, which let Erik write off the instance as not needing him to track down the fucker who had taken her first kiss.

"So you're not just a virgin, huh? You are entirely innocent." Liam pressed his lips to her neck in a gentle kiss.

"I'm not a child," she complained, though any heat was stolen from it when Liam teased his fingers beneath the fabric of her shirt in the space between the buttons. Her large chest, pushed out as it was in an unconscious offer, pulled at the buttons until the shirt gaped. She sounded delightful when she moaned.

Erik and Liam never minded a bit of dominance. Some girls required a firm hand. They got off on having someone there to lead them. Erik enjoyed that, though he had no love for brats who pushed just to push. Funny, given how hard-assed he was in general, but he much preferred a submissive woman who *wanted* to be taken, to please, rather than a woman he'd have to fight every inch of the way.

Ashley seemed just the sort girl he liked.

"Trust me, I know you aren't a child," Liam assured her as he teased the skin peeking through the tiny gaps in her shirt. He set his other hand on her hip and pulled her more firmly into his lap, and her widened eyes said Liam was making it clear how much he wanted her. "Though, I'm thinking a little show and tell might not be out of line right about now."

"Show and tell?" Confusion saturated her words.

But Erik knew *exactly* where this was headed, and he was all in for it.

And Ashley? She looked like the best snack he fully planned on devouring.

How could they do this to her *again*? It had gone from an innocent lunch to Erik locking the door while she was perched in Liam's lap.

She'd always been someone who took things slowly, who was careful. She thought everything through and *never* acted rashly.

So how was it that every tiny touch from these two could turn her to fire?

Erik slid off the jacket to his suit, and his shirt showed off his impressive physique.

Liam didn't stop teasing her with his touches, stroking along the bottom curve and side of her breast but avoiding her pointed, desperate nipples. She shifted, the action causing his rigid erection to rub against her.

She wanted to keep shifting, to grind down until she could get him to tease her clit enough to throw her over that edge.

She might have no experience with sex, but she could get herself off, and using him seemed a great idea. Except, she couldn't bring herself to do it, to admit she wanted that. It felt like a different woman who would do that, some vixen.

Erik undid the buttons of his shirt, and each one parted the material to show his tan skin. Scars sat there, tiny white lines that only made him more attractive. *How did he get those?* He tugged the fabric so it wasn't tucked into his pants, but didn't remove it. It hung open down the front and gave her a hell of a sight. When he reached for the fastening at the waist of his pants, her breath stilled.

"I don't think I'll ever get enough of that scent," Liam whispered into her ear. "You look and act like this naive, innocent little thing, but then you just warm up so fast. Are you wet, sweet?"

Yes. She was drenched and she knew it.

Liam chuckled as his brother worked down his zipper. "Of course you are. Don't worry—we'll take good care of you."

Erik parted the fabric of his pants and shifted them down, taking his boxers along with them. He didn't remove them entirely, just enough so his cock was free.

And the moan Ashley let out was so embarrassingly loud, she had to believe the other offices around could hear it.

Erik's cock was thick, the skin darker than the rest of him, and it curved slightly toward his body. He was long, with a thatch of dark, curly hair at his groin.

Her mouth watered at the sight. What would he feel like? Would the skin be warm beneath her touch? *How does he taste?*

Something wrapped around her wrist, and it took a moment to realize she'd reached for Erik. Liam's hand grasped hers, and he pulled it back, trapping both her hands behind her back. "It's look but don't touch," he said into her ear with no shortage of humor.

Erik didn't stop, didn't slow. He wrapped a large hand around his cock and stroked himself slowly, a deep groan leaving him as if the feeling were the best thing in the world.

"Look at you," Liam said. "So desperate, aren't you? I guess it isn't a surprise, being a virgin at your age. You must be pretty pent-up."

Ashley shifted in Liam's lap, her pride nothing compared to how much she needed some relief. She shamelessly rubbed herself against Liam's dick, her gaze locked on Erik's mouthwatering length.

Liam moved her hands so they crossed behind her back, then pinned her against him so she couldn't move her arms. He cupped her heavy, aching breasts in his large, strong hands, squeezing for a moment before working the buttons of her shirt loose. "You'd get yourself off just like this, wouldn't you? Rutting against me because you can't wait another moment?"

A spark of embarrassment started in her, but somehow it mixed with her want and only made her burn hotter. She *liked* that edge of humiliation, especially when it washed over her along with Liam's voice.

Her shirt opened beneath Liam's coaxing hands, and he hardly spared a momentary stroke of his fingers over the line of her bra before venturing beneath, into the cups to finger her pebbled nipples.

Liam rolled them between his warm, rough fingers and pushed the fabric of her bra out of the way.

She was sitting in the lap of an alpha she barely knew, her shirt open and his hands on her breasts while she was at *work*. Another alpha stroked his cock inches away from her, and the only reason it hadn't gone further was that they hadn't let her take it further.

Again, she questioned her sanity. She questioned the effect they had on her.

Not that any of it mattered, because she couldn't stop just how much she *needed* this.

Erik stroked himself faster, though he would stop at the base and offer a squeeze, as though for no reason other than her viewing pleasure.

And what a view it was. She'd watched porn before, knew what men looked like unclothed, but it hadn't ever sparked any interest in her. It had been clinical, like reading a book on biology. She'd even wondered if she was sexual at all, because she hadn't felt anything from watching.

Now, though? Despite Erik masturbating in front of her hardly being the most risqué thing she'd ever seen—at least in porn—it had her pussy clenching in want.

Erik's growl was dark, and when Ashley jerked her gaze to his, she went breathless. He reminded her of a wolf she'd seen in the woods once. Its golden eyes had glowed from the flicker of the campfire, wild and untamed.

Erik's eyes held that same fire.

Liam tightened his fingers around her nipples in a pinch that forced her hips to roll again, the delicious friction from his erection helping her get impossibly closer but not *quite* there.

"Do you need some help, sweet?" How could Liam's voice sound so coaxing and yet be so filthy?

"Yes." Her rough voice gave away just how badly she needed him. Needed *them*.

Liam released one nipple and moved that hand down. He tucked it between her legs, which she spread as if she didn't even have to think about it. He didn't reach for her pants button, bypassing that and cupping her pussy through the slacks instead.

"Fuck," he groaned. "She's on fire."

Erik's gaze drifted lower until he stared where Liam's hand covered her cunt. "I can't wait until we get her completely naked. If her breasts are this good, just imagine what she's hiding between those thighs of hers."

Their words were even more dangerous than their touches, or so Ashley thought, until Liam shifted his grasp so his fingers rubbed up her pussy to find her clit.

The shocking sensation of the strong touch made her jerk backward and gasp, as if her entire body were alive and drowning in lust.

Liam didn't stop, only choosing to chuckle at her response as he ground two fingers against her needy clit through her clothing.

Erik stroked his cock faster, his fist working up and over the thick head then back down. A glistening on his length said he'd spread his pre-cum over his shaft, and her tongue itched to taste it.

Not that she could do anything, with the way Liam had pinned her.

The muscles of her thighs twitched as Liam shoved her toward a frightening release. Everything inside her coiled tighter, as if Liam could wind her up from those simple touches.

Erik moved closer, close enough she could have leaned forward and touched him. He trapped her with his gaze, the cords of his neck standing out before he released a deep growl and came, painting stripes of white over her chest just as Liam released her breast and captured her chin, forcing her gaze to stay on Erik.

The heat and scent of Erik's cum were the last straw, the thing that stole away any ability she had to resist the pleasure coursing through her. She snapped, her release so powerful it crashed over her, stealing her breath, her thoughts, her power. Her thighs closed around Liam's hand, but he kept grinding his fingers against her clit, kept the rising and falling pleasure going until she feared she'd drown beneath it.

It was an epiphany, like the world opening up, or perhaps some part of her that she'd never recognized before waking. She dragged in a ragged breath as soon as all that tension inside her melted away, and she leaned against Liam's strong form.

His lips toyed with the side of her neck, the warmth of his breath helping her to slow her heart rate.

As the chaos in her body eased, as she opened her eyes to find Erik still staring down at her, as the lust from the moment of insanity drifted away, she had to face how monumentally stupid this had been.

And how much I want it to happen again.

Chapter Seven

Liam doubted their apartment had ever felt quite so much like *home*.

Which made him laugh, since they'd lived there a long time. When Kara had been there as well, for those short years before she'd moved out, it had felt more welcoming, at least. With only the three of them, though, it was somewhere to sleep, a place where their things stayed.

Suddenly, however, he'd been excited to get back. He wanted to see Ashley, to touch her again, to bask in her scent.

Which seemed fair, as he'd been the only one not to get off the day before. Good thing he enjoyed a bit of deprivation. The delicious want that coursed through him, that had grown all day, was worth a bit of discomfort.

They'd left her be after their lunch break, not wanting to crowd her. She'd taken the car home at a reasonable hour, but the alphas had far too many things to do still. It meant it had been over twenty-four hours since Liam had actually laid eyes on Ashley, and he found he missed her.

Erik, Liam and Torrin had finished their work and returned to the apartment, with Ashley needing to run an errand. Despite their offering to go with her, she'd declined.

Liam understood, though. She'd gone from living on her own to having three alphas constantly looking over her shoulder. She had worked at the bar already, so her going there to collect her final paycheck wasn't exactly dangerous.

Besides, she'd agreed to meet them for dinner at the apartment afterward. He didn't want to press his luck.

"Ashley seems to like Torrin." Erik tossed a tennis ball against the far wall then caught it on the rebound.

Liam cocked up an eyebrow, then turned a mocking grin toward his twin. "Jealousy doesn't suit you."

Erik threw the ball harder, and the smack as it struck his palm was sharp. "You know I'm not jealous. It's just…" He cursed softly. "Never mind."

Liam rolled his eyes. They'd never moved past that, past Erik being closed off and Liam trying to yank the truth from him.

Which was funny, because Liam was the only one Erik *ever* shared with. He told Torrin things, but never as much. Their bond was something no one else understood, but that didn't mean Liam wouldn't have to coax Erik to talk openly.

"Out with it," Liam said.

Erik turned a glare in Liam's direction then threw the ball once more. "Torrin won't give in, but he's going to end up leading her on."

"He's difficult, but do you really think he's stubborn enough to say no to her?"

Even as Liam spoke, he had to wonder. Torrin *was* hardheaded. Worse, he resisted because he thought he was protecting them. If it was just him generally being a stubborn ass, it would be different, easier to work around. Since his entire thought process was taking care of others, however, he'd grasp that self-imposed denial with everything he had.

"Do you remember back before Gilly?" Erik sat on the couch, switching so he just tossed the ball up and caught it.

Liam did, of course. It had been before Kara, before tragedy had struck. Things had been different.

They'd never been overly optimistic people. How could they be, with their history being what it was? All three of them had survived hell as children and doing so had taught them that life was rarely what a person deserved. Still, they'd gotten out from beneath the horror of their childhood. They'd started to build something. They'd been a real trio.

Then Torrin had found Gilly and everything had changed. He'd taken a mate, and for a short while, things had been happy. It hadn't lasted, though, and Torrin hadn't crawled back out from his grief yet.

"He'll never move past it," Liam said. "He doesn't even want to."

Erik cast a deadpan look his way. "Coming from you?"

"What are you talking about? I'm an open book. You both wear trauma like a medal of honor. Torrin has Gilly, and you have Beth. You have the brooding asshole thing down." Liam kept a far-too-wide smile across his lips.

Erik snorted softly. "Of course. That's why you kept sleeping with Kara."

At that, tension crept into Liam. He curled his lip up into a half-hearted snarl. Some topics were just off limits, and that should have been one of them. "She needed help. Not my fault I was the only one willing to do it."

"Right," Erik said, his tone full of *you liar*. "Maybe we're all too fucked up. Maybe we should send Ashley on her way to find people who don't have as many hang-ups as we do."

"Do you really think you can do that? Because I can't exactly bring myself to even think about sending her off." Liam leaned back, able to relax with the subject of Kara off the table.

"Neither can I, but where does that leave us? You know Torrin will argue."

"Yeah, but there are two of us. We've always been able to outsmart him if we work together."

Erik twisted to look at Liam, then huffed a soft laugh, the sound rare from him. "Well, I suppose we've done more difficult things."

The office door opening signaled that Torrin had finished his call, and Liam grinned.

More difficult, sure, but he suspected this might just be one of the most fun.

* * * *

Ashley blew out a hard breath while she waited in the bar she'd worked at only a few days before. *Funny how quickly things changed.*

Carla wiped down the counter, the hour being too early for many customers. Only the old regulars were there, which was the reason Ashley had picked that time.

She'd taken the car and driver to pick up her money from the last night and to say goodbye.

She almost regretted not bringing Liam along with her. The company would have been nice, and the bar didn't feel as safe as it had before. Still, she needed a little space, a chance to breathe on her own.

"You're here for your pay?" Carla turned toward Ashley.

"Yeah."

"Girls like you never last long in places like these." Carla reached below the bar and pulled out an envelope. "I already had this all made up and ready for you."

When Ashley reached out to take the envelope, Carla snatched it out of reach. "The thing it, I had an interesting visitor last night."

Ashley froze at those words. *A visitor? It can only mean…*

Carla leaned her hip against the bar. "Yeah. He gave me a pretty good offer if I could give him information about a pretty brunette named Ashley. He had a picture. Looked just like you."

"What did you tell him?"

"Told him I didn't know you."

That let Ashley pull in a rough breath. "Thank you so much—"

"Not so fast, sweetheart. He offered me a lot, and I could really use that money. I'd just as soon keep your secret, but money doesn't come easily."

Ashley wrung her hands together. "I don't have anything."

Carla tapped her fingers on the envelope. "Why don't you just have me keep what's in here? It's not all that much, but it's something."

Ashley tried not to let the hurt show on her face. Yet again, she'd been betrayed. She didn't consider Carla and herself friends, but that didn't ease the sting. The envelope would have had a few hundred in it, the money from her regular hourly pay plus the training hours. She really needed that, since she had access to nothing until her first check at the new job.

It was still an easy choice, though. Ashley nodded.

Carla tucked the envelope into the pocket of her apron. "Well then, good luck with wherever you're running off to now."

"You won't tell him anything?"

"Not a word."

Ashley tugged her coat around her and left the bar, trying her hardest to not cry as she was forced to remember the lesson she just seemed to refuse to learn. No matter how many times she went through this, how many times she suffered for it, there was one real truth to the world.

She couldn't trust anyone.

And that included the alphas.

* * * *

Torrin couldn't ignore the sense that Ashley was off when she returned from her errand.

She seemed on edge and distracted. According to Linda, she had settled in well to her job, hadn't had any issues there. Perhaps it was just the adjustments, the changes. He had found her difficult to read, which was funny, since she didn't lie well.

He sat at the table as they ate, though he'd been tempted to take his food to his office. Not because anything was pressing, but because it would limit his exposure to her, to his cousins, to what they all had that he was on the outside of.

He'd stared at his plate, however, as the others had sat and he hadn't been able to bring himself to leave.

"You're telling me you actually *like* cream of wheat?" Liam pointed his fork at Ashley. "No one likes that. They just eat it when they can't chew oatmeal anymore."

"Well, I like it," she answered, and despite the odd conversation, she smiled.

The ease of the conversation, of how they all sat together, made Torrin fidget. Things never came easily, and they certainly didn't end happily.

But what if it could?

"I'm telling the chef to never make that. Don't worry, we'll retrain your taste buds into something that works."

Ashley leaned over to push Liam's shoulder, the touch innocent and the sort of thing she seemed to do more and more. Was a playful touch like that easier for her to do? Easier to pretend it was nothing?

Liam didn't seem willing to allow the simple contact to go unchallenged, though. He caught her wrist and tugged her toward him until he could capture a kiss.

It was hardly the chaste kiss that often happened between partners at dinner. Instead, this was a prelude to something more. It was a claim and a tease all in one.

More than that, it was a *show*.

It was made all the clearer when Liam twisted toward Torrin after the kiss ended to offer a smirk.

And for Ashley's part, she looked smitten and slightly drugged by the action. Then again, she often reacted that way when confronted with any of the carnal pleasures.

Torrin wondered what she'd look like when she came. Her skin flushed when she was embarrassed, so he'd bet it would turn a pretty pink over her chest and cheeks. Would she cry out or go silent? Would she twist and thrash or would she freeze?

He tore his gaze away from her when she offered a startled look his way, a reminder that his wants were not quite as secret to her as he'd have liked them to be.

Omega noses were hard to trick.

He stared at his food instead, and tried to feel less like the interloper, the one who didn't belong, the one who *couldn't* belong.

"What about your family?" Erik's voice broke into the tension. "I know, no names. Keep your secrets but tell us how you grew up."

Ashley took long enough to answer that Torrin risked looking her way. She'd switched her attention from him, thankfully, and a smile full of pain rested on her lips. "My fathers raised me."

"Fathers?" Liam asked. "That explains why you didn't complain too much at the idea of more than one mate."

Mate. The word made everyone at the table go still, like something Liam shouldn't have muttered, hadn't meant to mutter, but had still loosed.

Ashley tiptoed forward with her answer, ignoring the title. "My mom died when I was too little to remember her, so it was just my fathers and me after that."

"How many would that be?"

"Five."

Liam snorted softly. "Five mates? Your mother must have been one tough woman."

"I wouldn't know. I don't remember her, and if you listened to my fathers, you'd think she was a saint. I don't think they ever really got over losing her."

"That's how bonds work," Torrin offered before his brain caught up to what his mouth was saying. "Death doesn't break them. It's like have a rope that ties around you and someone else. Even though the other person is gone, that rope still dangles, it still catches on things, it still trips you."

The silence in response told Torrin he'd said too much. He never spoke of Gilly, so why had he blurted that out?

Liam picked up the conversation before Ashley could ask, and it reminded Torrin why his cousins mattered to him. They saved him as often as he did them. "Sounds like a good family. Can't imagine why you'd have left."

"I didn't want to," she said, voice dropping low. "Sometimes things go in ways we don't want, though, and there's nothing we can do about them."

"Whatever the problem is, we can help," Erik said, mirroring Torrin's thought.

Kids ran away for many reasons, even from loving homes, from good families. Whatever had convinced Ashley that she had no choice could be dealt with, and Torrin was all for doing so.

Her expression said she didn't believe them. Then again, could he blame her? She knew nothing about who they *actually* were, what they could do. If she did...

He sighed. If she did, she'd likely run from them as well.

She was far too soft-hearted for their world.

Better to keep her in the dark and safe.

Liam rose and pressed a kiss to Ashley's head — the action surprisingly sweet — before he gathered her plate and his. "I'm thinking a movie. Comedy. Torrin, won't you help Ashley pick something while we clean the table?"

Torrin turned a less-than-subtle-glare on Liam.

He was not fooled by the flimsy excuse to get Torrin and Ashley alone, and to tempt Torrin to spend more time with them.

Yet, as much as he knew the ploy, as much as he knew he should ignore it, Torrin couldn't quite say no.

Instead, he found himself rising, gaze on Ashley, willing to do the menial task if it meant just a bit more time together.

Which was a very bad sign.

Ashley had to admit, she enjoyed the movie.

Well, not so much the movie itself. It was a comedy she'd picked, but she hadn't known anything about it. As it turned out, the plot was a thinly thought out rom-com, and the entire romantic vibe hadn't been what she'd wanted.

However, sitting between Liam and Erik had been far nicer than she'd expected. Their bodies were warm and solid, and it hadn't taken much before she'd leaned against Liam and Erik's hand found its way to her thigh.

Torrin didn't sit on the large couch, instead perching in an armchair to the side. That seemed common for him, to be near the group but not quite a part of it. In fact, she was surprised he'd even agreed to watch the movie. His desire to say no had been written all over his face, yet he'd stayed.

Liam's fingers distracted Ashley as they skimmed over her leg, drawing designs that she couldn't identify or ignore. They also moved up, toward the juncture of her thighs, and it was as though nothing else existed beyond those exploring fingers. The movie drifted away, the room, the worries, all of it disappearing.

He reached where her thighs pressed together, sliding along the crease there but not pressing in. Even that gentle stroke forced a thin, soft moan from her lips.

It wasn't even the touch itself, but the promise there, the reminder of how they'd made her feel before.

Not afraid.

It had been the first time in years she hadn't felt any fear, that she hadn't looked over her shoulder, that she hadn't been thinking about Gregory and her safety, and what she'd lost. She hadn't had to be anyone except herself.

They managed to chase those things away and replace them with something that felt dangerously close to hope.

Liam huffed a soft laugh at the sound. "Do you have any idea how sweet you are? Because, damn, that sound is addictive." He pressed his lips to her throat, the feeling already familiar. She *really* liked his lips. They were coaxing and reassuring. It felt like he was leading her, like his kiss was a crooked finger. It frightened her how much she wanted to follow.

Liam shifted so he could take her lips in the sort of kiss that could have talked her into anything. His tongue teased at the seam of her lips, and as always, she followed. She parted to let him in. He distracted her, and her thighs spread when she couldn't worry or think about it.

That gave Erik the access he seemed to want, the movie forgotten in the throes of their touches.

Erik stroked along her slit through the fabric of her leggings, and despite the layers of clothing, she felt it as though she were bare.

It drew a gasp from her, one that Liam swallowed before breaking the kiss.

A growl tugged her attention over, and her cheeks heated. *Torrin.*

She'd entirely forgotten him, unable to focus on anything beyond the twins. He sat in his chair, the room dark except for the movie, his eyes lit by the glow of the television. He looked like a beast, like a monster, especially with the deep growl that filled the room.

Despite him saying he wasn't interested, despite all his denials, the want in those glowing dark eyes said differently.

It rooted her in place, made her question what to do.

"I should go," Torrin said, his voice so rough she wouldn't have recognized it. He'd lost that elegant edge.

"Why?" Erik's fingers caught the bottom hem of Ashley's shirt, then he met her gaze, a question there.

Him giving her a choice helped her push aside her nerves, and she responded with a tiny nod.

He pulled the shirt up and over her head, then tossed it away.

A chill from the room ran along her newly exposed skin, teasing her as much as the stares of the three alphas.

That growl increased, and Torrin's fingers dug into the armrests of the chair.

So much for acting unaffected.

"You know why," Torrin said.

"Even if you *can't* touch, why leave?" Liam said 'can't' as though mocking Torrin.

The entire conversation didn't make a lot of sense to Ashley, but thankfully, Erik continued to slide his fingers in light strokes against her cunt, so she didn't care what they were talking about.

Liam reached behind her and undid the hooks of her bra, pulling it free and discarding it with the shirt. Her nipples responded, going taut from the cold and from Liam's hungry gaze. "Pretty," he all but purred before palming one of her heavy breasts and lowering toward it.

The first touch of his hot mouth felt like a baptism, like yet another time he'd broken her and reshaped her.

Erik moved his fingers to the waist of her leggings, and she lifted to help as he pulled them down her legs. She didn't worry about how she looked, but the thought of being naked still drew a shiver. It was yet another line she would cross, another risk she would take.

Liam huffed when he pulled away from her, and his look said he'd caught her hesitation. *How? How can he read me that well?*

He stroked his hands up her sides, his thumbs brushing the bottom curve of her bare breasts. "I'd tell you that you can trust us, but you won't listen. I guess we'll just have to prove it to you."

When he pulled back, Erik set a hand on Liam's arm to stop him. "I don't think so. You got to touch last time."

Liam laughed softly. "Are you really saying it's your turn? What are we, five?"

The bickering was almost funny, the two sounding like brothers for the first time.

Her laughter died, however, when Erik moved off the couch and dropped to his knees in front of her.

Again, she was reminded how different the twins were. Whereas every touch of Liam's was a tease, Erik moved into his spot with the single-minded focus of a man who planned to take.

And she *wanted* him to take everything.

Even so, she held her knees together, Erik kneeling in front of her, his hands on the tops of her thighs.

It was strange to be naked while everyone else was still fully dressed. It made an odd power dynamic that put her even more off-kilter.

And the entire time, Torrin didn't move. He remained on the outskirts, watching with an intensity that stole her breath.

Erik dug his thumbs into the seam of her thighs but didn't pull them apart. Instead, he stared at her. "Shy? Why is it that everything about you I shouldn't like, I do?" He leaned down and pressed his lips to where his thumbs rested between her thighs, peppering kisses along that line. His breath was hot against her skin as he spoke. "Not that I'm worried about you being shy. I'm rather persistent."

Ashley wanted to spread her legs, she really did. She wanted to feel everything he offered, to drown in what she knew he was capable of. Already the alphas had turned her inside out, had made her want things she'd never even thought about before. How much more was there to explore with them?

The answer rested in his dark eyes, but even then, taking the leap was hard.

"Spread your thighs, dove." Torrin's voice had that same wild edge to it, yet it held absolute authority, the sort she couldn't deny, couldn't refuse.

And Ashley obeyed. She didn't have to think, didn't question it. She let her legs fall open, with Erik's grip guiding them wide.

It was trust in a way she'd never felt before, a willingness to believe that she was safe.

This was what she'd never had with Gregory, the reason she could never really fall for him — well, other than the fact that he was a horrible person. He'd asked her once, when they were still friends, why she resisted him. She hadn't known what was missing, but now? Now she knew.

Even naked, even faced with three alphas who were so much larger and stronger than her, who she still knew so little about, she'd never felt safer.

Ashley met Torrin's gaze, his demand still simmering in her blood, her body lighting up beneath it. He didn't look away, except for the moments when his gaze would dip between her legs then return, his lips *almost* curling into a smile.

He offered the slightest of nods, and despite how subtle it was, the praise of it went right to Ashley's core as though he'd stroked his fingers through her hair and whispered 'good girl' into her ear.

He distracted her so fully, she wasn't prepared when Erik dragged his tongue up her cunt, the first direct touch she'd ever felt from another.

I am out of my element.

Liam had to admit, the sight of Erik's tongue teasing Ashley's pussy was the sort of thing he wanted to make sure he'd never forget.

112

Even better, Torrin had stayed.

Not just stayed, but when he'd ordered Ashley to spread her legs, it had been that tie to pull him in.

And Ashley? She'd reacted in a way that would have driven Liam to his knees, if Erik hadn't already taken that spot. She'd followed the command as though driven to, as if she couldn't *not* follow it, and the soft moan that left her when Torrin had nodded in approval?

Beautiful.

A naturally submissive woman was a work of art, and he'd seen none lovelier than Ashley.

Which reminded him again of the aching in his cock, which had been sorely neglected the last time.

Torrin might not be willing to join in and get any real satisfaction, but blue balls could do a lot to convince a man. Besides, that was *his* problem.

Liam undid the button of his jeans, then tugged them down enough that he could pull his dick free. He caught Ashley's chin, tugging until her gaze fell to his lap.

A sharp intake of breath signaled that Ashley had looked where he wanted her to, and a whimper said she liked it.

"Don't sound so surprised. I happen to know for a fact that you've gotten a look at a man's cock before." He held the base of his cock, squeezing tightly, more turned on than he expected by her hungry gaze.

The entire time he spoke, the filthy sounds of Erik punctuated the conversation. Erik had never been the sort to do things half-assed or to worry about being proper. It meant that when he finally got his tongue on Ashley, he no doubt planned to enjoy it.

And from the tiny gasps that left Ashley, from the way she moved, she was enjoying it as well.

Still, Liam had no intention of being left out. He caught Ashley's hand and brought it down to his cock. She wrapped her fingers around him as though by instinct.

Her warm hand was small, her skin soft and her grip gentle, tentative.

He reacted to her more than the most forward and skilled lover he'd had in the past, especially when she stroked him the first time with a single unsure motion.

Liam didn't keep his pleasure in, either. He groaned loudly at the sensation, and that seemed to help her continue. She kept her gaze pinned to him, to where his hard cock rested in her small hand, to where she stroked him, to where the drops of pre-cum escaped. It wasn't quick and dirty, not like what Erik was doing to her. Instead, it was an exploration that did more than steal his breath — it stole his heart.

It was sweet in the midst of so much lust, soft against the hardness of Erik's lips and giving in the face of Torrin's intense gaze.

A perfect dichotomy. The trio of alphas had always had too much hardness. They were all made entirely of sharp edges, and it had made allowing people close impossible. Anyone who came too near was undoubtedly cut by the viciousness the three had.

And yet in Ashley, he saw a woman who could withstand it not because she challenged them, not because she was tougher, but because she was soft enough to meld to them, to make them *want* to be better.

Liam groaned at the feeling of her hand, especially when she grew more confident. Her gaze was hot as she stared, as she pulled the pleasure from him out of sheer instinct. It wasn't that she was skillful, that she knew how to touch him, how to prolong, how to shove him toward a release. Instead, he was pretty sure she could have flicked him and he'd have come, because it was *her*.

What she did mattered less than the fact *she* was doing it.

"Please," she begged. Such a pretty sound, the plea on her lips. His twisted mind pictured her naked and kneeling and begging for his cock with those sweet eyes on him.

"Please what, sweet? What do you want?"

She cried out, and Liam grinned to see that Erik had latched his lips to her clit. It seemed he wasn't playing carefully anymore. Or maybe he just enjoyed the way her words were cut off by the gasping, needy sound.

Liam caught her chin, forcing her to bring her gaze to his, savoring how drunken her eyes were, how clouded with lust and need. "Please what?"

"I need you," she said brokenly.

Which was exactly what he needed to hear.

He knew what would send her over, and which of her firsts Liam wanted to claim for his own.

He rose to his knees on the couch, one foot to the ground. Ashley released him as he moved, her beautiful dark blue eyes lidded, her chest rising and falling in heavy, quick breaths that made her breasts sway.

She was *so* close, strung along that line but not quite there, and he loved watching her trapped there.

He slipped his fingers into her hair, grasping the soft brown strands to pull her closer. "Open your sweet mouth up," he said, voice soft. When she did, when the heat of her mouth enveloped his shaft, he let himself growl at the feeling. "Such a good girl," he praised.

He didn't hold back—he wasn't sure if he could have—and the first soft, tentative lick was enough for him to shudder in pleasure. He stayed shallow so his cum pooled on her tongue rather than hitting the back of her throat—he didn't need her choking, since he planned to do this again.

The intensity of his release was worth the wait, worth depriving himself the night before. He groaned at the sensation of claiming her, of filling her with his seed. It went deeper than the physical release and was something *more*. He could almost feel a bond snapping into place between Ashley and him, and the sensation staggered him.

He didn't have time to enjoy it, though. Instead, a soft warning growl from Erik woke him. A girl with as little training as Ashley would sure as fuck bite him when she came, and he'd prefer not to lose any inches of his dick to that.

So Liam, as much as he didn't want to, pulled away from the warmth of Ashley's sweet mouth. She swallowed without him even telling her to, and that drugged expression that took over her and the deep moan that escaped her humbled him.

She is fucking perfect.

Liam looked between her legs, to where Erik was dragging his tongue up Ashley's wet cunt. He locked eyes with his brother for a moment, enough for the message to pass between them, honed by years of taking women together.

Go in for the kill.

Erik offered what was almost a smile before he used his thumbs to spread her, to move the hood of her little clit out of the way. He offered one more hard lick, then latched on to her erect nub.

She jerked at the sudden, rough touch, but Liam's grasp on her chin kept her from going anywhere. He wanted to drink down each moment of her coming orgasm. The last time he'd not been able to actually watch, so this time he planned to enjoy it.

"Let go," Liam said. "He won't stop until you come."

Ashley whimpered at his words, actually *whimpered*. She was so near losing all control. Still, she seemed to fight it. Even as she begged for them, even as her body strove for that release, she couldn't seem to just let go.

What was it? What held her back? Why did she fight so hard against what she wanted so badly?

Liam didn't have time to ponder more before Torrin's voice rang through the dark room, carrying the same tone of absolute authority it always did. "Come for them, dove."

The nickname was sweet, but the hard edge of his voice said that was all the sweetness she'd get from him. Just as she had when she'd spread her legs for his demand, she heeded this one, too.

Her back arched and her mouth opened. No sound left her, not even a sharp inhalation as her body went rigid. It was as though she froze in time, her eyes closed, lost to the feeling.

It felt like a miracle, like a blessing he'd never deserved to watch. Where her swallowing his cum was a brand on her, a claim on her, witnessing her so undone felt like her claim on him. She went lax a moment later, gasping in a greedy breath.

Erik offered a kiss to her inner thigh, then another, like a line of sweet adorations to say what the man had no idea how to say.

She gave a tentative smile down to Erik. *Nervous again?* It charmed Liam to no end.

Except she lifted her gaze to Torrin, that openness on her face, a lovely flush on her cheeks, expectation there. Torrin *had* participated.

And Torrin did what he did so well, the bastard. He rose, managing to look entirely unaffected. "Goodnight, Ashley."

The wounded pride that washed over her features, the snapping shut of the openness that had been there — it was a withdrawal so fast it *hurt*.

Liam lifted his lip into a snarl as he watched his cousin leave the room.

He'd beat some sense into Torrin if that was what it took.

Chapter Eight

Ashley ached. She hadn't slept well, having tossed and turned all night after returning to her apartment.

Not that Erik and Liam had wanted her to go back. In fact, both had offered to join her if she insisted on returning to her own lonely bed.

And the temptation had been strong. She'd wanted to say yes, to curl up beside their strong forms, to fall asleep with her head clouded by their scents.

Except Torrin's rejection stuck with her.

And it *had* been rejection. If it had happened at the start, she'd have dealt with it. If he'd walked out from the first moment the other two had touched her, she'd have accepted it. Instead, he'd not just waited, not just stayed — he'd *participated*. His rumbled demands had coursed through her body. When she'd looked at him afterward, when everything she'd used before as protection had been chipped away by the alphas, when she was truly entirely and naked, he'd left as though she meant nothing.

Don't be a fool. Of course you mean nothing.

She slammed closed the scheduling book, frustration eating away at her. Why had she given in? Why be stupid enough to think there was even a chance for her?

She'd gone to work, because what other option was there? She had nothing to her name and nowhere to go.

At least if she kept working, she could save up money, create a nest egg. She could leave afterward.

Pain lanced her chest at the thought of leaving, Liam's charming smirks and Erik's ghost of a smile haunting her.

She'd seen none of them today. Already life had turned routine, with the security in the building recognizing her, with people smiling and talking to her as though she were important, as though she were a coworker they cherished.

The doorman had held the door for her when she'd left, had called her Miss Ashley, and the car and driver had sat parked and ready for her, since the alphas had already left. They usually left for work first and stayed later than her.

She could scarcely believe this was her life now.

Then Torrin's cold eyes came back to her and she wanted to throw it all away.

Her computer chimed, and she expected an email from a client.

Torrin's name mocked her in the 'from' line before she opened the email.

Ashley,
I am sorry for last night. It was a mistake.
Torrin

The words were so straightforward that she could almost hear him in her head, that flat, uncaring tone he liked to use.

She deleted it.

Of course he was sorry. Of course it had been as mistake. Not that he'd rejected her, but that he'd been there at all.

Another chime.

Perhaps we could speak over lunch?

Again, she sent it to the trash.

Maybe ignoring her boss—one of the alphas who were responsible for her having a place to live—was a bad idea.

Still, sitting through lunch with him while he explained he didn't want her sounded like as much fun as pulling out her fingernails.

Her cell phone rang, and when she lifted it, she found Torrin's name across the front.

The man has no patience, does he?

She knew damned well that if she didn't answer, his next step would be walking to her office, and while she felt tough a few floors away, she knew she'd crumble if she faced him.

It prompted her to answer, trying for her best *I don't care that you rejected me and made me feel like shit* voice. "Hello."

"You are ignoring my emails."

"No, I wasn't."

"You should stop trying to lie, dove, because you are horrible at it. Our email servers tell me when you've opened one and when you've deleted it. Are you avoiding me now?"

"You were the one who seemed to want to avoid me."

They both went silent at that. She didn't normally call people out, but the wound still felt too fresh.

His sigh was low and drawn out. "About last night —"

"Please, don't. You don't need to explain."

"If I didn't need to, you wouldn't be so angry."

"I'm not angry."

"Angry seemed a kinder word than hurt."

That shut her up. It wasn't fair that he could read her so easily, that he knew how much his reaction mattered to her.

"It's fine," she said, her voice having lost the edge. What was the point in being defensive if he saw right through it? "I really don't want to have lunch with you, though. Please don't push it."

He hesitated before answering. "Then talk to me on the phone, at least. You said once it was easier than face to face."

"What do you want from me?" She hated that her voice sounded pleading, but that didn't change that it was true.

He didn't want her, but he seemed drawn in. He tempted her then rejected her. He drew closer then fled. She had no idea how to deal with any of it.

Worse? He was so connected to Erik and Liam, she had no idea how to form something with the two of them and not with him in his half-in-half-out thing.

"I want you safe and taken care of and happy. That hasn't changed."

"I can't do this," she whispered. "I don't understand you."

He didn't respond at first, and for so long a time, she feared he'd hung up. Finally, he answered, voice even flatter than usual. "I can't have you, Ashley, no matter how much I may want that."

"Why not?"

"My life is dangerous. I…" Another sigh drifted across the phone line. "I lost someone once because I wasn't careful enough. People who wanted to hurt me hurt her. I can't risk that. I can't risk you."

"And you don't think that could happen anyway?"

"If I never touch you, if I never carry your scent and you never carry mine, no one would think to use you to get to me."

"What if that isn't enough for me?"

"Come to dinner tonight, please. We'll discuss it." She knew by his words that 'discuss' meant 'explain it to her so she agreed, so she *understood* his reasoning'. "Please, dove."

The nickname crumbled her resolve. Besides, what other choice did she have? Yet again, she was backed into a corner.

"Okay," she whispered.

They hung up quickly, probably because Torrin was afraid she'd change her mind.

Her phone rang again, and she put it to her ear without looking. "I said I'll be there."

"Hello, Ashley." Gregory's voice snatched the breath from her lungs.

It only took those two words for her to feel as though the floor had disappeared and she were choking in the vastness of space.

He found me.

"Breathe, love. You have always frightened so easily."

She hated herself for it, but she pulled in a breath at his order. Or perhaps her body had simply demanded it. "How did you find me?"

"I told you before, you can't hide from me. Your old employer was helpful, and once she mentioned a driver and handed over her security videos, it wasn't hard."

Carla turned me over? Even after I gave her all my money, she still betrayed me?

"Just leave me alone," Ashley whispered. "Let me go."

"You know I can't do that. You are my mate."

"I'm not."

"You are." He spoke with absolute certainty, with the sort of fanatical belief that had always terrified Ashley. "Have they sullied you, love?"

Those words reached into her like icy tendrils to grasp her heart. *They.* He knew about the alphas? "What do you mean?"

"Those alphas who think you're theirs. Have they taken your innocence?"

His insanity dripped through the line. He hadn't ever pushed her for anything physical, even before she'd run, always accepting that she wasn't ready. The one kiss he'd tried for had turned her stomach, and he'd backed off. Small wonders, she supposed, to be spared that.

"No," she said, afraid to upset him and frustrated by her own cowardice.

"So they have, then? I can hear it in your voice. Don't worry, love, I don't blame you. It isn't your fault."

"They haven't," she swore, afraid now not of them but for them. "I haven't..." Even still, she couldn't say it.

"You are saying you are still untouched?"

She chose to decide that meant sex, made sure to believe it as she spoke because, as had been pointed out to her many times, she was a terrible liar. "That's right."

He let out a soft sound, that almost-purr that he did as if it should calm her, as if she should trust it and relax because of it. "I'm glad. I would hate to have our first time soiled, whenever you're ready for it."

Her stomach twisted and churned, and despite not having eaten anything, she wanted to vomit at the thought of his hands on her, of him touching her. It was almost worse that he spoke to her with such softness.

It was what had frightened her so much. Gregory had seemed perfect. Rich, sweet, well-spoken. He'd seemed to be exactly what she was supposed to want, despite that passion and lust never occurring in her.

Her fathers hadn't liked him, but teenage rebellion only meant that made her surer Gregory must have been the right choice.

Then things had changed, slowly at first, with him calling more, wanting to know where she was all the time. She'd found people following her, and when she'd reached out to him, frightened, he'd assured her they were for her protection.

Except they hadn't *felt* like protection. They'd felt like a chain he'd placed around her neck.

The more she'd pulled, the more he'd pulled. Never with any meanness, never by yelling or calling names. Instead, he'd spoken calmly, as though she were the hysterical one, the foolish one. He'd speak to her as if she were a child who needed lessons.

She'd questioned her sanity at times, wondered if he wasn't right, if it wasn't all in her head.

"You get lost in thought so easily," he said. "I've set up a place here in town. I thought perhaps we could stay for a while if you like it so much. From what I've seen, you have created a name here, gotten a proper job.."

Ashley gripped the phone, her heart pounding. "I'm afraid."

"I know, love, but you are always afraid. I'll see you later."

The line went dead, and the phone clattered to the desk when it slipped from her grasp.

She remembered every other time she'd run, each time she'd had nothing, when she'd left because he'd gotten too close or threatened something.

She thought about what he could do to Torrin, to Liam or to Erik.

She only had one choice.

She had to run.

* * * *

Erik tapped his fingers against the railing as he stared out over the city. Liam was inside talking to the chef about dinner plans, and Torrin had retreated to the balcony for some quiet.

That was the exact reason Erik stood out there, with his cousin seated in the place he knew smelled of Ashley, the one she'd fallen asleep in.

How could someone so obvious be so oblivious to the truth?

"You'll have to give in," Erik said to break the silence.

Torrin answered without hesitation, as though he'd expected the statement and had prepared for it. "I can't give in. Why can none of you see that?"

"Because it's bullshit."

"Gilly—"

"We were young, still learning. You can't let her be the reason you hide forever."

"You don't understand. You've never lost anyone like that. Think, for just a moment, how you would feel to walk into Ashley's apartment, to see her carved to pieces, to know it happened because of you, that if she'd never met you, she would have lived a long, happy life."

A shooting pain ricocheted through Erik's skull, as though his mind objected to the very notion of such a thing.

He shook his head. "I get it, I do, but we have to deal with things from where we are, and where we are is with an omega you are clearly bonding to. Even if she doesn't carry your scent yet, she's still your mate."

He waited for a denial, for Torrin to say Erik was seeing things that were not there.

Instead, Torrin leaned forward and carded his fingers through his hair, looking more disheveled than he had before. "I know she is, damnit. Don't you think I feel it? It is torture to keep a distance, but what other choice do I have? As a mate to you and Liam, she'll be protected. As mine, she'd only be in danger."

"So how do you see this going? Because you being some sort of weird voyeur each time isn't going to work—not if her reaction last night means a thing."

Torrin turned his gaze to the dark skyline, the shadows making him look even older than he was. He'd always been older, not much by years, but by responsibility? *Always.*

"I'm going to move out."

"What?" Erik sat straighter, a rare panic going through him. After almost forty years of them all living together, he couldn't imagine a life that didn't involve his cousin. Of all the things he'd expected Torrin to say, that had been the last.

Torrin didn't turn back to him, didn't acknowledge Erik's reaction. "Not far. I thought Ashley and I would switch residences. She would move in here and I would take the apartment. Business would then go on as usual. I would have space, would be able to give you privacy, and Ashley would be safe."

"You can't be serious. That is the worst idea I've ever heard."

"It isn't. You simply dislike change. It's the best outcome for everyone. You and Liam have your mate, Ashley is safe and content, and I am near enough to still watch out for you all but not so near as to be tempted or to put her in danger."

Erik twisted away, gripping the railing with his hands, staring out into the same vast sky that Torrin was watching.

They'd always loved the sky, all three of them. Maybe it was because of their upbringing, because it always felt free.

"I think about that night," Erik whispered into the darkness.

"I believe we all do."

What did it say that it could only mean one night? That a single evening had shaped their lives so dramatically, that they both knew of what he spoke.

Erik wanted to shut his eyes, but that wouldn't stop the memories. "I've always wondered why. Why that night? What changed?"

Torrin sighed and the seat creaked as though he moved. "People sometimes believe things happen all of a sudden, that they snap and give way. That isn't true, though, at least not most of the time. It's never just one thing. Anger grows like sand in an hourglass. It goes just one piece at a time, growing heavier, but each only a speck. That night it grew too large."

There was more to it. There always was with Torrin. "So tell me the speck, that last one that pushed you over."

"I was sitting awake the night before, listening from the darkness of the backyard. Your father was drunk to the point of nearly toppling out of the chair. Our mothers were seated at that rickety old table, playing cards. I'd already put you and Liam to bed, had snuck you both what little food I'd found."

The memory of how hunger had gnawed at his sunken stomach made Erik wince. It was likely why he and the other alphas always went overboard with food now. They knew what it was like to have none.

Still, Torrin's voice pulled him forward in a story he was no longer sure he wanted to hear. "I watched them because I couldn't sleep, and because get-togethers always riled up your father. The night went on, they all got drunker, got higher, until near two a.m. your father wanted more meth. The problem was, he lacked the funds. His dealer wouldn't give anything more, so he laughed and said 'I have a couple of brats who could work it off.'"

A chill went up Erik's spine, especially when he considered Liam and himself at that age. They'd grown into strong, powerful alphas, but back then? At seven? They'd hardly been capable of protecting themselves.

Torrin had been fourteen, not even close to an adult yet still somehow responsible for all of them.

Erik couldn't bring himself to say a word about it, about the horror that had never happened, all because Torrin had acted.

Still, Torrin continued. "Our mothers laughed, this thin, ugly, hollow laugh, and I knew it was only a matter of time. They all passed out shortly after, and the next night, I made sure that would never happen."

Erik tried to consider making that choice, doing the things Torrin had at that age.

It reminded him of Torrin's limp, of that pain he endured and never spoke of, the one no one knew exactly how he'd gotten. The night they spoke of, Torrin had woken them, taken them outside and sent them off with a friend of his. They hadn't seen him for two months, though word of a fire that had consumed their old hovel of a house—and their parents—had come the next day. When Torrin had returned, limping, they'd never asked.

Now, he wondered.

"Your leg."

"I think that's enough story time for one night, don't you?" The set of Torrin's tone said he wouldn't offer more.

Fair. Where Erik had flashing memories of that life, Torrin had to live with it all. He could keep a few pieces to himself if he wanted.

The slider opened and Liam came out, his expression missing the normal humor.

"What happened?" Erik asked.

"Ashley's late."

Erik brought his wrist up to find the time. Sure enough, she'd missed dinner by thirty minutes. "Maybe she was caught up."

Liam crossed his arms, a tic in his jaw. "No. Her driver just called. She asked to stop at a store on her way back to pick up some wine to go with dinner, except she went out of the back door of the store, and she isn't answering her phone."

Erik pressed his lips into a thin line at the idea that she'd bolted. Sure, she'd been annoyed with Torrin, but that didn't excuse her trying to run off.

"Well," Torrin said as he rose, dusting off his pants as though they had a speck of anything on them. "It seems dinner will have to wait. We have an omega to catch."

And by the time they were finished with her, she'd be far too exhausted to run anywhere.

* * * *

Ashley leaned forward in her seat at the bus station, the chill of the air made worse by something she couldn't shake.

Not fear. Well, she *was* afraid, but she'd grown used to that. Instead, it was a dreadful sense of isolation.

She'd been isolated before, but it had been something she'd known, accepted. Now that she'd felt something different, now that she'd had a moment of having more, of that isolation being driven out by the warmth of bodies she missed horribly, she struggled with its presence.

It was like always being sleep-deprived, then going on vacation and sleeping twelve hours a night. Going back to real life, back to the nights where she couldn't sleep, was a hard transition.

One she hated to make.

But she *had* to. Not only for herself, but for the alphas.

Whereas before she hadn't said anything because she was afraid they'd turn her over, that they'd sell her out, she now feared for them.

Gregory didn't anger easily, but the undercurrent of it in his tone as he'd asked about them had terrified her. He'd kill without a second thought, and it would forever be her fault.

It was what had gotten her to run the first time, that fear for her fathers. It was what was getting her to run this time, too.

She couldn't have them die just because she wanted what she should have known she could never have.

Her phone rang again. The alphas had called a number of times, but she'd ignored each one. She'd need to ditch the phone. They'd be able to track her calls, so it wasn't safe, but she didn't want to cut that one last tie.

She figured she'd leave it on the bench when her bus got there. She'd bought her ticket with the money from the driver. It was all the money she had, but she'd started over with nothing before.

How did she always end up like this? Broke, homeless, alone.

Her eyes burned, but she refused to be that girl crying at a bus station.

The phone rang again, and she twisted it to find not the alphas, but a restricted number. *Gregory.*

She answered, the same terror he always sparked in her forcing her to.

He didn't wait for her to speak. "My darling one, why do you play games I always win? You run and I find you. I've offered you a life here, a life wherever you would want. Stop running. Just sit there and wait and I will come to collect you."

The future he offered overcame her. She'd have the finest things and no freedom. He offered to live wherever she wanted because it didn't matter where they lived — it would always be a prison. She'd be his. Nothing but his little trophy, the thing he owned.

She'd die every day with him until nothing but an empty shell remained.

After so long on her own, the thought of giving in, of doing what he wanted, of admitting failure, made her chest tighten until drawing breath was difficult.

Though at least she wouldn't have to run anymore. She'd be settled, wouldn't have to live in fear.

Sometimes she felt like her life was avoiding something that would eventually happen. She lived in that fear before a strike. If she just let the hit happen, maybe it would be better than avoiding it.

Except then she remembered how Liam had kissed her, his soft lips, the heat that grew inside her from it. She recalled Erik's strong hands, the way he offered her that almost-smile that felt rare and precious. She even thought about Torrin, about how no matter what happened, she felt *safe* beside him, how when he told her to do something she could relax into the command and let things go.

The idea of giving that all up was too much. For the first time in so long, she'd glimpsed a future worth not giving up.

Sure, she might not get *that* future, but it was worth at least trying for.

* * * *

Liam couldn't stop the soft growl as they entered the bus station. Tracking Ashley's cell phone wasn't something they'd do normally, but these weren't normal circumstances.

He wasn't controlling.

Bullshit.

So maybe he wanted to be controlling. A fear inside him wanted to know where she was at all times, and yes, it was easier because with all the security in place, they had a good idea where she was much of the time. However, he had no problem with her having privacy, either.

He'd have never tracked her phone if he hadn't known damned well she'd run off.

Worse, since they hadn't set up any of the financials yet, she didn't have more than the hundred the driver had given her from their discretionary fund.

If she really wanted to leave, she needed to do it right. They'd help her get set up wherever she wanted, but she wouldn't end up in another roach-infested apartment building. That was not about to happen again.

They entered the bus station, with Torrin in the center and Erik on the other side.

Her being ready to get on a bus and expecting to just disappear without a word had his temper sharp. The tension running through Erik and Torrin said they shared the sentiment.

"I will turn her ass so red," Erik snarled, the same threat he'd made before.

"Please. You're too soft-hearted," Liam said.

Erik snorted softly. "I am when she doesn't take off like this. The girl deserves a reminder that we aren't so easy to throw."

They passed the ticket area, since a call placed on their way had let them know she'd purchased her ticket.

Las Vegas. That was where she'd been headed, probably because the price of the ticket was about what she had in cash.

The thought of her stuck out in Vegas without anything had Liam's hands drawing into fists, his knuckles aching.

On the back bench, something caught the light of the overhead florescent bulbs. *Her cell phone.*

He picked it up, frowning at her leaving it behind.

Had she realized they'd been tracking her?

The bus she'd gotten the ticket for hadn't left yet, especially since Torrin had made sure it would be delayed.

Had she figured out the delay was due to them?

Where the hell is she?

A security guard stood at the back corner, so Liam headed his way.

"I'm looking for a young woman. Long brown hair, blue eyes. She was wearing…" *Damn it, what was she wearing?*

Torrin spoke up. "Black slacks and a white blouse."

The guard nodded. "I remember her. She was sitting back there"—he pointed at the bench where the phone had been—"but she left about ten minutes ago."

"Do you know where she went?"

The guard hiked a thumb toward the left. "She went out the back exit. It lets out into the parking garage."

Liam thanked the guard then took off toward the back. However, he slowed his steps when he was reminded by the click of Torrin's cane against the floor that he couldn't keep up as well.

Normally he didn't forget Torrin's limitations. They were simply a part of life.

It seemed he was more thrown off by Ashley's behavior than he'd realized.

They went through the back door that opened into the large, multi-level parking structure.

"She could have gone anywhere," Erik said.

Liam closed his eyes and inhaled, catching a trace of her scent. Not enough to follow—he wasn't a fucking bloodhound—but it at least eased him. *If I was trying to run, where would I go?*

"She's out of money and has no phone. She can't call a rideshare. She has no friends to call. She must have gone toward the street," Liam said.

Torrin pointed away from the exit, toward the back. "She wouldn't take the street, because she knows we'd come looking. It's why she wouldn't have gone out the front door. There's an alleyway that way, but no exit for cars."

Liam side-eyed Torrin, again reminded that while he might pretend he wasn't involved, he knew the omega well.

He paid more attention than he liked to let on.

Torrin's idea made the most sense, so they took off that way. Through the back there was a door, right where Torrin had claimed. Through there sat a quiet alleyway, only a single car wide, with the parking structure on one side and what looked like a warehouse on the other.

And down the path, sitting on a half wall with her head in her hands, was one wayward omega.

Misery clung to her, and when her back shuddered, his anger melted away.

Damn, that girl would be able to get away with anything if she could steal his anger this easily.

"Hey there, sweet."

Ashley wasn't shocked to hear Liam's voice, and worse? It made her feel better.

She'd gotten about a block away from the bus station before her feet had frozen and she'd realized...she had no idea where she was headed.

What was she supposed to do? Where was she supposed to go?

It had all become too much, and she'd sat down, just crumbled onto the low half-wall beside an empty lot and dropped her head into her hands.

She didn't acknowledge Liam, or Erik and Torrin, who she could smell even if she didn't lift her head to see them.

Warmth pressed against her side as Liam took a spot beside her. "You make it hard to be mad at you when you look so miserable."

"So I know how to get out of trouble?" Her joke fell flat the moment she said it.

"If you don't want to be in trouble, how about you explain why you ran off." Erik sounded dramatically less friendly than Liam, but that didn't shock her.

She sure as hell wasn't going to look up, though. She'd meet Torrin's gaze and she was sure that was pure ice.

It had been too trying a night to be faced with that.

"Come back," Liam said. "Come home and we'll figure it out. We'll deal with whatever the problem is."

Home. The word made her want to cry again.

Even if she hadn't made it far — since when had her plans ever really worked out? — she still couldn't stay.

They didn't know.

"You need to let me go," she said.

"I don't see that happening," Erik answered. "Talk to us and we'll resolve whatever the issues are, but if you think we'll accept you simply walking out, you clearly don't know us very well."

"I figured I'd be gone before we had to worry about it."

"So why'd you stop?" Liam bumped her arm with his.

She peered down the alleyway, still avoiding where Torrin stood. "It just seemed too far all of a sudden." *And isn't that the truth?*

"Come on, dove. Let's get you home." Torrin's voice held no room for argument, and it made her eyes burn more with a desire to listen.

She wanted to fall against him, to look into his face and trust that he'd take care of it all.

Sure enough, she rose to her feet, and the heat of his body was so close, it chased the chill from the front of hers. His shoes, black and without scuffs, were in her line of sight along with the end of his cane.

His strong fingers caught her chin and forced her gaze up, the caress sizzling through her, the first time he'd actually broken that touch barrier.

Everything else drifted away as she met those dark eyes—all the hurt, all the reasons she had to go, couldn't stand against the absolute certainty there.

What would it feel like to have that sort of certainty? To feel that sort of control?

She wanted to borrow it, to wrap herself up in it and trust in it.

"Why did you run?"

"It's too dangerous," she whispered back.

Her words came a heartbeat before something shattered the quiet moment, when her stomach sank and her heart froze.

First one bullet, then another, then a grunt and a body hitting hers.

A heavy weight knocked her to the ground as everything she feared came crashing down around her.

Chapter Nine

Everything went so fast, Ashley struggled to keep up. The blasts of sound from a gun firing made her ears ring, and the scent of the body on top of her said Torrin had taken her to the ground.

He was heavy, and his body blanketed her like a shield.

Closer shots said someone was firing back, as Torrin cupped the back of her neck and pulled her face against his chest, keeping her tucked there.

Cursing, shouted responses and, after a few moments of silence, the weight on her lifted.

Hands on her arms pulled her up from the ground, and Ashley forced herself to open her eyes.

Blood on the ground said someone was hurt, and she lifted her gaze to find it dripping from Erik's fingers. His black coat hid most of it, but then she found the damage to his left shoulder, the coat shiny as blood soaked into it.

Liam appeared unharmed, as did Torrin, though both Erik and Liam held pistols she hadn't noticed before. They didn't look like the sweet, kind alphas she'd grown used to.

They looked angry and capable and dangerous.

Then Erik turned a furious look at Ashley and she took a large step backward, away from it.

He turned his face away, though the frustration there didn't leave.

"Let's get off the street," Liam said. "It seems we need to get somewhere safe, then I think our little omega has some explaining to do."

Her stomach dropped at the idea of doing it, which seemed almost more frightening than what had just happened.

* * * *

Erik gritted his teeth as the doctor prodded the wound.

He rarely got hit, which meant he wasn't used to bullet wounds. Him letting his guard down chafed, that he'd not only risked himself but Ashley, all because he'd been distracted by her.

He knew better than to ever relax, yet he'd done so around her. Worse, there was no sign of the shooter. The man must have run.

And now, back at the apartment, they'd contacted a local doctor to treat his wound. A hospital would have to report the injury, but their own doctor had more discretion.

Not that Erik had sat still. Upon reaching the apartment, he'd immediately upped their security safeguards. Even as the doctor had examined him, he'd been on his phone.

Ashley sat on the couch, and she hadn't said a word. Erik was on a stool over the tile in the kitchen so he didn't stain anything while the doctor worked, and Liam stood near the window, tension lining his body. Torrin was on his phone, pacing, the click of his cane against the floor loud as he dealt with the increased security needs.

At least they didn't need to worry about securing the other apartment, because there was no chance that Ashley would be sleeping alone there.

Hell, after the close call, she'd be lucky to get to sleep in a bed alone.

The bullets hadn't been near her, so he doubted she was the target.

Still, they'd been too close. Accidents happened and stray bullets could claim lives.

That fear drew a snarl from him, even when the doctor stitching his skin together didn't.

It took longer than he would have liked before the doctor placed a bandage on the front and back of his shoulder and declared him well enough. He left a prescription for antibiotics to avoid infections and pain meds before he left.

As soon as the door shut, when they were alone, Erik twisted in the stool to stare at Ashley.

She hadn't spoken, her knees drawn up to her chest, her gaze on the floor.

She looked exhausted.

The way she'd stepped away from him hurt. He'd been pissed, sure, given the secrets she'd kept that had clearly been dangerous. The terror in her eyes had taken him back, though, back to when the last female he'd risked feeling anything for had done the same.

He'd dealt with distrust, had used it and even enjoyed the power it gave him, but he didn't like to see that on the face of someone who had no reason to fear him. He'd never escaped that same wariness in Beth's eyes, the way she'd never let her guard down with him.

He pushed that aside, because they had more important things to deal with than his wounded feelings.

Liam turned around as Torrin hung up his call, all their attention returning to Ashley.

A nod from Erik let Liam know to take the lead.

He was the best at coaxing, and Ashley needed a gentle touch to get her to speak.

Liam took a seat beside her. "You didn't run because of us, did you?"

She shook her head. It was an obvious answer, but that was how interrogations worked. Ask small, easy questions, and once they answered, a person was more likely to answer the harder ones.

"What's after you, sweet?"

"Gregory." The name was whispered with a fear that made Erik's alpha side snarl. He didn't like her being afraid of *anything*.

"Who's that?"

She sighed, dropping her gaze to follow the lines of tile as if that made it easier. "I met him when I was seventeen. I thought he was nice."

Given that she was a virgin, he couldn't have been a serious boyfriend.

Still, she kept going. "We were friends, even though he made it clear he wanted more. He kept getting pushier, more controlling. I tried to tell him I didn't want him. I thought I could let him down easy and it would be okay."

Her hesitation said it wasn't okay, but Erik could have guessed that.

"What happened when you told him?" Liam coaxed.

"One of my fathers got into an accident. His car was almost pushed off a bridge. Gregory met me at the hospital and told me the world was a dangerous place. He said it would be less dangerous if I accepted his proposition."

Erik lifted his lip, keeping the sound of his reaction in despite the rage that swamped him at the idea of anyone threatening Ashley.

Liam set a hand on her knee and gave her a squeeze but let her go at her own pace.

She shuddered as if the support were enough for her to continue. "That was when I ran, at eighteen. I couldn't stay and risk my family. I've picked up and moved over a dozen times, changing states, leaving nothing behind, but he always finds me."

Erik frowned as he did the math. She'd run at eighteen, which meant she'd been going on her own for six years. The thought of that sweet girl being alone for all that time broke him. She *needed* affection. She was the type to thrive on that.

"Did you ever go to the police?" Torrin asked.

"I tried at the start. I sat in an interrogation room for hours talking to them, trying to get them to understand. After that, one detective handed me a phone and Gregory was on the line. I figured out then that he has people everywhere." The bottomless hopelessness of her words bled through, and suddenly her hesitation and fear made sense.

She'd had no one to trust for so many years, no one to rely on, nothing but herself and what seemed like an endless, fruitless race.

"And you didn't tell us because you were afraid we'd sell you out like that police station did?" Liam asked.

She nodded. "I've learned that Gregory has a long reach. Every time I've let my guard down, he's made me pay for it."

Fuck. Erik's chest ached, his anger dissipating.

He'd deal with this Gregory soon enough. He'd remove that problem from her life—slowly and painfully—but right now it wasn't the priority.

Instead, what mattered was the fragile omega who sat on the couch looking defeated. Despite the fact that she'd outrun and outsmarted someone who had proven to be a brutal and dangerous male, she seemed to feel as though she'd failed.

Which was stupid. After all he'd done, Gregory must have money, power, connections and an unhealthy obsession, yet even with all that, he hadn't managed to get Ashley beneath his thumb.

Erik considered that one a hell of a win.

Liam caught her chin and turned her to look him in the eyes. "You're going to give us all the information you have on Gregory."

"You don't understand how dangerous he is."

And she didn't understand how dangerous *they* were. Though, given her history with Gregory, Erik doubted it would be good for her to know that. If he'd been sure she wouldn't react well to their truth before, that had only been cemented because of what he'd now learned.

Liam curled his lip into a smile no doubt meant to reassure. "We know people who can help. First, though, we need more information. So, you will tell us everything, then you will eat, then you will sleep."

"And tomorrow?"

"Tomorrow we'll deal with you trying to run out on us," Erik said.

She turned to meet his gaze, the first time she'd looked directly at him since she'd stepped away. There was still a wariness in her eyes, one he wanted to wipe clear, but that wouldn't happen then.

Liam leaned in and brushed his lips to hers, recapturing her attention. "You'll need your strength, omega, so make sure you rest up. I don't feel particularly interested in going easy on you."

And Erik was on board with that plan.

The night crept in on Ashley.

She hadn't talked about Gregory in so long that recalling their long and unhappy history felt like ripping scabs off festering wounds. Those spots on her now ached, burning as she thought about the man who had stolen so much from her.

The alphas had listened without chiming in other than to ask questions.

Much of it she didn't know.

Gregory had always been an enigma to her, a mystery she couldn't quite figure out.

From all the people who seemed to do what he said, she knew he had some amount of power, but she didn't know what he did, didn't know anything specific.

The more she spoke about him, the more she realized how little she actually understood about the monster who had chased her. They'd met by sheer chance at a small shop she had worked evenings at. He'd kept coming around, kept showing up where she was, until they'd turned into friends. If she ever asked about his work or his life, he'd side-step the question. She knew his last name was fake, because when she'd first run, she'd tried to search for it without luck.

By the time they'd finished the conversation, during which Liam had given her something to eat, it had been three in the morning.

When she'd been ready to head back to her own place, they'd made it clear she would instead be staying with them.

It was safer, she knew, yet it still felt like a large step she wasn't sure she was ready for.

There appeared to be four main bedrooms in their apartment, each with a bathroom and office. When she used the one that didn't smell of the alphas, one with a faint scent of an omega she didn't recognize, she struggled to feel comfortable.

Whose room was it? Fresh flowers sat on the side table as if they expected whoever stayed there to return at any time.

She lay there for nearly an hour, but by the time the clock hit four, she was done.

She went to the slider, figuring sleeping on that outside sofa again would work well. She could curl up, breathe in the comforting scent of the alphas instead of an omega she didn't know, and manage a little shut-eye.

The door opened and she took herself to the balcony. The first breeze that caught her hair and ruffled it eased the tightness of her chest.

"You shouldn't be out here." *Torrin*. Of course it was him. He was the shadow who was always there, yet always just out of reach.

"I couldn't sleep."

"If Gregory has people who are watching, then being outside in the open is unwise."

Ashley turned to look at the slider to the room she'd stayed in and took her lip between her teeth.

"Ask for what you want."

"Can I come to your room?" She lifted her gaze to his, throwing it out there.

And she expected him to turn her down, to tell her that if she wouldn't sleep in the room they'd supplied her, she should go to Liam or Erik.

Except his shoulders dropped and he nodded, then held his hand toward a slider farther down. "Come along."

Torrin's room was different from what she'd expected.

He was so well put together, regal and proper. She'd expected black and white silk bedding with bare shelving, everything minimalist and expensive. She'd expected it to reflect the rest of the apartment.

Instead, the room was full of warmth. A faded leather chair sat in the corner, the seat and back worn from obvious use. The bed was unmade, with the beige comforter thrown around and a crocheted throw in a rainbow of colors.

It was comfortable in a way Ashley hadn't expected, but between that and his scent, she relaxed.

"If it's so dangerous, aren't the big windows a problem?" she asked as he closed the door.

"Who do you take me for? This glass is bullet-proof. Anything short of a missile attack, they can easily withstand, and since he doesn't seem to want you harmed, I suspect that won't happen."

Ashley turned toward Torrin and gave him a smirk. "That's why you let me come in here, isn't it? I'm your human shield."

He didn't smile, but he didn't *need* to. Ashley could spot the slight crinkle beside his eyes, the lightening of his gaze. "As I recall, when we were in danger, it was I that shielded you."

That reminded Ashley of how his body had fit against hers. She hadn't really felt him before, given the distance he always kept between them.

His body was lean and strong. He wasn't Liam or Erik, with a lot of bulk, but that hadn't hidden the hard lines or just how much she wanted to see and feel more of it.

Which was foolish.

She tore her gaze away, trying to still her reaction, to hide it.

"Eyes on me." His tone brooked no argument. He didn't speak harshly, didn't raise his voice, yet it never failed to demand her compliance.

She met his dark eyes.

He pulled her in with his intense gaze. "Why are you here? You could have sought out my cousins. They've offered you everything. Why do you look at me the way you do?"

Ashley was drawn toward him, to where he stood beside the closed slider. "I don't know. I can't explain it."

He crossed the touch barrier again when he slid a hand behind her neck, the heavy weight of it reassuring. "I can't give you the things you want, dove, the things you deserve."

"Why not?"

"Because it isn't possible. Now, get in the bed or go back to your own room, because you need sleep."

When she didn't move, he used his grip on the nape of her neck to get her going, and her choice was easy. The bed looked too welcoming to ignore, and she was sure the best way to get any shut-eye would involve being surrounded by his scent.

She crawled into the bed, the warmth of it implying he'd been lying there before coming out to the balcony to check on her.

The tap of his cane against the floor had her rolling to face him. "What happened to your leg?"

He didn't tense, didn't seem as though talking about it bothered him. He did look down as if he'd forgotten, though. "I shattered my hip in my teenage years. It never healed right."

"Car accident?"

He shook his head. "No. An angry man with a baseball bat."

The words had her rising. "How? Who would do that?"

"My uncle. Now, would you like me to sleep in the living room?"

His words scraped along her, so sharp she had trouble accepting or believing them. Her family had been so important to her, her fathers a source of strength. To think of her own family being the ones to do such a thing…

She shuddered and took a moment to say a silent thanks for her own life. The set of his jaw and short words made it clear he'd say no more on the subject, so she let it go.

"Stay, please." She patted the bed beside her. "I'll sleep better if I'm not alone."

He didn't look happy with the choice, but after a moment, he slid into the bed carefully. He moved surprisingly well given his injury, but then again, if it had happened as a teenager, he'd had a lot of years to grow accustomed to it.

"Lie down," he ordered her.

Ashley did so, and under the coaxing of his hands, she rolled to her side, her back to him. He didn't move against her, though he kept one hand on her hip.

Only a thin layer of cotton rested between them from her shorts, and the heat of his palm soaked through it and into her skin.

She moved her thighs, the action forcing her shorts to rub against her, reminding her how badly her body begged her for release.

Funny, since she'd never *needed* sex before. She'd masturbated, of course, but it hadn't ever felt like this. It hadn't ever made her thirst for it before.

His sigh was hot and made her hair rustle. "You're not going to sleep, are you?"

"I'm trying. I just can't..." She flushed at the idea of telling him that the problem was that she was horny. "I can't relax," she settled for.

He let out a soft hum, as if he knew better.

She waited for him to tell her to go to sleep anyway, to scold her for feelings he didn't return.

Instead, his deep, smooth voice rumbled through the darkness of the room. "Take your shorts off, dove."

Nothing could stop the shot of arousal she felt at that command.

The increase of Ashley's mouthwatering scent screamed what she thought about Torrin's idea.

Not that he needed anything to tell him that. He had eyes—he could see how much she wanted him. It thrilled him as much as it scared him.

He *wanted* her. Hell, no, it was worse than that. He was pretty sure he *needed* her.

And yet despite her requiring sleep, that her body would be dragging come tomorrow if she didn't lie down and rest, she wouldn't relax.

His nose was more than good enough to know the reason for it. It had been written in the hungry stare of her eyes, in the way her thighs had rubbed together.

The omega was beyond needy. Her body screamed out for satisfaction he wished he could give her.

He wanted nothing more than to part her soft, warm thighs and slide into her wet heat. He wanted to worship every inch of her perfect body, to indulge in each curve of hers, each delectable spot on her form, until she couldn't even imagine keeping her eyes open for another moment.

However, he hadn't been lying about that not being possible. Even if he'd risked crossing the touch barrier, he still couldn't really have her.

Each time they were in close contact, she would carry some of his scent on her skin. However, it was the exchange of fluids that would truly make him a part of her. If he came inside her, if he licked her, if he left any of himself on her like that, then he would change her scent.

Enemies who got close enough to either of them would be able to tell, and that was a danger he couldn't risk.

That didn't mean he couldn't take the edge off for her, that he couldn't at least help her get to sleep.

"Excuse me?" Her question made him want to chuckle, from the innocence of it, the surprise.

Torrin sat up, then leaned to his dresser to pull out the vibrator tucked away there. It would provide a barrier, to reduce the risk of her carrying too much of his scent.

"You heard me, dove. You need sleep, but if you can't, then we'll have to remedy that. So, your choices are simple. Go to sleep, go see my cousins for relief or remove your shorts."

He waited as if the answer didn't matter, which was absurd because it sure as hell did. He wanted her to slide that bit of cloth off herself.

She wore another pair of silly long socks, these with cartoon dinosaurs, and despite the fact that they shouldn't be sexy, he seemed to have lost his mind when it came to her, because he found everything she did a turn-on.

When she moved, his breath caught, waiting to see if she'd leave. Instead, she slipped her thumbs into the waist of her shorts and worked them down her legs.

Fuck. He lost his train of thought when he spied all the bare skin, since she wore nothing beneath the shorts.

He'd gotten a look when Erik had gone down on her, but now she was all his.

He allowed himself to growl softly in appreciation at the sight of her on her back, her thighs falling open.

Beautiful. He shook himself back awake, the weight of the vibrator in his hand a reminder. It was a wand style, which would be perfect for getting her where she needed to go quickly. He'd kept it in his nightstand like some sort of strange desire for a partner that he didn't really believe would happen.

It had paid off, it seemed.

Torrin remained seated beside her, not wanting to miss a second of the view. His hip complained at the angle, but too bad. He slid a hand along her thigh, feeling just how soft her skin was, how she melted beneath his fingers. His body was all hard muscle, but hers gave so beautifully.

"You are stunning," he whispered without even meaning to.

Except, when he did say it, she whined and lifted her hips.

So, she likes praise? It didn't shock him, and he planned to praise her until she understood how amazing she was.

He moved his hand up over her hip, then slid it along her stomach.

She tensed beneath the touch, which he rewarded with a sharp growl. She had no reason in the world to be self-conscious, and even that second of worry annoyed him.

He didn't pull away, caressing over her soft stomach and up to her full breasts beneath the loose fabric of her shirt. When he teased her nipple, she seemed to forget her worries, because she arched into his palm.

Which seemed the perfect time to take it another step further. He flicked the button on the vibrator and it came to life. He brushed it against her clit, its power meaning he didn't need to be as direct.

She gasped at the sensation, moving away from the intensity.

"Be still," he ordered.

Ashley whimpered but tried to comply, despite the way her muscles twitched beneath her skin. Remaining still was one of the hardest things, so seeing her try to follow the order had his cock hard and desperate.

He teased her clit with the vibrator by easing off then pressing again to tease her. Meanwhile, he toyed with her nipple beneath her shirt, the hardened peak begging for his attention.

He wished he could take it between his lips to toy with it with his tongue. He wanted to lavish attention with his mouth, to bathe each inch of her body with affection.

Since that wasn't possible, he shifted the vibrator to hit the bottom of her clit so the hood couldn't buffer the sensation.

Ashley rolled her hips up, and he could only picture how that would feel had he been over her, how her body would move and her little nails would dig into him.

"You are beautiful like this," he said even as he told himself he should remain silent. Then again, after the day, after worrying he might have lost her, he had no intention of leaving things unsaid. "Surrender to me," he said. "Give in and trust me."

She writhed, but he kept the vibrator on her, even as she twitched, as she whimpered and moaned and drew ever closer to bliss.

Her hand shot out, grasping his thigh, digging in when she came, as if she needed him to keep her safe.

He swore then that he would, that no matter what happened, she'd never feel fear again.

She arched off the bed, her legs snapping shut around his hand despite him keeping the vibrator against her. He teased her through the waves of pleasure, his cock aching, ready to have her himself.

Not going to happen.

When her legs fell open, he turned off the vibrator and pulled his hand from her shirt. Her cheeks were flushed pink, her breathing erratic.

He leaned down and pressed his forehead against hers, breathing her into his lungs, wanting her to soak into him even if he couldn't claim her like he wanted to.

She shifted, and her still-hard nipples brushed his chest.

Instead of what he wanted, he moved away and settled in behind her. He pulled the comforter over them, rewarded by her scooting back against him.

Ashley's breathing evened out as she fell asleep and gave in to the exhaustion that plagued her.

Before Torrin closed his eyes, he allowed himself the smallest of tastes by pressing a gentle kiss to the back of her head, a safe way to offer and take the affection he was driven to express but knew he couldn't.

He had no idea how he would deny them both, but he had to.

Her life depended on it.

Chapter Ten

Liam sat in the home office as he rubbed his eyes. The time was approaching four in the evening and they'd found little that was useful.

Erik groaned from his spot at the side of the room, seated on the couch. Lines were etched between Erik's eyebrows, the only real signs of discomfort.

Not that it was a surprise. No one got shot and went on without any pain.

Liam pulled a bottle of ibuprofen out of the desk, then tossed it over.

Erik hissed when he tried to lift the arm in a sling and the bottle landed in his lap. "Asshole," he muttered before holding the pills in the hand with the sling, then pinched the top and opened it. He dry-swallowed at least two pills.

"How could he be this far off the map?" Liam shut the drawer especially hard. "We've tracked down gangsters and fucking special ops with less trouble than this."

They'd tracked the phone number he'd called from, but it had been a dead end of fake names. The name she knew, Gregory Dice, had no information, no background, nothing. Clearly, another fake.

A knock on the door brought their gazes up. There would only be one person who would knock. Torrin would just walk in and they'd canceled cleaning services for the day. Until they had a better handle on the situation, they'd rather not risk people coming and going.

"Come in," Liam called.

Sure enough, Ashley walked in, dressed in jeans and a sweater, her hair damp and braided back. She'd slept late in Torrin's room, well past the time he'd come out.

Torrin, for his part, had only offered a blank look before telling them they'd work from home that day.

Still, it felt like a win. The pink on her cheeks said she hadn't minded her night in his bed.

"Hey, sweet. How are you feeling?"

She tugged at the sweater sleeve. "Good. You should have woken me up, though."

"You needed the sleep."

She shuffled her foot against the ground, then cast a quick look Erik's way.

Ah, that's the problem, then.

"He's fine," Liam assured her.

At that, Erik lifted an eyebrow as though he'd just caught up. "Were you worried about me?"

"You got hurt because of me."

Erik shook his head and held his good hand out to her. He waited until she took it before he pulled her closer and into his lap. It probably jostled his shoulder, but he showed no sign of it. "I was hurt because someone shot me."

"The only reason you were there was because of me, and the only reason they shot you was because of me."

"Did you hold the gun? Pull the trigger? No? Then it wasn't your fault." He wrapped his good arm around her and had her lean against his uninjured side.

Despite it having to have hurt, Erik appeared entirely content having Ashley in his lap.

And Ashley? She seemed uneasy but cautiously optimistic, as though she enjoyed the position but couldn't quite silence all her nerves.

"What are we supposed to do now?"

Liam answered her question. "I'll be honest, sweet, we haven't found much so far. Thankfully, we can work from home for a few days until we hire extra security."

"And I'm supposed to just stay trapped here forever?"

Erik leaned forward and nipped her shoulder. "You will behave yourself for as long as you need to, yes. However, it shouldn't be forever. We'll take care of it."

"Would it be so bad to be trapped here with us?" Liam asked.

Ashley bit her bottom lip as if thinking about it. "Maybe. You are rather bossy."

"Yes, but you like that. Don't forget we can smell how wet you get when we order you around. If you want to lie about it, we'll just have to have you walk around naked, then we can check whenever you deny it." Liam grinned at the thought of Ashley nude, at how he would be able to reach between her curvy thighs and press his thick fingers into her tight heat.

He let his groan escape and echo in the room, not bothering to hide any of it from her.

"I don't know what you're talking about," she said, the lie as obvious as any of hers were.

"Really? Should we check now, then? Because I wouldn't mind a nice examination."

She sucked in a breath that was part embarrassment and part excitement.

Except, before he could act on it, a phone rang. He frowned for a moment, not recognizing the tone.

It was the fear on her face that let him know what it was. He rose and snatched her phone, the one she'd left at the bus station that they'd picked up, and tossed it to her. Erik reached around her and pressed the answer button, then put it on speaker.

The click of Torrin's cane came through the hallway just before the alpha appeared. He must have heard the ring and suspected the same.

"H-hello?" She stumbled over the greeting.

"My darling," came out a voice so calm it nearly drew a shudder through Liam. "Have you not learned your lesson about getting others involved?"

"I didn't get anyone involved."

He released a soft tsk through the line. "I assume the three are there, listening, are they not? Come on, we're gentlemen. Let us speak, man to man."

Torrin picked up the phone, always willing to be the face of the trio, or in this case, the voice. "This is Gregory Dice, correct?"

Gregory hummed softly. "Yes. And this is Torrin Kansas, no doubt. Your bodyguards are with you often, but I doubt they speak for you."

Torrin's hand tightened on the cane, his knuckles blanching. "Yes. I'm giving you one chance to walk away from this. Ashley is under my protection."

"She is mine." Gregory said it with no doubt in his voice, with the same certainty as though he were saying the sky was blue or that the earth circled the sun. "I don't care if your bodyguards have taken a liking to her. I don't care if you wish to keep her. I have chased her for a long time and no one, least of all you, will keep her from me."

"You have no idea who you are dealing with," Torrin threatened. "Trust me when I say I can make things very unpleasant for you."

A pause, then a chuckle. "I was about to say the same to you. Since this is going nowhere, I suppose I'll speak to Ashley once more. You can hear me, dear, right?"

Ashley trembled in Erik's lap so hard, her teeth almost chattered. "I'm here."

"Very good. Don't worry. You'll be back with me soon, safe and sound, and I will remind you why you belong there. You can't escape me, love, not ever."

The line went dead, and that shaking grew in Ashley. Liam was over to the couch a heartbeat later, catching her hand. He'd heard the insanity in Gregory's voice, had gotten a taste of the sort of obsession he had.

He wouldn't let it go, not ever. That disease was too deep inside the man for him to ever let her live any sort of life. As long as he breathed, she'd never be free.

Liam met Erik's gaze over her head, a question there.

Erik nodded back to Liam's unvoiced question.

If Gregory would never let her go, the solution was obvious.

They'd track down and kill Gregory.

* * * *

Ashley expected being stuck inside to bother her more than it did. After so many years of feeling as though someone were following her, as if she couldn't ever let her guard down, she'd thought going through that same fear in an enclosed space would eat at her.

Instead, she found an odd sort of freedom in it. Maybe it was the alphas that helped her relax, that helped her to feel as though the walls of the apartment were a fortress rather than a cage.

The men worked, though it seemed there was usually one who was 'taking a break' to keep her company.

Not that she needed company. Liam had set her up in the office off her bedroom with everything she needed to do her job as well. She called clients, scheduled meetings — though none for at least a week — and passed the day without thinking much about Gregory.

There was freedom in that.

It wasn't that he wasn't a threat — he was — but for the first time, she had something other than him to think about.

She thought about Torrin's story, about the mate he'd lost. She thought about the three of them, about the life they must have had before her. They'd hinted at a less than happy childhood, but they'd grown into smart, successful businessmen.

Still, she couldn't shake the feeling they weren't being entirely honest.

You're just paranoid because of Gregory. Stop it.

But...the way Erik and Liam moved, the way they watched things, the ease they'd had taking down the men who had attacked her, with exchanging fire with whoever had shot Erik—it all screamed there was more to them than she'd realized.

They'd said they were bodyguards. So, they *would* be comfortable with those sorts of things.

Guilt clawed at her for even questioning them. They'd taken her in, helped her, had kept helping her even after one of them had been wounded and all were in danger.

Hadn't they proven themselves?

"Hey there, sweet." Liam looked up from his laptop when Ashley entered his office.

Torrin was in his own office and Erik had gone to the lobby to check in on the workers they'd hired to install extra cameras. Erik didn't seem to trust people to do their jobs without him overseeing.

Ashley held up her offering, which won her a smile from Liam.

She handed over the cup of coffee, made the way he seemed to like it. She'd watched him drink it into the late hours, and almost smiled at how she'd already started to memorize their preferences and differences.

Liam was the one who liked sweet drinks, so he poured an ungodly amount of sugar into his. Erik enjoyed his black, whereas Torrin liked a bit of heavy cream but no sugar. Ashley had filed all those details away.

Liam sipped the hot liquid, then closed his eyes and let out a moan that reminded her of other, much less appropriate things. "Thanks. It's perfect."

The praise made her breath catch. Why was she so susceptible to that? One little compliment and she melted like butter for them.

Like it even takes that.

Fair. She had to be the sluttiest virgin who had ever lived.

Liam caught her by sliding two fingers into the front of her skirt and tugging softly until she stood just between his thighs. His gaze was hungry, and she doubted it mattered what he wanted — she was on board.

He took another sip of the coffee before he set it on the table beside the couch. "You know, one of these times I'll need to get you in a bed. Gotten you off in your office, in the living room, but never in a bed."

She recalled Torrin from the night before, how soft and warm his bed had been, how his scent had wrapped around her as he'd reached between her thighs and —

"Have I told you how much I love that your face is an open book? Anything that crosses your mind dances right across your features, too. Makes me want to play strip poker with you."

Ashley chuckled at the joke. "Yeah, I was never really the poker type."

"Not surprised. What type were you? Before the running, before just surviving, what were you like?"

Ashley tried to think back, feeling like it was almost another lifetime ago, like it had been a different girl. "I was happy. I did well in school, had everything set up to go off to college."

"Yeah? What were you going to study?" Liam pulled her forward more until she crawled into his lap, straddling him with her knees on each side of his body.

What were we talking about? "Business," she said after having to think far too hard for the answer. "I was going to get a business administration degree."

"Not a surprise. You're already damn good at it. Not sure I've ever seen our clients sing anyone's praises quite so high. I mean, you had Hardwitch happy, and he's never been happy since Erik broke his thumbs."

Ashley laughed at the stupid joke. Leave it Liam to always try to humor her.

He spoke again, quickly, as if trying to wipe away the joke. *Afraid I'll take it seriously?* "What else, sweet? Were you an AV nerd sort of girl? Couldn't have been drama, not with how easy you are to read."

Ashley shifted, unsure she wanted to say the next part. As she'd grown older and tried to be taken seriously, some things seemed...childish. The alphas were tough, full-grown adults with real lives. Still, they'd already gone over her not lying worth anything, so she dropped her gaze and muttered her answer. "I was a cheerleader."

Silence met her for a heartbeat, before his dark chuckle ended it. "Oh, sweet, why'd you have to go and say that? It probably isn't right at all, but now I can't think of you in anything but one of those cute little cheerleader skirts." He set his large, strong hands on her hips and pulled her down against him. His hard cock stroked her, stealing her breath.

Ashley went on instinct, tired of waiting for things, and leaned forward. She took a kiss, wanting it more than she cared about looking stupid.

Liam offered it, seemed to offer anything. Even as they kissed, he kept the hold on her waist and rocked her down against him, a reminder of everything he wanted—everything *she* wanted right then.

She wasn't afraid—hell, she wasn't even nervous. He could have lifted her skirt and she'd have happily let him slide into her.

Sure enough, he moved one of his hands to her knee, to where the skirt had ridden up, then slipped it up her thigh. His fingers teased her, drawing goosebumps where they trailed along the soft, sensitive inside of her leg.

Liam broke the kiss only so he could move his talented lips to her neck. He drove her crazy with the stroking of his tongue over her pulse and along her collarbone.

Though all of that paled from where her attention was mostly focused, which was how near his fingers were to her bare cunt.

He let out a feral sound when he brushed naked skin. "No underwear?"

Her skin flushed, but Ashley still answered his unasked question, feeling like she wanted to deny it had been some plan. "I didn't have anything nice, and I was sick of you all seeing my plain cotton ones."

Liam barked out a laugh before dragging his tongue up the side of her throat. "You could wear a paper bag and I'm pretty sure I'd still get hard just looking. Besides, I've got a thing for those cute little panties of yours, the ones with the silly cartoons on them." He slid his fingers up the center of her pussy, the action enough for her hands to fly to his shoulders and grip tight. "Now, Ashley, you think I could slide into your tight cunt? I bet it'll squeeze around my fingers so well."

He made her breathless. Every word he spoke, filthy and direct, made her hotter. She'd only dealt with boys before, with people who used euphemisms. She'd never had a man who was willing to tell her exactly what he wanted.

And even better? One willing to ask.

Ashley brushed her forehead to his, an oddly intimate caress. "Yes, please."

She trusted him. Trusted him not to hurt her, to only bring her pleasure, to take her somewhere she'd never been before.

He licked along her bottom lip, the action as drugging as the praise he offered, then pulled his hand away.

Before she could ask him, or worry that he'd changed his mind, Liam licked his fingers in a slow and unbelievably sexy motion. He quirked his lip up into a smirk. "I would usually have to do that to help, but you're drenched, sweet, absolutely *dripping*."

"So why?"

"Because I haven't gotten to taste you, yet. Figured it was my turn."

She tried to look away from the intensity of his dark eyes.

"Keep looking at me." He didn't hold the same snap that Torrin did in his tone, yet she still followed him, her cunt squeezing around nothing. "I want to see those eyes when I get my fingers inside you. You've got the prettiest eyes, Ashley, the most expressive. I want to see it all." As he spoke, he lowered his hand beneath her skirt again. He went to her pussy, pressing softly at first, until he sank one thick finger into her.

The unfamiliar stretch of her body made her squirm, made her dig her fingers into his shoulders.

"Easy," he coaxed. "You have a body *made* for this. Trust me."

Ashley tried, but when he moved his hand, when he teased the walls of her cunt with his careful finger, she gasped. Her body squeezed, but he only waited. She relaxed after a moment, and he took that chance to sink deeper then retreat. He didn't stop, only pausing when she tightened down, and before long, his finger was buried all the way inside her, his hand pressed against her pussy on the outside, as deep as he could get.

"I knew you'd feel perfect," he said. No doubt he'd meant his voice to come across as soft and reassuring, but instead it sounded rough and wild, as if he was walking some difficult line himself.

Ashley sought his lips again, to distract herself with them. Liam gave what she wanted before he started to thrust that finger into her. He withdrew then plunged deep, and each time he did, she wanted more.

She'd always assumed she'd want gentle, sweet sex, except when he touched her the way no one else had, she wanted more, deeper, *rougher*.

She'd have sworn Liam was a mind reader, because he chuckled against her lips and gave her what she wanted. He didn't just tease her—he fucked her with that finger, until he withdrew once and two pressed against her.

Ashley didn't have time to worry, not when he plunged his two thick fingers into her.

He brought his other hand to his own pants. It took a moment to shove her skirt out of the way, but he undid the button of his jeans and managed to free his cock.

Ashley rose up, ready for him to shove into her, wanting it more than she had wanted anything else in her life.

Liam let out that dark laugh again. "Eager, huh? Your sweet little cunt isn't quite ready, but I'll be damned if I don't get to come, too. Shift a bit, hmm? I want a good look."

She rose up again, this time grasping her long skirt and pulling it so it bunched at her waist. Her cheeks felt as though they were on fire, but the lust in Liam's eyes said he was taking in the view.

And Ashley did, too.

Liam's cock rested so close, and he plunged his fingers deep into her. Of course, the size of his cock gave her a moment of pause she hadn't had before. He was right — two fingers weren't nearly the same girth or length.

"Don't worry," he assured her as he went about stroking his cock with rough motions and fucking into her with his fingers. He did them in time, as if he were imagining it was his dick inside her. "We'll train you up plenty before you take us. Hell, the work we'll need to do to get your ass ready —"

Her gaze shot up to his at that, and it seemed to cut off his words.

He laughed, hard. That felt strange, the way they could be in the middle of something so passionate, yet he still laughed, still had fun... It made it feel like something they were doing as two people, not just animalistic lust.

"How exactly did you think fucking two alphas would go? Don't look so shocked, sweet, but you do have three perfectly good holes once they get trained up."

Again, the way he spoke so easily made her jealous, since she'd *never* been able to talk about sex like that. Still, the idea of anal sex made her wince. What if she hated it? What if she couldn't do it? They weren't exactly small, from what she'd seen.

Liam curled his fingers inside her, rubbing against a spot that knocked aside the conversation. Not that he seemed willing to let it go. "Never met an omega who didn't end up loving having her ass fucked, and I doubt you'll be the first. Stop worrying, because I want to see that beautiful cunt of yours come, then I'm going to paint it with my cum."

And Ashley gasped as the orgasm washed over her, his words pulling it from her so fast, it surprised her. Somehow, being filled made it better, though he pulled out too quickly. He flipped them, setting her ass on the couch and crouching above her.

She had a spark of fear, just for a moment, that he'd press into her anyway, even though he'd said he wouldn't.

A stupid fear, she realized, when he only stroked his cock over her spread legs, then came with a rough growl. His warm seed struck her cunt, and even that against her clit felt overwhelming.

He had a hand on the couch beside her, his body so close she slipped her arms around the back of his neck, clinging to him.

When his hand slowed, when the tension melted from him, Liam brushed his lips against hers. He moved his hand from his cock to her, gathering the cum that sat on her skin and rubbing it into her, pressing some deep inside her. Each touch sparked lust, but he didn't seem to be trying for that.

Not that he ever had to try. None of the alphas ever had to look seductive, to do anything except be there, and Ashley seemed turned on.

"That was..." Nerves got the best of her. It was what? What was the right thing to say?

Liam seemed to understand her hesitation, because he only let out that same laugh she already knew so well. "It was amazing."

When he pulled back, Ashley stood, noting that she felt a bit less sticky than she'd expected. Still, Liam must have thought it wasn't a good enough solution, because he grabbed a rag from the bathroom and used it to wipe off any residual cum.

"I should shower," she said, his scent still strong enough to cloud her mind. She rose, her skirt falling down. Being covered helped her to form sentences that at least meant something.

Liam swatted her ass playfully. "Not a chance. I like you smelling like me, sweet. Now, go on, you've distracted me for long enough."

"I can't go around them smelling like you."

Liam's dark eyebrow lifted, a mocking curl of his lips. "Why not? I'm pretty sure they know we're involved. Besides, I figure it's a little like sending a lamb into a wolf's den with a steak tied around them."

"Don't lambs in that case get mauled?"

"Absolutely. But I think you'll enjoy the mauling you get, so run along, little lamb."

Ashley left at the gentle pushing of Liam's hands, his words echoing in her ears.

That was exactly how she felt with them, like a prey animal, so why exactly did she feel safe?

I should know better.

Chapter Eleven

Erik would have preferred to go alone.

That was how he worked, how he'd always worked. Sure, when doing basic jobs, he'd have Liam along. Many times, his twin was helpful, given how good Liam was at dealing with people. However, when handling these shadier aspects, Erik preferred privacy.

Maybe it was because a part of him hated to be seen in that light.

It was easy to play the bad guy part, to be used to people fearing him, but having others actually witness the atrocities he committed for the greater good — well, those he preferred to do without others.

However, given Erik's shoulder, there was no chance of that happening. He needed backup because he didn't have a death wish.

While he still had no idea who exactly Gregory was, he did know where the man was staying. Sometimes it wasn't about looking for what was there but for what wasn't.

Hotels were a no-go, because few had security a man like Gregory would trust. It meant he had to be renting something, especially because he'd claimed that he would remain in town if Ashley wanted to.

That had led to far too many hours on the phone with contacts until Erik had found the right one, the one who went silent when he would normally have talked.

Gregory had holed up in a large three-story house, the sort people normally rented when celebrities came into town.

It sat with neighbors on both sides, but with a small amount of space either way to give privacy. All the buildings around it had been split up into apartments already, and it stood like the last of an old dynasty.

Erik had his eyes closed as he sat in the living room, relaxing before he had to go, taking a moment to collect himself. He'd have preferred to be out on the balcony, but again, no death wish. One bullet was more than enough for him.

"Is your shoulder hurting?" Ashley's soft voice still held guilt, which gnawed at Erik.

He'd taken a bullet for her happily, and he'd rather shoulder the guilt, as well. Unfortunately, there was no strike to jump in front of for that.

"No," he said as he opened his eyes. How did she manage to surprise him each time he saw her? It was as though he picked up some new facet of her, a new thing he liked. This time it was that her hair had a curl in the front, amidst the slight waves, that brushed her eyebrow. Perhaps he hadn't noticed before because she often tucked it behind her ear.

He patted the couch when she seemed unsure of her welcome.

She took the seat he offered, tucking her legs beneath her, a long skirt billowing around her.

And she was *soaked* in Liam's scent. It sprang up more than a few filthy thoughts, made him want to add his own scent to her, especially before he left.

Instead, she turned toward him, her hands folded in her lap. "How long have you been with Liam and Torrin?"

He sighed, because talking wasn't his strong suit and talking about ugly subjects was the last thing he wanted to do right then.

Somehow, though, he found himself unwilling to deny her anything. "A long time. We grew up together."

"I didn't have cousins or siblings." Such loss in those words.

"Torrin's mother was Liam and my mother's sister. Torrin's father was never in the picture, so our father took him and his mother in. We've lived together all our lives."

At times, it took saying it for Erik to grasp how much his brother and his cousin meant to him. He knew it, of course, but given that they'd never known any other life than as a trio, it was his normal.

At rare moments, he'd think about losing them. His chest would go tight and he couldn't even consider it, as though his brain lacked the ability. They were more than family. They were like organs he relied on, that he needed to live.

"That must have been nice," she said, pulling him from his musing. "I had my fathers, which meant our house was full, but I didn't have any other family, anyone my age. Would have been nice to grow up with other kids."

'Nice' was not a word he would have used to describe his childhood. He tapped his foot, a nervous habit he'd never managed to break.

He'd learned to curtail it when it mattered, like when on jobs where it could be a tell.

Somehow, he couldn't seem to stop it when his least favorite topic of conversation came up.

"Erik?" Her voice was soft, a question there.

He rose, trying to play off the conversation. "Sorry. My mind wanders. You should sleep soon. Will you take Torrin's room again?"

Her cheeks flushed, that lovely show of unease. "Shouldn't that bother you?"

"You grew up with five fathers. You already know alphas are more than capable of sharing mates without fighting." Besides, it wasn't as though Erik could offer his bed up for the night.

He wouldn't be in it, and even if he were, a part of him wasn't sure if he wanted her there.

He disliked letting his guard down, and he'd never been a sound sleeper.

As petty as it might be, he suspected he wanted her to *want* to sleep in his bed. He didn't want to allow it, but just the desire from her would go a long way toward soothing him.

Which was ridiculous.

He went to take a step toward her, but stilled.

He'd been careful, more so after she'd backed away from him in the alleyway. It made him risk a question he hated to ask. "Are you afraid of me?"

"What? Why would you ask that?"

"Because you've backed away from me. You wouldn't be the first to be afraid." Bitterness nipped at his words.

She came forward, and though her steps were slow, she did it of her own free will. No coaxing, no demands. "What do you mean, I wouldn't be the first?"

He sighed, allowing her to near. "The last female I was close with never trusted me. She looked at me like you have, as though I could never fully prove that she was safe around me. She ended up walking away over it. I don't care for people to be afraid of me, to not trust me, but I have grown used to it."

He left out the rest, that she'd seen him kill, that when, during a walk, two men had leapt from the shadows, Erik had ended them without thought. He'd never shaken the way she'd stared at him, as if he were a worse monster than them.

"You make me nervous," she admitted. "Then again, you all make me a little nervous."

"But you don't retreat from Liam or Torrin."

She set her hands on his chest, careful to avoid his shoulder. "You're…"

Erik didn't pull her closer, didn't move at all. He let her go at her own pace, as much as he hated the slowness of it.

Finally, she sighed and moved to her toes, brushing her lips to his. She whispered against the kiss. "You're quiet, and sometimes I see this other thing inside you, like you're capable of things that would make me shiver. It isn't fair to blame you for it, but I can't help it. It just makes me nervous. I know it isn't you, though. It's just my own fears, my own past."

But it is me. She isn't seeing her own ghosts. She isn't running from her own past. She's seeing what I really am.

Erik gave up fighting it, even as memories swamped him of the last time a woman had feared him, when she'd run from him, when she'd seen the truth of him.

It had nearly destroyed him.

He just had to hide it from Ashley, had to keep it locked away so deeply that it didn't even peek from behind his eyes.

Because if she ever caught a real glimpse, if she ever saw what he was capable of, what he'd done, she would run so far, he'd never catch her.

* * * *

Liam smiled at the way Ashley had plastered herself against Torrin despite the man's obvious discomfort.

She reminded him of a cat who didn't much care if people liked her or not.

Of course, Torrin liked her. It showed in how his hand curled around her, in the rare softness in his dark, stern eyes.

Physical affection wasn't something Torrin had much experience with, however.

Liam remembered back to Gilly. Even with her, Torrin had been stiff, uneasy. He'd cared for her, of course. In fact, Liam had no doubt the two had bonded, that they'd been mates, even if it had been a short relationship. She'd had no desire for additional mates, though, so Liam and Erik had pursued their own relationships.

Well, Erik had.

Liam, despite being the best with women, was also their eternal bachelor.

It was harder to miss something he'd never tasted.

Still, Ashley's hair falling in sweet waves over Torrin's chest, her body curled around his on the couch, was endearing. She gave everything, which was something none of them had ever really experienced.

Their lives consisted of people who took, who stole, who would sell a person out at the first chance if there was something in it for them. Ashley wasn't like that, and while it was exciting, it scared him.

She didn't fit into their world.

Too soft. Too sweet. Too unaware of the real dangers out there.

She shifted, and a familiar tension in Torrin said she'd moved in a way that aggravated his hip.

Not that the stubborn man would say a word about it. He never complained, never bemoaned the injury. In fact, even when Liam thought back to the start, back to when Torrin had taken care of them when he'd returned, when that hip had to have been agonizing, he'd said nothing.

Just as Liam was about to say something — not to bring it up directly, it would only annoy him and upset Ashley — she seemed to realize it as well.

Observant girl.

Ashley shifted away. "Oh, sorry," she said quickly.

Torrin waved off the concern, though that same gentleness in his face said her worry had chipped away at his walls.

Still, Ashley remained sitting up instead of retaking her spot against his side.

"What are you thinking?" Liam smiled at her sharp look — or the sharpest the sweet girl could manage. "I know that face. You want to ask something."

"Erik said you three lived together all your lives."

An arctic chill took the room, the same temperature drop that happened each time the topic was broached.

She sighed, setting her hands in her lap. "Never mind."

Liam swallowed down his discomfort. "Sorry. It's just not a topic we much care for."

"Neither was Gregory for me, but I still told you."

"We needed to know about him. There's something that can be done. Our past has no resolution, so no point in discussion," Torrin said.

She deflated, shoulders lowering, body hunching.

How did she managed to tug at Liam that way? He'd always been the one to manipulate others, yet he continuously did what she wanted despite his best intentions. "It was an ugly time, sweet. Let's just say that our parents cared more about getting high than they did about raising children. We got out as quickly as we could. Can we change subjects?"

Her face said she didn't care for the avoidance, that she wanted to understand more, but she only nodded. "Then I want to know about the omega whose room I'm staying in."

Well, fuck. Liam wasn't sure that was any better a topic.

Torrin looked at her. "Is that why you didn't want to sleep there?"

She nodded. "The room's set up and taken care of like you expect her back. Am I just taking someone's place while you all wait for her?"

Torrin cast his gaze to Liam, but Liam only offered a short jerk of his head.

Of all the conversations he could have, he did not want to do this one. If he did, he'd have to decide whether to tell the truth or lie, and he didn't know which was worse.

"The omega's name is Kara. We met her when she was a teenager and took her in," Torrin said.

"Where is she now?"

"She has mates she lives with. We kept her room out of a silly nostalgia. She's grown now, hasn't lived here in a long time."

"So she wasn't your mate?"

Liam stared at the floor, not at her. If he looked at her, she might read the guilt.

Which was stupid, because he shouldn't feel guilty. He'd slept with plenty of females and had no problem with it. Just because she was a virgin didn't mean he was expected to be one as well. He didn't regret the sex he'd had, the women he'd enjoyed.

But Kara had been different, and he damned well knew it.

While neither of them had enjoyed the sex, there was still a connection between them, and keeping it from Ashley, especially since she was staying in the same room Kara had, felt wrong.

Not that Liam would change it.

Secrets were part of life, and he couldn't imagine that one was any worse than any of the others they were keeping from her.

You can lie to others, but don't lie to yourself.

"Sorry, I was being jealous," she said.

Her apology burned Liam, because she had no reason to apologize, unlike him.

Instead of dealing with that, he turned on the charm he used like a weapon and hid his real feelings away until they collapsed beneath the weight of his false mask. "Jealous, huh? Well, sweet, I actually sort of like jealousy on you."

She gave him a glare.

He only turned his look to Torrin. "Did you know she was a cheerleader?"

Torrin groaned, a break from his stoic act. "Dear god, I feel like a pervert thinking about that. I am fairly sure I am too old to like the idea of you in a cheerleading costume."

She flushed, the praise doing what it always did, as though it watered parts of her that had withered over time, like it soaked into her soul. "You can't keep a secret," she said to Liam.

"No, I really can't. To be fair, omega, I think the three of us have to work together just to deal with you. You seem to wrap us around your finger if we don't."

She stuttered for a moment. "I do not! As I recall, I said no to the furniture, to moving into the apartment, to the job and even tried to run away. You keep getting your way, not me."

He huffed a soft laugh at her sullen tone. "And good thing we do, because you don't look so bad off. You can't say this isn't better than being alone in some roach-infested apartment somewhere."

She took her lip between her teeth, but her expressive eyes said it all. This was *far* better.

"You're impossible," she said instead of fighting any further.

Liam moved from his spot to the couch beside her. He grasped her shoulders to rearrange her—despite her hands that swatted at him—so her head was in his lap and her legs rested over Torrin's lap.

It wouldn't aggravate the other alpha's hip, and Liam rather liked her belonging to them both like this.

Liam stroked his fingers through her hair until her breathing evened out, until she drifted off to sleep.

He liked that, liked the trust she must have in them if she could let down her guard enough to be so vulnerable with them.

Claimed by the Alphas

Torrin stroked his fingers over the knee-high socks she wore—this pair without characters, just stripes of bright colors—his gaze curious.

"So, are you giving in, yet?"

"She slept in my bed last night, did she not?"

Liam shrugged. "Sure, but she still doesn't carry your scent, so you clearly kept enough distance to stop that from happening. How long do you really think you can walk this line?"

"As long as I need to."

The stubborn alpha was often too difficult for his own good—or anyone else's.

"Don't bullshit me. I know you too well. You're going to give in, because you can't help it. None of us can."

Torrin's long fingers traced the stripes on the socks in slow, gentle caresses. "I feel like this is temporary. We're balancing things that won't stay, and we are doing so at her risk."

"She needed help. Were we supposed to turn our backs on her?"

"No, but we also didn't need to get involved. Do you really think she has a place in our world? Be honest, Liam, not about what you want, what you wish, but about reality. Do you truly think that this could last?"

Liam twisted one of her soft tresses around his finger, marveling at how every part of her gave so easily. She was like water, able to meld to anything. She was the thing missing in their lives, the thing they didn't deserve but wanted so badly.

She was the softness to all the hardness their lives had been.

But Torrin's question refused to be ignored, knocking at Liam's skull as it had since he'd met her, since he'd first set eyes on the beautiful, gentle omega who was so much more than they'd ever expected to find.

He forced himself to answer, no matter how painful the words were, as though ripped from his throat and jagged. "No. I don't see how it could last."

"Then how can we put her through this? How can we do it to ourselves?"

Liam sighed, letting go of that mask he wore, letting Torrin see how tired he was from it. "Do you remember that treehouse we built? The one that was mostly just random pieces of found wood leaning in that huge old pine tree?"

"As I recall, I told you two it would never stand."

"And Erik and I still built it and sat up there. The first good windstorm that happened, the pieces went flying. Erik and I ended up cut up—"

"And I got a black eye from a piece that fell down," Torrin reminded him. "It seems I was right."

"You were right that it would fall, but you know what? When we were up there, even if it was a short time, even if we paid for it, we were free. It was a break, a moment of something good in the middle of all that shit. Ask Erik and I bet he'd say the same. It was worth the pain, even if it didn't last."

Torrin didn't acknowledge the lesson, his gaze dropping to the sleeping omega stretched out between them.

He could see the question in Torrin's eyes.

Will the pain be worth it?

Was it ever?

Chapter Twelve

Erik waited in the dark car parked across from the house Gregory was staying in. He'd yet to catch sight of the man himself — Ashley had given him a general description — but the movement of figures across his lines of sight signaled guards.

It all said the man was connected, though he doubted it was much past a trust fund kid. Everything he'd heard thus far had screamed of a man who had never learned the meaning of the word no, someone who had been denied nothing. That sort of egotistical asshole had caused Erik plenty of problems, but nothing a sharp blade couldn't fix.

The door to the car opened, the light remaining off, as his backup slid into the seat beside him.

"We should kill people more often." Kara spoke in the same voice he suspected children used about going to a carnival.

"I'm surprised your mates let you out." He didn't bother to hide his distaste for the three she'd chosen to settle down with. Kara was vicious — Erik, Liam and Torrin had taught her to be — and she'd somehow decided to bond with three goody-two-shoes private detectives.

However, he'd long since learned he couldn't control her. If the alphas she'd picked annoyed her too much, she would bury them herself.

"I snuck out. I've gotten six text messages since I left."

He shook his head and remembered that as much pity as he had for her, he should probably have more for her mates.

Still, she kept up that dreamy tone of voice, as though talking about a future romantic date. "Maybe they'll spank me later."

"I do not need to hear that," Erik assured her.

She only laughed, the pleased reaction she gave whenever she managed to annoy someone enough. "Okay, fine, so you were vague on details here. What are we doing?"

"You don't normally care why you're hired."

"And I don't especially now, except you smell like an omega and your arm is in a sling and I heard there's a female staying with you all. That's the only real reason I came out tonight. I need details."

Kara was a consummate liar. Few words left her mouth that weren't at least partly untrue. She'd have come out no matter what, because, despite her flippant attitude, she cared for Erik and the others as much as they cared for her. However, the tiny blue-haired girl also wouldn't let it go until she had answers.

"Her name is Ashley."

She waved her hands to get him to keep going.

Frustrating woman. I should have let her bleed out the first night we met instead of saving her. He chose to keep the subject on the task at hand. "She's been stalked for years by the man who lives here. She's had to move from place to place since she turned eighteen to avoid him. When he knew we were involved, he had someone take a shot."

"*You* let your guard down and got shot? Are you getting old, or is it love?"

He gritted his teeth against the invasive and unwelcome question. "The easiest way to handle the situation is to remove Gregory. Do you have a problem with that?"

"With offing some stalking asshole who is preying on young omegas? You know that's like Christmas for me." She rubbed her palms together, excitement seeming to thrum through her.

Which again reminded him how different Ashley was from Kara.

The only two omegas who had been in his life for any amount of time and they were nothing alike. Of course, his only other attempt at a relationship had been a disaster, and it had been with a beta female whose personality was like Ashley's.

The truth was, women like Kara did better in his world. They survived it, were tough enough to handle it.

But that was the thing—Erik had never wanted a woman like Kara. She was strong, capable, but drenched in as much blood as he was.

Maybe it was stupid, desiring someone unlike him, but that was what he'd always wanted. He craved a woman who would ease him, who would make him feel like something other than a killer.

"That's a pretty sour look," Kara said, her voice surprisingly soft. "What's rattling around in your thick skull?"

"You settled down with men who were nothing like you."

She nodded, sitting back in her seat as if content to let the talk take as long as it took. Perhaps her time with her mates had done her some good, because never before had she been able to actually communicate. "I've spent enough time with myself. Let me guess, your little female you're doing all this for…she's a sweetheart, isn't she? She must be, if you're here playing hero while she's home safe and sound."

Erik cut a sharp look her way. Her digging under layers of his secrets had always been an annoying habit of hers.

She only kept speaking. "I've learned something that took me a long time. People, for the most part, hate themselves. We tend to want something totally different. Soft people want tough ones, bitches want gentle people, dominants want submissive. We always want what we don't have because that's how things fit. If we wanted to spend our lives with ourselves, why try at all?"

It all sounded good, but none of it soothed his worries. "How can someone like that accept—"

"Someone like you?" Was that pity in her voice? "Look, I'll deny it if you ever repeat this, but you're not so bad."

"I'm a killer."

"Everyone is a killer if given a good enough reason. Even your little wallflower. If she's still there, willingly, then she must not mind you too much, especially if her scent all over you says a thing."

He shook his head. "You don't understand. She doesn't know about us. She thinks we're simple businessmen."

Kara snorted softly. "There's never been anything simple about any of you. How about you take some advice from me, huh?"

"Because you're an expert at relationships?"

"I've done better than you, asshole."

Erik had to concede that point, so he gestured for her to continue.

"Don't lie to her. We females take that personal, and we *always* find out the truth eventually. Then you have to deal with not only the problem — which might not have been such a big problem to start with — but with the fact you're also now a lying douchebag. So come clean, deal with the fallout then move on and have little crotch fruit or whatever it is you do."

He went to open his mouth, to argue, but she pointed a finger at him. "One had better be named after me, but I will not babysit."

Before they could go further with the conversation, the lights on the upper floor went out, signaling that Gregory had gone to sleep.

It put the conversation on hold, which Erik was thrilled with. He hadn't really considered children, considered that life.

It made his chest tight. If having a mate was a risk, he couldn't imagine the danger to his offspring.

Thankfully, Kara didn't dwell on things. She was already sliding from the car.

They made their way easily through the dark house, entering through the back door when one of the guards went out for a smoke break. They didn't kill any of the guards, since he preferred not to leave bodies when it wasn't necessary. Silence and quickness let them put down the four people inside the house. Because of Erik's arm, Kara did a lot of the heavy lifting. Still, it was amazing how willing to be gagged and zip-tied a man was when faced with Erik's blade.

It put them on the top floor in only about fifteen minutes, with no one the wiser. They crept into the last room, the large master at the end of the hallway, the place Gregory had to be.

Once in place, Erik flipped the lights on.

The bed lay empty.

Erik searched the room, unease pricking him at.

Sure enough, in the far corner, leaning against a desk, stood a man who matched the description Ashley had given him.

Late-thirties with short, neatly styled black hair. Blue-eyed and impeccably dressed.

Gregory.

Kara kept her gun trained on him, but his lack of reaction didn't bode well.

"So, it seems you were right. I didn't know who I was dealing with," he said. "I had expected Ashley found some simple alphas, too dumb to be a true problem. Who would have expected she'd have found *you*?"

Erik narrowed his gaze, wanting to rip her name from his mouth so the man could never utter it again. "You made a mistake by targeting her. At least it will be your last."

Gregory crossed his arms, appearing as if the threat meant nothing to him. "I don't make mistakes. I'm impressed you not only found me but made it up here. Did you kill the guards?"

"They're fine," Kara said.

"Pity. They were useless, and I'll kill them anyway. I can't abide useless people." Gregory's eyes found Erik's shoulder. "The man who took that shot did not make it another night. He should have killed you, not merely wounded you. I guarantee, the next person I send will not miss again."

"You won't get the chance for another."

Gregory's smile lacked warmth when it slithered across his lips. "You truly think I wouldn't be prepared for this? Nothing escapes me, nothing goes without my planning it. Ashley should have explained that."

"To me, it looks like you're unarmed, and we have you in our sights."

"Yes, but if I die, Ashley will never be safe. I've already set up a contract on her."

"So much for loving her," Erik snarled.

"Oh, I love her dearly, but if I am dead, she ought to join me. In the event of my death, I have people who will be paid handsomely to ensure she doesn't survive the night."

Erik bared his teeth, a sense of impotence surrounding him.

A bang down the stairs caught his attention. *Reinforcements.*

Gregory chuckled. "The moment you breached the back door, I had more men on the way. You didn't really believe I would be so easily caught unaware? I recognized your friend there immediately. How did you get pulled into this, Kara?"

Kara had lost her smile, a rare event. "I didn't realize it was you we were coming to kill."

"And if you had?"

"I'd have set the building on fire and roasted marshmallows."

Heavy feet on the first story stairs told Erik where the reinforcements were, and Erik doubted they'd come in friendly.

Kara shrugged. "Well, this was a clusterfuck. Until next time." She offered a mock salute then brought her elbow back, shattering the window.

Erik growled softly. Kara was the type to act first and think never, but she wasn't wrong in their limited options.

She ducked through the window onto the short ledge outside. Erik followed, though his shoulder made his balance substandard.

They shifted to the left, moving as quickly as the thin space would allow. At the corner sat the narrow space between buildings, along with a balcony attached to the next-door apartment.

Kara went first, leaping over the short expanse, and landed on the balcony. Erik went next, though his useless arm made it more difficult. He hit the ground of the balcony hard and toppled forward a few steps. Kara steadied him.

Kara pulled that slider, rewarded by it opening. Then again, the owner probably thought the second-floor balcony to be a fairly safe entry point.

Amateur.

The place was dark, but Erik followed Kara through the room — an office, it seemed — then down the stairs. In the living room, a man sat in front of a television that ran infomercials. He jumped up, face masked with fear, wearing nothing but boxer shorts.

"Sorry, just passing through," Kara said as though it were the most normal thing. Still, the man didn't seem up for tangling with them, because he lifted his hands as if threatened and let them pass.

Erik and Kara went out through the back door, into the small back yard. The slam of a door from the next yard said the reinforcements were trying to play catch up.

However, Erik and Kara had spent enough time together over the years to be faster than most.

At the back fence, Kara laced her hands together. The need for help chafed but Erik used the boost to help him over. She hopped the thing without a problem, and they went through that front gate to the street.

A block over gave them some space, and before long, Erik and Kara had disappeared into the night.

The car had been stolen, so there was no worry about it.

"We need to talk," Kara said, her voice more serious than usual for her.

Erik stopped short, the words less chilling than her tone. "Who is he?"

"Let's get back to your place before I explain how fucked you are."

Chapter Thirteen

Torrin didn't care for waking to find Erik still gone.

At times he felt less like an equal and more like an exhausted mother trying to keep her unruly children in line. That feeling was only intensified when Erik and Kara were together.

Torrin loved Kara as a sister, but no matter what the problem was, she could always make it much worse.

Still, for what needed to be done, there was no better choice. Liam could be taken to help on such jobs, but his talents were mostly wasted there. He was better for face-to-face work, when coaxing was needed. This particular job would be all teeth.

And no matter how much Torrin might worry for Erik and Kara, he also knew the two were exceptional at their skills.

Still, with the sun rising and no word, he couldn't help but worry.

His hip ached from sleeping on the couch, though he'd not have given it up for anything. Somehow, with Ashley near him, he always slept with more peace.

Nightmares didn't come, or if they did, he pushed them off with ease. An ache in his hip was a small price to pay.

The door opened, and Torrin was already prepared to complain about not hearing from Erik. Except, when he came in with Kara on his heels, both looking worse for wear, it stopped anything he'd considered saying.

Their expressions said it all.

It hadn't gone well.

"What happened?"

"I had to walk for two miles. I jumped off a building. Also, Erik is a horrible date because I didn't even get a meal out of it," Kara said, her humor helping to ease the tightness of Torrin's chest.

If she was making jokes, she was fine.

Erik cut her a dry look. "If you want food, you have two hands. Go to the kitchen and make some."

"Worst date ever—"

"Get to the point," Torrin snapped. Normally he took Kara's bickering—and she fought with everyone—in stride. Right then, however, he couldn't find his usual calm.

Not with his life on pause. Not with Ashley at risk. Not when faced with what was an obvious failure.

Kara whistled low. "He's smitten, isn't he? I don't think I've ever seen him yell like that, not even when I wrapped his sports car around that lamppost."

Torrin pressed his lips together but didn't answer.

"Fine," she said on a sigh. "Look, Tor, this is bad. I know Gregory."

"What do you mean, you know him?" True, Kara had more than her fair share of odd acquaintances, but Gregory seemed even further out of her normal group.

"Well, I don't know him personally. We don't go for frozen yogurt or anything." At Torrin's sharp look, she continued, "He's one of the top guys in that slavery ring that's been going around."

That had been among the last things Torrin had expected to hear. Dealing with spoiled rich kids was one thing. Going up against the sort of people who worked with slavery rings was quite another.

Torrin and his cousins were not good people by a long shot, willing to skirt more than a few ethical lines to do what needed to be done. However, slavery was evil of an entirely different sort.

Omega trafficking was the lowest level of foul, and the people who engaged in such a business were beyond ruthless. It was one of the many reasons omegas so often went into hiding. Some alphas cared little who their mate was as long as they had one, and were willing to pay handsomely to be given one.

"You're sure?" Erik asked.

Kara nodded, crossing her arms. "I had a job about four years ago to steal some files for a client from a big office building in Arizona. As usual, I took a look at what they were before handing them over. It was information on a few of the smaller cells, on recent abductions in that area. In addition, it had a file on Gregory Tansin, along with a picture. The files were from a private eye the father of the family member had hired."

"What did you do with the files?"

"I left out the file on Gregory and washed a few other files before turning them over. Don't look at me like that. It was pretty obvious that the asshole who hired me wanted to see what the father and PI knew. If they'd realized the PI had found out that much, they'd have killed them both." She shook her head. "Not that it mattered. Wasn't a week after I handed the files over to my client that I heard both the father and the PI were missing. I didn't think Gregory would have known about me, but I guess he was more involved with hiring me than I realized."

Kara's gaze held that spark Torrin had always envied. She felt so much, and while it could hurt, she also had a passion Torrin lacked. He'd assumed it had been his past that made him like he was, yet Kara hadn't lived so different a life and she retained her fun, her ability for things to matter.

He'd thought, at first, that perhaps having that sort of life around him might somehow soak into him. It was one reason he'd taken Kara in when he'd had every reason to turn away the wild, undisciplined kid who had broken into his apartment, trying to rob him. It had never worked, though.

Until he remembered the way Ashley made him want to smile.

He cut short that line of thought, focusing on Kara instead.

"Is there any chance you still have what you found?"

Kara nodded. "I'll get it sent over today. It isn't much, but at least you'll have a start. Now, please tell me you still have some of my things here."

Torrin gestured toward the room that had been hers—*funny that I already see it as now being Ashley's.* "Ashley's sleeping in Liam's room. Your things are still in the far closet, though I suspect we will have to consider moving them."

She paused, curling her lips into that smirk he knew so well. "So, it's that serious? Good for you."

She left, moving a bit slowly, telling him she had to be sore.

He focused his attention on Erik, feeling freer to talk without others around to listen. "Anything to add?"

Erik's gaze fell to the floor, the way he did when thinking. "I spoke with him, looked into his eyes and talked to him. We are not just dealing with a man willing to trade omegas like cattle — we are dealing with a man who believes with all he is that Ashley is his due, that she's already his mate. I think the bastard is bonded to her somehow."

"I'm surprised you didn't kill him."

"He put a contract on Ashley. If he dies, we have to deal with assassins. It seemed a better option to deal with him. At least we know he's coming. Plus, he's after us. Easier to protect ourselves than keep Ashley alive."

Torrin didn't disagree with the choice. He would far rather have a target on his back than Ashley's.

A phone rang, the one that had been Ashley's, which sat on the kitchen table.

Only one person that might be.

Torrin crossed the room and answered. "Hello, Mr. Tansin." He used the name Kara had given him.

"Well, I suppose it's only fair we are on an equal footing, isn't it? I've spent some time after the close call tonight looking deeper into you and your cousins, and wasn't I surprised to discover we are not so different."

"I would disagree. I don't sell human beings into slavery."

"So righteous, aren't you? You have quite the body count to your name, Mr. Kansas. Through your career, from what I could find, I see drug sales, arms sales and no shortage of corpses in your wake. You might think of yourself as being better than me, but you're not. I'm only more successful."

"But you're in our city."

"So it seems. I came here for Ashley, and I will leave with her. Make no mistake about that. Have a nice day, Mr. Kansas."

When the line went dead, Torrin lowered the phone to the table.

This had just become a far more dangerous situation than he'd have liked, and for the first time, he feared they might not make it through.

* * * *

Ashley yawned as she entered her room, having left Liam sleeping. Not that she could blame him for being tired. She'd woken in the early hours as he'd carried her to his room, not hers, and she couldn't fault his choice. He'd ensured she'd gotten to sleep afterward, something he seemed to excel at when he'd put his smart mouth to good work, driving another orgasm from her.

It wasn't just the sex that drew Ashley to the trio, but she had to admit that was a bonus she'd never expected. She'd been so shut down for the years she'd run from Gregory that she hadn't been sure this part of her had survived, the one that enjoyed touch, that craved passion. However, the alphas had woken it and had somehow allowed it to grow until she felt fundamentally different.

She slipped into her room, wanting to get a comb through her hair, brush her teeth and dress.

Her room felt almost silly, now. She hadn't slept in it for a single night, instead sleeping beside the alphas. Alone, she always waited, listening, fearful. With them near, her body relaxed into a sleep she'd not felt since leaving home.

The door to the bathroom opened, and Ashley jumped when a woman she didn't know exited the bathroom.

No, an omega. Her nose caught that first and a few moments later, she figured it out.

It was the omega who had lived in this room.

"Kara," was all Ashley said, the name she'd heard them say.

Kara stopped in her tracks, her gaze raking over Ashley like a predator sizing up prey. It was then that Ashley realized just how different they were.

Ashley was soft where Kara was much more like the alphas.

They said she wasn't their mate. She's like a sister.

Still, it was hard to shake the nerves, especially with Ashley staying in the omega's room...

"Ashley, right? Sorry to scare you, but Torrin said you were sleeping in Liam's room."

Liam's name on Kara's lips felt strange, but Ashley couldn't quite identify why.

"I let him sleep in," Ashley said as though to defend herself.

Kara waved her off, her smile not unfriendly but not exactly warm, either. "I wasn't trying to blame you, just explaining. I needed a quick shower and change before I head home, and I still have a few things here. Didn't mean to disturb you. I was just going to go check in once more with Torrin before I head out. Nice meeting you." Kara was out of the room before Ashley could gather anything else to say.

She got herself dressed quickly, pulling her hair into a ponytail as she considered the strange woman.

Kara was strong, confident and more than a match for the alphas. So why *weren't* they mates?

Once Ashley felt human again, when her mouth tasted of minty toothpaste and she'd dressed in her favorite pair of jeans, the ones she wore that made her ass look good on days when she needed that sort of pickup, she exited the room.

Torrin stood in the kitchen, his gaze finding her in an instant, as if he'd been waiting for her. Liam was at the table, Kara seated beside him.

They were talking, smiling, *laughing*. Something about it gnawed at her, something she couldn't write off. There was a strange connection between them.

Ashley walked into the living room from the hallway, until Kara reached over and set her hand on Liam's arm.

That was when it hit her.

It was obvious in a way Ashley couldn't deny.

They'd slept together.

It was written in the comfort between the two, and somewhere in their scents, she could identify it. *But they said…*

Ashley flinched. No. Torrin had said *he'd* never slept with her, and they'd said she wasn't their mate.

Liam hadn't admitted to sleeping with her, but the carefully worded conversation made it clear he'd purposely left it out.

"Ashley." Torrin's voice, careful yet strong, made her lift her gaze toward the kitchen, to where he stood.

It also made Liam turn, so engrossed with his conversation that he'd not even noticed her.

Of course not. Who would with Kara there?

She didn't even dislike Kara, which made it worse. Kara seemed honest, and she didn't strike Ashley as someone who was conniving. She had her own mates, but that didn't stop the hurt.

Liam didn't speak, though his face said he'd read her reaction.

Kara rose, appearing uncomfortable for the first time. "Well, I think I'll take myself home. I've ignored three calls from my mates and three is the limit before they start getting really mad. Nice to meet you, Ashley."

With that, Kara all but ran from the apartment, leaving Liam, Torrin and Ashley there.

"Hungry?" Liam's question was soft, like he knew he was bullshitting her but hoping she wouldn't call him on it.

"Not really." Ashley pulled at the hem of her shirt, cursing herself for thinking the jeans would make some huge difference.

Foolish child.

"Sit," Torrin said from the kitchen. "You need to eat even if you don't want to."

Ashley followed Torrin's order like a lifeline, all the time avoiding looking at Liam.

She took the seat at the far end of the table, then picked at the paper napkin already set out. She tore little pieces off it.

"Look at me," Liam said.

She didn't. Even when he sighed, even when he used that sweet voice of his to repeat himself, the one that melted her although she wanted to be stone, she ignored him.

Torrin set a plate in front of her, but her stomach lurched at the idea of food.

How could she have been so stupid? She knew better than to trust them. The first people in so long she'd put her faith in and already it had been shattered.

A soft growl brought her gaze up, but neither alpha looked at her. Instead, they were staring at one another, and the sound had come from Torrin. The warning there, the anger, the message, was clear even if he didn't use words.

Fix this.

Liam rubbed his hand over his head, then took a deep breath. He didn't speak until Torrin left, however.

Once alone, he switched chairs so he sat just beside Ashley. "It didn't mean anything."

"Of course not."

"I'm serious. Kara and I were never together."

Ashley finally lifted her gaze, and the weight of his eyes made it difficult to keep looking at him. "So why keep it a secret? Why lie to me?"

"I didn't lie—"

She snorted softly and dropped her gaze again.

A snarl brought her eyes back up quickly, the sound a surprise from him.

He caught her chin, his fingers impossibly warm. "Fine, I left it out on purpose. I knew you'd think it meant something, that you'd be uncomfortable, especially because Kara will always be a part of our lives. I didn't want you to be hurt or to cause any tension between us all."

"So you lied."

He let out a slow, long breath. "Yeah, I lied. Kara has a condition that makes her go into heat often. I slept with her because I didn't want to see her hurting, because I was afraid of what could happen if she kept going to strangers. It wasn't romantic, it wasn't anything more than that and quite honestly, we both hated it."

Ashley searched his expression for a lie, for something to help her believe the story he was telling. Men told tales for all sorts of reasons, and Liam had already proven he'd say what he thought he needed to.

It was true, but…there was a shadow there, something that said he was holding something back.

"You said you and Erik never took females alone."

"Erik didn't agree with my choice. It caused some problems at the time, but we moved past it. I'm sorry I didn't tell you, but it was only because it really didn't mean a thing."

Ashley tried to let go of the tension, but a gnawing ache inside her wouldn't quite release.

"I haven't been able to trust people in a long time," she whispered. "My life has been being betrayed by one person after another, always looking over my shoulder, always waiting for the next person to screw me over. I thought I'd found something different here."

"You have. I screwed up, and I'm sorry, but you *can* trust me. I'd do anything for you, sweet." He sounded so earnest, as if he needed her to believe him.

That was what got her to ignore the unease she couldn't kick, the one she chalked up to her past making her paranoid. She leaned forward and offered him a soft kiss, as if that sealed their agreement, like it was their own make-up. It didn't erase the hurt, it didn't fix that horrible little pit in her stomach where she struggled with the idea of him and Kara, but it was her promise to try to let it go.

"Don't lie to me again. I won't be with people I can't trust."

A shadow crossed his eyes, one gone as quickly as it came, and Ashley told herself to forget it.

I won't let paranoia ruin everything.

Chapter Fourteen

Ashley stretched as she got into the apartment, grateful to be home…and puzzled by the fact that it *was* home.

Already, so quickly, it felt like her space. She'd realized it that morning when she'd gotten ready, her things in the bathroom off her room. Liam had moved Kara's things from the room and into the apartment across the hall, going as far as to have new bedding brought in.

He was making an effort, trying to send a message, one she appreciated. *You belong here.*

It had helped, though she couldn't quite kick her unease. She chalked it up to a mixture of paranoia and her own fears about her inexperience.

Somehow, going slow with them, being a virgin — it all made her question herself. It was hard to think they could actually want her above Kara, who, from what Ashley had seen, was some sort of funny, sexy rebel.

A sting at her ass made her yelp, and she turned a glare on Liam, who only offered an unrepentant grin after he'd slapped her ass. "You have this look on your face when you're putting yourself down. I've finally identified it, and any time I see it, I'll swat that lovely ass of yours."

"I'm not a dog you can train," Ashley argued.

"I don't know about that. You seem to fall into line pretty easy. I'd call you praise-driven."

She flushed, the words feeling insulting even as she thought back to the *training* he meant, the way his fingers had slid into her, stretched her, especially as he'd reminded her he'd done it to prepare her.

Erik came up behind her, leaning closer to inhale loudly near her throat. "You smell amazing. Whatever you're thinking, keep thinking it."

She waved them both off, taking a few steps away. They always did that, stood too close, made her forget herself.

Even during her workday, they'd stop in, and with just a few words, with a promising look, she'd find her breath quickening and her panties becoming damp.

It was downright embarrassing how quickly she reacted to them.

Torrin sighed as he passed them. "You three are like teenagers. I'm going to order dinner. Any requests?"

"Anything that can be drizzled over her naked body and licked off," Liam said.

Torrin huffed, though a certain tension remained through his shoulders, as if he had pictured that. "You've lost your vote. I'll call down and decide."

With that, Torrin went to his office. While they'd stopped their chef and housekeeping from coming, they had kept the concierge who handled the entire apartment building. It meant that they only needed to call the number they'd shown her to order anything they wanted. The items would then go through the extra security they'd hired and be delivered to the door.

Ashley missed doing her own shopping, but she had to admit, it was safer.

Still, Liam and Erik stood there, both staring at her expectantly.

What are they expecting, exactly?

"What?" She crossed her arms, hoping the action hid how hard her nipples had become.

Liam's lip curled up at the side, that half-smile he often wore. "We're going to fuck you tonight, sweet."

Ashley's mouth fell open at the boldness of the statement, the way he said it without any doubts.

It wasn't a threat, and yet for a moment it *felt* threatening. And promising. And sexy.

What the hell is wrong with me?

"What if I'm not ready?"

Erik shrugged, as though the conversation were about less personal things. "We'd never force you, but don't forget, we can *smell* you. You're more than ready."

"I've felt you loosen right up for my fingers, sweet. Don't worry, you'll take a cock just fine."

Ashley set a hand on the table for balance, her knees weak. It wasn't just what Liam said. It was the way he said it. He had no doubt in his voice, the words saturated with lust and certainty.

She'd never felt more seen, more desired. While she wasn't sure she understood why exactly they wanted her, it still reached inside her and made her want them, too.

Well, that and a million other things.

"Okay," she said, as if his statement had been a question, as if they couldn't read on her face that she wanted this as much as they did.

Or maybe more, which shocked her most of all.

Her agreement was met by Erik coming closer, taking only two large steps to end up right in front of her. He took his kiss, passionate and deep and enough to make her dizzy. His lips were solid, taking control just as he slid his hand into her hair and grasped tightly.

He stole her breath and her thoughts until she struggled to get closer, until her hands seemed to wander on their own and find their way under his shirt, to the hard, hot skin beneath.

Except he pulled away then, an unhappy groan leaving him.

Ashley's lust-filled brain couldn't keep up and she wondered why he'd pulled away. A list started in her head of all the things she might have done wrong.

And, just as he had last time, he swatted her ass hard in response. "You worry too much," he reassured her.

"You said—"

Liam chuckled from behind Erik. "I know you're eager, sweet, but dinner will be here shortly. What we have planned will require a lot longer than the little time we have."

Heat danced across her skin at the reprimand, at the amusement, at how she'd completely forgotten about food and everything else because she'd wanted them that badly.

Erik caught her chin, rubbing his thumb over her jawline. They all liked to do that, to force her eyes to theirs, to take that tiny bit of power and turn her to jelly with it. The more Gregory had pushed her before, the more he'd tried to run her life, the more she rebelled.

So why, every time these alphas took control, did she fall into place? Worse, it was a place she felt comfortable in, a place that fulfilled her in a way nothing else had.

Liam chuckled darkly, the sound that said she was in far more trouble than she was prepared to deal with. "Oh, sweet, you're begging for it, aren't you? Don't worry, you'll have all you can handle and more tonight."

She'd finally not be a virgin anymore. She'd finally understand something she'd been missing.

Forget dinner, Ashley would have been happy for them to pull her to the bedroom right at that moment.

Erik twisted his lips into that rare smirk of his before he dragged his thumb across her full bottom lip. "Don't pout. We'll have you knotted in no time."

Fuck food.

Erik couldn't concentrate on the Mexican food Torrin had ordered. Even with the scent of chilis and spices in the air, he could focus on nothing but Ashley.

Her cheeks retained the slight glow from earlier, and he knew each time she thought back to what they'd said. Her eyes would lift to either one of them and she'd take her bottom lip between her teeth, shift in the seat then jerk her gaze back down to her food. Even if her face didn't scream it, the blooming of her delectable, tempting scent did.

They'd taken their time, eased her into the idea, waited until she was nearly begging for them.

There was no doubt in his mind that she'd be knotted before the night was out. Perhaps it would ease them all. Alpha territorial impulses were nothing to laugh at, and having her unclaimed put them all on edge. Some foolish, primal part of him worried about a challenger coming in and trying to take her.

I'd tear their throat out.

He scoffed at his own thought. Not that he wouldn't do it — of course he would — but he didn't need to be thinking about it.

Still, having her smelling of him, of Liam, of Torrin — if that stubborn asshole got out of his own head long enough — would relax them all.

This whole thing felt temporary until then. Sure, Erik knew he was bonding to her. He could feel that pull she had, that she'd had from day one if he were being honest. The more time they spent together, the stronger it grew, until he wasn't sure how he'd ever let her go.

She *was* theirs, and they'd make sure she had everything she could ever want for.

Except the truth.

If she knew about them, it was over. He stilled as he thought back to Beth's face when she'd realized what he'd done, when she'd seen the blood on his hands. She'd flinched away when he'd reached for her, fear covering her features.

Erik dragged his hand over his face, trying to wipe away the memory that haunted him.

He couldn't handle seeing that look on Ashley's face. While he had no doubt he'd never hurt her, he also knew people were fickle. She'd see the worst in him and assume that was all he was.

Maybe it is all you are.

"Erik?" Ashley's sweet voice was like a rope tossed to him at the bottom of a well, something he could grasp and climb up with, something to pull him to even ground.

How could she do that? It was as if those dark places inside him withdrew at the sound of her voice, fled from her when they fled from nothing else.

"Sorry, lost in thought."

Her smile held hesitancy. "I said thank you, for the new pajamas."

"Oh. Of course. When things are more settled, we'll take you shopping for some actual clothes. Until then, dial nine on any of the phones here and you'll reach the concierge. He can order whatever you need and have it delivered." Erik had personally picked out the pieces, though he'd never admit it. He'd selected a nice mixture of items, with many similar to the colorful and cartoonish things she opted to wear.

Never had he thought such silly pieces of clothing could be so sexy, but leave it to her to prove him wrong.

In addition to them, though, he had included some more risqué items. White lace would look stunning against her tan skin, making her look like the innocent creature he knew she was.

And part of him liked that. It was like giving in to his predator side, to think of her as prey who willingly embraced him, who allowed him to devour her.

"Are you wearing any of it?" His voice came out rough.

More red on her cheeks signaled yes.

Liam chuckled from his spot, the man always an interesting dichotomy. He could chuckle, seem disarming, and yet his eyes held no less lust, no less promise. "Well, seems like that will be a very pleasant surprise for me. I never saw what he ordered."

Again Ashley shifted, no doubt aching for friction against her swollen clit. Not that she could get what she needed sitting there. *Why is it such a turn-on to think of her needy and unfulfilled right now?* Probably because Erik knew damned well she'd get what she wanted after dinner.

Possibly sooner, if she kept smelling like that.

A quick glance around the table told Erik the same. Liam and Torrin had barely touched their food, far more interested in the omega than anything else.

It seemed dinner had been mostly a bust. Ashley had eaten some, though that had been likely because they'd pushed her, reminding her to take bites, and she'd obeyed like the sweet omega she was.

Torrin breathed in deeply, his eyes closing and lines of tension appearing between his eyebrows. No doubt he was as affected as the others by that delectable scent. "Are you finished eating, dove?"

She nodded, and Erik needed no further welcome. He stood at the same time Liam did, the strange connection the twins had, that not even they fully understood.

"Good, because I'm starving for something else." Liam pulled her from the seat as Erik took her plate, piling the barely touched food and discarding the plates on the kitchen counter to deal with later.

He turned when Ashley's gasp called him, then couldn't stop the grin as he found Ashley seated on the large dining table. The sweet, naive little thing looked entirely confused.

"Show me what you're wearing," Erik ordered, his mouth watering at the thought of what she might have picked.

There had been no shortage of options, but he secretly hoped she'd picked the white lace, the one that would allow her lovely skin to peek through the holes, that was thin enough to show her nipples.

She trembled and grasped the hem of her top, then pulled it off.

Perfection. The white, just as he'd hoped.

And as he'd imagined, she looked like the best virgin sacrifice.

"Fuck, Erik, you picked this out? Who would have thought you had good taste?" Liam's voice held mocking fondness as he traced his fingers along the bottom edge of the bra, teasing the skin there.

Torrin hadn't moved yet, was still seated in his spot, eyes rapt to the sight before him.

No longer was it a question of if, but merely when. Torrin walked a line no man could keep from toppling from. He touched her now, but never an exchange of fluid. It was a boundary that could not continue, that was impossible to keep.

And once they had crossed it, once Torrin had no more reason to avoid it, they would all be the better for it.

However, they'd never been able to push Torrin anywhere, which meant temptation was the only option.

And there was no better place for that than here, with Ashley displayed on the table like the best feast.

One he planned on fully enjoying.

Liam was going to devour every luscious inch of Ashley's perfect body. He wanted to suck her breasts until she cried out his name, to spread her soft thighs and feast between them until she begged for him to stop, until she pleaded for someone to fill her.

A nod at her bottoms had her following the unspoken demand, shimmying off the pajamas to reveal matching white lace panties.

She shifted, and he groaned. Not just panties, but a thong that revealed her luscious ass.

At which he had to remind himself that anal was not on the table just yet.

He scolded himself for the stupid pun, trying to keep his head in the game.

Liam pressed a hand to the center of her chest — her heart thundered there — and pressed her to lie flat.

Maybe he should have taken her for the first time in a soft bed, but they weren't soft people.

Best she knows that from the start.

She was spread out before him like a sacrifice on an altar, like the best lure that could trap any man.

And he wanted to be trapped. He wanted this perfect creature to dig her claws into him and never let him go.

He ran his hands up her thighs, savoring the curves, the responsiveness of her trembling body. He brushed his thumbs over her lace-covered pussy but didn't pause even when she moaned.

Instead, he continued, up over her hips, up her soft belly, her ribs, her succulent breasts. Every part of her was made for pleasure, made for *him*.

Not an inch of it failed to excite him.

Erik had stripped out of his clothing, no doubt eager.

Liam allowed himself a moment to lean down and drag his tongue against her nipple, the lace thin enough to feel the already hardened peak. Ashley gasped and reached for him, carding her fingers through his hair to keep him close, to urge him to continue.

But he wanted her surrendering entirely.

Liam caught her wrists and met her lust-drunk gaze. "Hands up, sweet. Grasp the edge of the table and don't let it go. Can you do that for me?"

Her chest rose and fell rapidly, but she nodded.

"Such a good girl," he praised as she lifted her arms and grasped the top of the table, her body lying across the short length.

It stretched her out, made her chest lift as if on display. He'd never seen a better sight, one that made him want more. He reached beneath her to unhook her bra, then pulled it up her arms and left it on her wrists like cuffs. Her panties went, too, as he tugged them down her long legs.

Liam slid off her to undress as well, needing to feel Ashley's warm skin against his own.

Torrin hadn't moved from his spot, though he had undone his pants, his cock in his hand. He sat where her hands grasped the table, giving him the perfect view down her tempting body.

Ashley's moan stole Liam's focus, his hands frozen on his own pants as he turned to see Erik between Ashley's supple thighs, the sweet girl still gripping the top of the table even as she shifted and writhed on its surface.

Damn. What a sight.

Liam could almost enjoy himself right there, taking in the show, the way her breasts moved, the way Erik slipped two fingers into her cunt.

Liam could imagine her squeezing down, knew how tight she was, how her taste lingered on his tongue.

Erik drove her hard. Her muscles twitched beneath her skin as if the distrust inside her warred with what she wanted, with what Erik seemed determined to pull from her.

His pink tongue appeared as he circled her clit before he pressed his lips to the hardened nub.

She gasped, the cry cut off, her back arching impossibly off the table and her knuckles turning white.

Torrin groaned, and Liam had to agree.

That was the sort of sight he never could picture getting tired of. Hell, the more they did this, the more he thought about a future, about waking up beside her, about how after an especially taxing job he could come home and wash away the day with her curled up to his side.

If we can deal with Gregory. And if she doesn't leave us.

Ashley's eyes fluttered open, Erik having moved to more gentle affection, offering soft kisses and nibbles to her folds as she came down after her orgasm — her first but certainly not last one that night.

Her blue eyes drew him in, the honesty there, the offer of something real he'd never experienced before in his life.

It chased away his fears, made him resolve to make it work somehow. How could he lose the way she looked at him?

"You ready, sweet? Because it's time to fuck you, now."

Liam's words stole what little of Ashley's mind was still working worth a damn after the orgasm Erik had given her. His eyes, brown with those green flecks that caught the light, were mesmerizing.

It was really happening. No more waiting, no more wondering.

She shouldn't have had to answer, the truth in her trembling body, in her scent, but still the alphas waited.

They wanted to *hear* her say it. Was that their way of making sure, or did they just enjoy the power of making her say it?

And why did she like that? When they pushed her, when they made her do things she wasn't sure she wanted to, her pussy would clench and her breath would quicken.

"I'm ready," she said, pleading with her eyes to not demand more.

The curl of Liam's lips said it was enough. He came forward as Erik shifted between her thighs. A tug at her waist made her yelp. Erik moved her on the table until her ass almost hung off the edge, but his warm body was there.

What is he —

The teasing of his cock against her pussy made her moan and reminded her that the table put her in the exact right position.

Had they picked that table for that reason? She could almost picture Liam—because he was the one who would have done that on purpose—at a furniture store, walking up to tables to see if they'd place a woman at the perfect height for him to fuck.

The position made her arms stretch, but she still could reach the top of the table, just barely.

The blunt head of Erik's hot cock stroked her.

She knew without a doubt they wouldn't hurt her. They'd proven it to her time and time again, giving her only security and pleasure.

So when Erik teased her, she let her thighs go lax, giving in.

Erik rumbled out a soft growl along with a *good girl*.

The table groaned as Liam hopped onto it. The sight of him on his hands and knees made him look even more predator-like, making his body bigger and more threatening, especially since she was lying on her back, stretched out and so vulnerable. His shaved head and sharp features did the same.

He moved closer, sliding his leg over her so her sat above her, over her ribcage.

Never had their difference in size and strength been as obvious as right then, when she stared up his strong, muscle-covered body, his thick, hard cock resting against his lower stomach.

"Do you have any idea how fucking pretty you are?" Liam grasped her breasts, not a moment of hesitation, as if he had every right to do so. That sort of comfort only made her burn hotter, especially as Erik kept grinding his dick against her still sensitive clit.

Ashley swallowed hard, the praise doing sinful things to her even as her brain tried to deny it.

Liam slid his hands, fingers pressing into her heavy, aching breasts until he had each nipple trapped between his fingers. He squeezed and pulled, the bite of pain sizzling through the electricity already coursing through her, mixing with it, sparking into flames together. "You don't have any idea how sexy you are, but you will. We have all the time to teach you, and we are damn good teachers. Do you feel Erik? Feel how much he wants you? Well, you're going to feel more in a moment, sweet, when he stretches that tight, wet cunt of yours for the first time."

Right at that moment, Erik seated his cock against her and grasped her knee, pressing it up and out. Even without a line of sight, she *knew* he was staring at her pussy. The weight of his gaze was as intense as another touch, another teasing stroke.

Liam didn't let up on his torment of her breasts, lessening the pressure for a moment before squeezing again, before pulling again, and it scattered her thoughts.

At least, it did until Erik sank into her. The pressure of his cock overcame any resistance, her body drenched enough to make the slide easy. She parted around him, a delicious, primal stretching of her body making her toes curl and her eyes flutter shut.

It was better than she could have imagined, each inch of space he took ramping up her pleasure. She'd thought it would hurt—had expected it to.

That was what girls said. They talked about the pain, but that was with fumbling teenage boys who wanted what they wanted and gave little care to their partner.

These alphas—*her* alphas—knew what they were doing. Erik rocked his hips, forward and retreating in tiny advances that had her moaning in need.

She wanted him to fuck her fully, to feel the way his dick would plunge into her and take her entirely.

She wanted wild, untamed passion.

Liam chose that moment to again pinch hard at her sore nipples. "If one cock is this good, imagine when we have you trapped between the three of us. Your cunt full, your ass full and another cock between your pretty lips? You'll be a good girl and do that, won't you?"

Ashley nodded. *Yes. Fuck, yes.* Anything they wanted, she wanted.

Erik let out a growl, dark and crazed, before he thrust hard and his pelvis pressed fully against her. He massaged the knee he still had hold of, keeping that leg out, and Ashley wished she could see what he was doing, that she could see how her cunt was stretched tight around his cock, the sight of his pubic hair against her body.

Instead, she could see nothing but Liam, his smirk the only thing to hold on to.

"So, sweet, how do you feel? So full of cock, finally?"

Ashley opened her mouth, but Erik pulled back and snapped his hips forward again, harder than before, and no words came out. Only a strangled, desperate sound left her lips.

Liam chuckled. "Well, I guess that sound will answer." He winked before shifting his hands so the palms rested on the outside of her breasts. "You know, I've been thinking about these tits since day one. Not all girls have enough to do this, but I've been dreaming of this since I first saw you."

Ashley didn't need to ask what he meant as Liam leaned forward slightly, tucking his impossibly hot cock into the valley of her cleavage, then using his grip on her breasts to push them together.

His groan was masculine and deep, rumbling from his solid chest, his gaze pinned to where his dick was trapped between her breasts. "I was wrong, I guess." He gave her that devastating smile of his. "*This* might just be the best sight. Now, be a good girl and let us use this luscious body of yours for a bit, hmm?"

Use. Why did that word do so much for her? It made her think about sweaty, breathless pounding, about the sort of sex she'd always dreamed of but had long before figured wasn't in the cards for her. It was the sort of thing that happened with sultry, sexy women. Not for virgins who were awkward at the best of times.

Liam pinched down tightly on her left nipple, a reprimand in his expression telling her he'd somehow caught the type of thought on her face. Even still, he said nothing else before shifting forward and back, running his cock between her breasts. His pre-cum gave enough lubrication so there wasn't any painful friction, allowing him to slide easily.

She wanted to touch, to grasp his thighs, to feel the soft, dark hair that covered them, to dig her nails into him.

When she loosened her grip on the table, something stopped her.

She looked up to find Torrin holding her, his hand covering her wrists, pinning her in place. It was a restraining touch, one that kept her still, yet it also made her feel *safe*. It was sweet in an odd way, like a reminder he was there and she was fine.

His other arm twitched, and she realized the rhythmic motion was him jerking off.

It pulled a wanton moan from her, a desire to see him, but the steel in his heated gaze said he'd not give that to her.

Liam growled above her, drawing her attention back just as Erik let her leg fall open more and chose to stroke her clit instead. "You'll come again for us, sweet."

What? It seemed too much, but she wouldn't argue.

She wanted to please them, wanted to see more of that pleasure on their faces, wanted to hear them praise her, to call her a good girl.

Besides, it wasn't as if they couldn't make her if they wanted to, and they seemed determined.

Erik's touches were focused as he stroked his thumb against her clit. All the while, he pounded into her, taking her harder, giving her what she'd always wanted.

Liam thrust, the head of his beautiful cock in sight each time he slid all the way forward, the head shimmering from the pre-cum that she wanted to lick from him.

Not that they seemed willing to let her do anything she wanted. Instead, they were content to give her only what they chose to.

Erik closed his fingers around her clit in a hard pinch just as he slammed in deep, and it overloaded her senses. She tried to move, but Liam's body over her kept her in place, forced her to lie there and take the pleasure that twisted through her.

Torrin's grip didn't move, keeping her still. She yanked against the hold, against the overwhelming feeling that she wasn't sure was entirely pleasure anymore, but she could do nothing.

Erik pounded into her with his cock, Liam trapped her with his body and Torrin pinned her with his hands.

It all worked with the orgasm, making it stronger, sending sparks of pleasure through her, so intense, that they frightened her.

Even as she tried to catch her breath, as Erik gave her a slight reprieve by leaving her clit alone, she squirmed.

Liam's strong grip and heavy body didn't let her go far, and he groaned as he fucked between her breasts in the filthy display she loved. It was messy and wonderful and perfect and she never wanted it to end.

At least until Erik went after her clit again.

"Too much," she gasped out.

Liam's smirk widened, an almost sadistic glint to it. "No, it's not. You can take it. You will take it for us, won't you, sweet?"

No. Yes. She didn't know.

Even still, she nodded. Wetness tracked down her cheeks, everything too much.

Erik didn't press as hard against her clit, but it didn't take much. In fact, each drag of his cock against her overworked pussy walls made her feel as if she was nearing that edge again, as if the abyss there called to her. The third orgasm washed through her exhausted body, ripping away defenses and worries.

Liam growled before releasing her breasts and shifting forward. He slid his hand beneath her head and pressed his cock to her lips. "Swallow me down, sweet," he said in a rough and desperate tone.

Ashley did as he asked, parting her lips to take him into the heat of her mouth. She lapped at his cock as if it were an instinct, the taste of him sinful and everything she'd wanted.

"Such a good girl," he whispered just as his dick jerked and the first spurt of cum landed on her tongue.

It was so hot it felt as if it seared her, but she greedily swallowed, needing more, sucking as if to milk him dry, to take all he could give her.

Too quickly, it was gone, even the clinging taste inside her mouth disappearing, especially when he pulled back.

He looked sated, happy, tired. He dragged his fingers across her cheek in a soft caress.

Just then, Erik's thrusts turned erratic, losing their steady rhythm as if driven by something deeper now, by a primal need inside the alpha.

At the same time, his finger brushed her sore clit.

Not again.

Liam scooted back so he could lean forward, his lips to her forehead. "Hush, sweet. You're fine."

But she didn't feel fine. She felt adrift and helpless and so raw it was as though all her skin had been scraped off.

Erik released a snarl that would have frozen her blood, that might have made her recoil if Liam and Torrin hadn't been there, their soothing touches helping ground her. Erik plunged in, the base of his cock growing, stretching her even more.

She would have sworn there was no more room inside her, that she was stretched and full to the brim, and yet when he rocked his hips forward as though to get deeper, when that growing knot locked inside her, behind her pubic bone, he somehow fit.

When he could no longer pull out, when the unfamiliar feeling of being stretched like that overcame her, she cried out. Liam's lips found hers, swallowing down the small, panicked noises she made, coaxing her through the brutal orgasm as Erik knotted her.

Everything was too much. Erik's knot pulsed slightly as he came, stimulated by her exhausted body. Liam's lips were soft against hers, and Torrin's strong grip on her hands never faltered.

Everything washed away with that final orgasm, the world shrinking to the four of them, and she felt bare in a way that was so much deeper than her naked body.

Erik stroked along her hip, over her thigh, a reassuring touch she needed, especially after the sound he'd let out.

Liam pulled from her lips. "You did so good," he told her. "You're perfect, you know that?"

She was too tired to argue it, for her brain to even try.

He grinned as he moved off her. "So that's the way it works, huh? Just have to force a few orgasms out of you and you start listening. Good to know."

Erik shifted, and it made his knot tug at her overworked body.

That wasn't pleasure. She wiggled, hands yanking at Torrin's grip.

Torrin spoke this time, his voice like warm water rushing over her, easing her sore body and frazzled nerves. "Try to relax. The more you fight it, the more you tighten up, the more you'll feel it."

She twisted, wanting to see Torrin's face. His eyes were soft in that rare way she'd catch glimpses of now and then.

"You know, you could help her." Liam nodded at Torrin's lap as he crawled off her.

Torrin lifted his hand, his eyebrows drawn together. Cum sat on his fingers in tempting white stripes, and her mouth watered at the sight.

Except Torrin's eyes did that thing where they changed, going flat and empty, the rejection as obvious as if he'd said it.

He released her hands, then dropped his beneath the line of the table. *Zipping up, no doubt...*

He left without another word, the sight of his back painful, yet she couldn't drag her gaze away.

The shutting of a door signaled the rest of his retreat, and she just stared at the empty hallway where he'd gone.

A hand at the nape of her neck drew her to sitting and against the strong chest of the alpha still locked inside her. He made a soft, soothing sound from his chest.

It was the sound Gregory had tried to make at times, to ease her, to relax her, and yet it had never done either from Gregory.

Against Erik, though, it helped. She closed her eyes, resting against him, choosing to snuggle into the warmth and safety he offered.

At least there she could pretend that Torrin's rejections didn't hurt as much as they did.

Chapter Fifteen

Liam groaned when the light shone in his eyes. He had blackout curtains in his room that allowed him to wake up when he damned well wanted to.

It meant he opened his eyes, a frown on his face as he wondered why the hell he hadn't shut those miraculous draperies.

A mutter from beside him, along with a shifting body, only brought up more questions.

The answers came as he glanced down to find Ashley curled against him, her head on his chest.

The night before came back to him, and that he'd crashed in Ashley's room rather than returning to his own. Her warm, naked body had been far too tempting.

Erik had thought the same, it seemed, because he was stretched out behind Ashley, on his side and facing her.

His eyes were already open, not that it shocked Liam. Erik had always woken earlier, had always been the lighter sleeper.

When was the last time they'd fallen asleep beside a female?

Liam's lips tipped down. Had he and Erik ever done so? They'd fucked plenty of women together, spent hours driving away whatever they needed to between the thighs of countless partners, but he didn't think they'd ever slept afterward.

That required some level of trust they'd never managed.

Erik had slept beside Beth, though Liam had never done so with any women. Even with Kara, after their quick flings, he'd returned to his own room after a long and very hot shower. It was only after she'd found her mates, once he'd known she was cared for, that Liam had been able to take a deep breath and admit how much he'd hated what they had.

However, the night with Ashley had helped chase those memories away, helped scour them off and replace them with something infinitely more pleasant.

Ashley snuggled closer, an unhappy mutter on her lips that spilled over his bare chest. The movement caused the light to hit her in the face, too, and lines appeared in her forehead a second before she opened her eyes.

"Morning," Liam said, unable to stop the smile that tugged at his lips, especially at the unhappy look on her face.

So, not a morning person?

"What time is it?" Sleep saturated her voice.

Erik reached over for his phone on the nightstand. "Eight-thirty."

She twisted, gaze landing on Erik as though she'd just recognized she'd slept beside not one but two men. The point at which she recalled she'd done a lot more than just sleep beside them was clear when she went red and covered her face with her hands.

Adorable. She was unfairly cute, and for a man who had had little of that in his life, Liam found he couldn't get enough of it.

"You do realize that covering your face when you still don't have a stitch on you is sort of useless, don't you?"

She rolled to her back and groaned. "What was I thinking?"

Erik dragged his fingers up the center of her chest in a soft, teasing stroke. "Whatever it was, I think we can get you thinking it again."

Her stomach grumbled, a loud complaint that reminded Liam none of them had really eaten dinner.

As tempting as her naked, sexy body might have been, that alpha side of him couldn't ignore her being hungry. "Come on," Liam said as he sat up. "Let's see what Torrin wants and order breakfast."

Torrin's name broke the comfort of the morning as surely as if he'd snapped the safety on it. Ashley's expression fell, her hands moving from her face.

Liam sighed. Torrin wasn't a conversation he wanted to have, but he had to admit, he'd thought the stubborn fool would have given in the night before, too.

Leave it to Torrin to be the only alpha stupid enough to turn down a wet and desperate omega like Ashley.

"About Torrin—"

She shook her head and sat up, curling up into one hell of a defensive position. "Don't. It's fine."

"It clearly isn't fine."

"He's made it clear that he isn't interested in a relationship with me. I need to stop hoping for something he'd already told me no about."

Erik set his hand on her back and rubbed gently. "Torrin is difficult."

She snorted softly, as if the word 'difficult' didn't come close to explaining it. It didn't, really, but she also didn't understand.

She hadn't been *there*.

Liam twisted so he could look at her, needing her to understand that it wasn't her. The way Ashley reacted to praise said she needed that build-up, and Torrin rejecting her over and over was tearing her down. She attributed it to her own failings, and only because she didn't know the story.

"Ashley," he started, voice soft. "Torrin lost his mate a long time ago, and he never really got over it."

When her eyes met his, the empathy there stunned Liam. He'd never been great with things like empathy, with understanding people, with being able to care all that much unless they were in his direct circle. Even then, he didn't want them to hurt, but he didn't *feel* that hurt.

Ashley's eyes said she did, right down her core. *What a treasure she is.*

"He said he lost someone but wouldn't tell me about it. What happened?"

Liam tore his gaze away, so Erik picked up the story. "His mate, Gilly, was murdered by people who were unhappy with Torrin. They tortured her first, wanting to make sure he understood the message."

That wasn't the full story, of course. It left out the reality of their lives, that they had made their fair share of enemies. Not just another business who had outpriced them, or stolen a contract, but the sort of enemies who didn't mind burning down homes with the people still inside.

Still, it was vague enough that she should understand the problem.

Erik kept rubbing her back as he spoke. "He blames himself, of course. It's why he doesn't think he can have you, why he's afraid of claiming you, of you carrying his scent. He doesn't want history to repeat, doesn't want to risk you."

She frowned, so much pain on her face as she seemed to hurt for Torrin, for a wound long passed. "And the person who did it?"

Telling her the gruesome way Torrin had dealt with the men responsible would not have been a good piece of information for her to have. Liam chose to answer that one, treading that line between lie and truth. "Justice was served, but he's never let go of it."

She let her shoulders drop, as though that understanding helped her to see that what was going on with Torrin at least wasn't all her fault. "He's used to taking care of everyone around him, to bearing the weight of their safety. I can't imagine what someone he loved being killed because of him would do to him."

Liam froze, with Erik doing the same.

She'd picked up on some truths to their dynamic that not many saw. Normally people never saw beneath Erik and Liam being heartless bodyguards and Torrin being an unfeeling, ruthless tyrant.

Yet Ashley saw deeper, recognized that there was more to them all.

She straightened her back as though their staring unnerved her, so they both looked away. Liam rose from the bed, trying to shake the strangeness away. It was one thing for him to understand others, for him to have a view into them, but he wasn't sure he cared for Ashley knowing *him* so well.

It felt as though she'd peeled off his skin and peeked beneath.

Instead of saying that, because he doubted there was any way to do so and have it come across well, he leaned forward for a quick kiss to break the tension.

He pulled away just when she started to lose herself to the kiss. The darker places inside him enjoyed how she chased it with her lips when he broke apart from her. "Get ready, sweet. I'll see what our fearless leader wants and get food ordered."

Torrin groaned as he rubbed at his hip. It hurt so much more than it had when he'd been younger.

Maybe he'd just had more energy to deal with it then, or perhaps survival had been more important at the time. Maybe he'd simply thought it would get better, that time would heal it.

Now, though? It was an ache he could never quite rid himself of. He'd had imaging done, seen specialists, and all had said the same — some injuries never quite healed.

They'd offered different methods of pain relief, but he preferred not to take anything that might dull his mind.

It was all he had anymore.

Well, that and what he'd built with it.

He sat on the balcony, trying to stretch out the aggravated injury to relieve the tightness there.

How many had he taken down to build what he had? Strong men who were so much more than he was in so many ways. Men who had had everything handed to them all their lives, who expected to win by some birthright, and Torrin had outsmarted them all.

He wondered at times what his uncle would think of him now. Torrin didn't know his father, so he never thought of him. His uncle, though? Liam and Erik's father? The only father-like figure he'd ever had?

He'd be proud, and that left a dirty taste in Torrin's mouth.

Not enough to stop what he was doing, though.

He'd been on the bottom before, knew what being stepped on felt like.

Torrin dug his fingers into his hip, massaging as if that would help, as if it ever helped, as he closed his eyes.

Ashley's face haunted him.

It wasn't the hurt, not exactly. Sure, that killed him, but what stuck with him was the absolute certainty that he'd put it there. It was knowing she'd endured it because of *him*.

The ends justify the means. Solid advice he'd always lived by, yet hard to swallow when the means included hurting her.

But a little hurt now was better than a lot of hurt later, wasn't it? A little heartbroken now was better than her mangled corpse later.

Not that it removed his guilt, but he'd long ago learned to live with that. It was his constant companion, like a pet forever trailing at his heels.

He'd claimed work obligations during breakfast and lunch. It wasn't entirely a lie. He could always find work that needed doing, even on the weekends.

Besides, there was plenty for him to deal with now that they had plans for Gregory. Kara had come through with some information, as usual, and Erik's contacts were trickling in useful tidbits.

Nothing substantial enough for a plan yet, but they had a direction at least.

It was more than they'd had days before.

With the extra security, they had a bit more freedom.

Gregory had moved from the place he'd rented, and finding his new location was proving far more difficult. It seemed he realized how far their information network reached and had chosen to remain more anonymous. At least it meant he recognized them as a valid threat.

Erik might hate to be seen as a threat, but Torrin enjoyed a bit of fear.

People were either feared or afraid.

He knew which he'd prefer to be.

The pain in his hip drew him back, like it always did.

The ringing of his phone offered a distraction, one he desperately needed. "Hello?"

"Mr. Kansas." Torrin didn't recognize the male voice on the phone, but it held the sort of self-assured power that always made him tread carefully.

"I'm afraid you have me at a disadvantage."

A soft laugh came through the line. "That's how I prefer to do business. I'd like a meeting."

"I don't meet people when I don't even know who they are. That isn't how I prefer to do business."

"Fair enough. We have a mutual friend. Gregory."

"'Friend' is a rather large stretch," Torrin pointed out.

"I'm pretty sure it's a stretch for anyone who deals with him. You see, I've heard your name come up a few times recently, and at first I thought you were a business associate. Come to find out, you're nothing more than another piece of his little obsession." The man's words turned sharp, sounding as though he often ranted about the very subject.

Torrin let him continue without interruption. Sometimes it was best to let them work themselves up.

"I would like to speak to you about something that could potentially help us both out."

"That's rather vague. It would be a large risk for me to show up anywhere when Gregory is currently intent on killing me."

"I'm not trying to trick you, and to prove it, I'd like to meet you on Friday at six in the evening. You can choose the place, so you know you aren't being set up. Send me the address at five, so you can already have your people set up to ensure it isn't an ambush."

Torrin tapped his fingers on the armrest of his chair. He doubted there could be a better deal. The risks would be limited, and security would be easy to attend to with those guidelines. The biggest threat would be to Ashley during that time, when he and his cousins would be conveniently drawn away from her...

Even that could be managed, however.

"Give me some hint to what you want. I do not walk into meetings blind," he pressed.

The voice let out another one of those soft laughs, as if the conversation pleased him. "You sound like you might be the right man. You want a hint? Very well. Come to the meeting, Mr. Kansas, because we both have the same problem—Gregory—and it has a very obvious and permanent solution. I hope to see you Friday." The call ended, leaving Torrin there in the darkness of the balcony.

There were so many unknowns, so many moving parts. His hip ached, but he tried to ignore it as he sat back in the chair, hearing the laughter from inside.

Ashley and Liam seemed to be playing some game, and Erik, while he didn't join in, watched from the sidelines with a smile across his face.

Torrin couldn't fail. Of all the choices he'd made in his life, all the times the stakes had been high, none had mattered more than this.

He swore to himself that he'd find a way to keep them all safe, no matter what the cost, and ignored the pain in his hip from what he'd paid the last time he'd made such a promise.

Chapter Sixteen

Ashley had crawled out of bed early, sliding over Liam and away from Erik's coaxing hands. Both men had suggested she stay a little longer. She'd been tempted, of course, sure that she could spend the last bit of time before she had to rise in comfort.

However, falling back asleep wasn't something she'd ever done well, and a nice hot shower before heading off to work sounded worth the hassle of leaving them.

She went to the kitchen, dressed only on her robe, because facing five in the morning required at least a cup of tea.

Sounds from down the hallway caught her attention, from the direction of Torrin's room.

She hadn't seen him for more than a few seconds since Friday night, when he'd watched her while she was on the table, the night he'd walked away.

Since then, he'd taken his meals in his room.

They couldn't continue like that.

Guilt tugged at Ashley. She was the new one in the situation, yet she'd chased him off. The three alphas were clearly important to one another, having lived together their entire lives, yet she'd managed to break apart their trio with her presence and her demands.

Which wasn't fair.

I'm as bad as Gregory, forcing someone who doesn't want me.

The thought made her wince, so she sighed and decided to deal with the problem.

She knocked on the door to Torrin's room, but no answer came back. When she peeked, she realized what the sound was.

Torrin was in the shower.

She should go back, but she struggled to do so. Sure, part of it was that she wanted to see more of him. She'd seen Liam and Erik stripped down so many times that it was normal, but Torrin? He'd never disrobed at all around her.

She justified it by saying that she didn't *have* to look, but if he was in the shower, he'd have to listen to her at least.

She couldn't get her feet beneath her when dealing with Torrin, so maybe she needed the bit of extra help surprising him would grant her.

The bathroom had no door into it, with the toilet set off in its own room and the large separate shower and bath identical to the one in her room.

Steam filled the bathroom, telling her that Torrin took his showers hot. The vapor fogged the glass enclosure so she could only make out a general outline of his body, but it was what she'd expected — lean but still much larger than her.

He was washing his hair, head tipped back, water streaming over him with his fingers rubbing his scalp. She could see his basic figure, but the details were denied her.

"Torrin," she called, not wanting to startle him.

The figure stilled. His deep voice rose over the falling water. "What are you doing here, Ashley?"

She swallowed at what his voice did to her, at how easily it teased her. "I wanted to talk to you."

"It would be best if our conversations happened when we were both fully clothed."

Sweat beaded on her forehead, and she realized she could smell him. Aroused alpha had quickly become her favorite scent, and the spice of it from Torrin was magical. Still, she tried to focus. "You've been avoiding me for days. I thought you couldn't run away if I talked to you right now."

His growl was unhappy and dark. "There needs to be no conversation. I will be more cautious from now on. Clearly, I'm untrustworthy when it comes to being around you."

"You can't just hide all the time."

"It's for the best. I can take the other apartment if need be, give you privacy with Liam and Erik." His voice had that flat quality, a sure sign he wanted that no more than she'd bet anyone else did.

Frustration gnawed at her. "I get that you lost someone. I get that you're afraid—"

"You don't understand."

"I've been running for years. If anyone gets what fear does, it's me," she argued when he refused to listen.

Sure, she'd come there to apologize, but yelling at him seemed to be the way the conversation was going to go.

Mostly because he wouldn't get out of his own way.

"I lost everything over and over because I couldn't stay in one place. Trust me, I get it!"

He didn't answer right away, as if the words had wounded him as well.

Great, more guilt.

He sighed softly, and his voice had regained its careful and straight-to-the-point tone. "I'm sorry, Ashley, but we can't happen. I'll move and take the apartment."

That was it. Ashley lost the temper she'd held. Normally she was easygoing, but after being rejected and ignored all weekend, she had less patience than usual. She walked over and pulled open the glass door that kept the shower separate. "There's no way you're going to—"

She sucked in a hard breath as she got her first look at him naked.

It wasn't a gasp of pleasure, not when she found it hard to pull in breath.

She'd known he limped, even if he hid it. The ever-present cane was a pretty good reminder.

What she hadn't expected was to see the burns on his body. The skin was damaged on that leg and side, from ribs to knee, gnarled and twisted.

Her gaze locked on to the damage and her mouth went dry, her brain unable to make sense.

She'd assumed his hip had been something simple, like a break that had never healed right.

"What happened?" she asked, her voice weak.

Torrin twisted away and turned off the shower. He moved past her, using the shower wall for balance, his cane nowhere in sight, before he pulled a towel around his waist.

It covered some of the damage, but when he turned, it let her see the burns on his back as well.

"You should go," he said, his voice devoid of any feeling, doing that flat thing his eyes did when he was hiding whatever he was thinking.

Her feet wouldn't move, wouldn't take her away from the scene.

"What happened?" She repeated the question.

Torrin sighed, turning to face her again. His hair was wet and pushed back out of his face, and his eyes seemed impossibly darker. "I made a choice and paid a price."

"How—"

He offered a sharp look that stilled the words in her throat. "It doesn't matter."

"It does to me," she snapped back.

At that, his lips tipped down. His expression shifted just a bit, as if, try as he might, he couldn't quite keep the same level of annoyance. "It happened when I was much younger."

"Does it hurt?"

"The hip does. The burns don't."

"How did it happen?"

"There was a fire," he said, voice slow, as though he wasn't sure how much of the tale he wanted to tell.

Ashley didn't speak, could only stare at the burns as if she could understand what had happened, how it could have happened.

Finally, he released a deep breath as if settling in for the full story. "You already know my cousins and I didn't exactly have a charmed life growing up. We lived in this tiny shack of a house out in the middle of nowhere. Erik and Liam weren't there when the fire started, and it spread fast. On my way out, my uncle ran into me in the hallway. He'd always hated me. He didn't care much for any of us, but at least Erik and Liam were his blood. Me? He viewed me as an outsider, a threat. He was sure I had started the fire, and he attacked me."

Ashley hurt as she listened, as she tried to think about the life Torrin must have lived. It was hard to believe he'd ever been small, that he'd ever been at the mercy of anyone.

His gaze remained pinned to the floor, but shadows in his dark eyes said he was reliving the event as he spoke. "He hit me with a bat before I ever saw him, shattering my hip. He was a beast of a man, and I was a fourteen-year-old kid. It wasn't much of a competition. He got on top of me and wrapped his hands around my throat, even as we coughed on the smoke that filled the house. I got my fingers around the bat—he'd dropped it so he could choke me with his hands—and slammed it against his temple. He was lying there, unconscious, the smoke filling the house, the air so hot it stung my eyes, and I left him there to burn. I crawled, clawing my way out, my hip and leg useless. On my way out, one of the ceiling beams came down, knocked me over. That's how this happened." He waved down at his side. "I was there, on the ground, and I remember not knowing how I was going to get up again, how I was going to move. I thought for a minute, 'This is it. It's over.'"

Ashley swallowed hard at that, an echo of the hopelessness still ringing in his voice. "Why did you get up?"

Torrin's gaze went to the door, his eyebrows drawn toward one another. "Because Erik and Liam still needed someone. I'd left their father to die in that hallway and our mothers were most likely dead, so I was all they had."

She struggled to believe the story, not because she couldn't see Torrin doing exactly that but because she hated the idea of it. He shouldn't have had to do that, to be that at fourteen. She'd bet that was one reason he never mentioned the hip, even when his face pinched into lines that had to be pain. He'd never put that on anyone else to bear.

Torrin shook his head and turned, walking from the bathroom. That got her feet moving, following as he went to his closet.

His steps were slow, careful. "What do you want, Ashley? If you wish to sleep here until later, you're welcome to. It's still early." He nodded toward his bed.

"Why are you still pushing me away?"

He twisted so he could see her, a droplet of water streaming down over his chest catching her gaze for a moment. "Maybe this was for the best, really. You refuse to listen to me when I talk about the danger you could be put in by being with me. Perhaps seeing for yourself is best."

"Seeing what? I understand danger just fine. Burns don't change that."

He stood tall, every muscle rigid as though it were a fight to just get his words out. "No. Best you see how I actually look. I'm not a foolish man, Ashley, not someone who refuses to see the reality of situations.

This" — he gestured down to his side, to the places where his skin was twisted — "is not what any female hopes to find on a mate. I know what I am and what I am not. I'm a ruthless and driven businessman. I'm intelligent and an excellent planner. I can offer you a lot out of that, and I intend to give that to you. That is all, and perhaps seeing me helps prove it to you, will help you get over this fascination with me you've had."

Ashley frowned and pressed her lips together while she tried to figure out what he was saying. "Why would that change anything?"

"Because I can't protect you," he said softly. "I'm not ever going to be like Liam and Erik. I'm a damaged alpha, and that is the truth we both need to accept. I didn't accept it with my old mate, with Gilly, and she paid the price for it. I couldn't keep her safe, no matter how hard I tried. She never saw me like this. I kept it from her, hid the truth from her, didn't want her to see it. She didn't know enough to walk away. No omega dreams of bonding to a cripple with burns."

The self-hatred in those words made Ashley's stomach churn. The most telling part, though? The way Torrin's gaze darted to the floor. He always met her gaze, held it firmly, even when speaking of difficult things. Instead, he'd hidden. It wasn't manipulation — it was Torrin being sure that she'd leave. It was written in his expression, in his stance.

He expected her to reject him, to walk out and leave because he wasn't perfect.

Pushing her away was for her safety, but it was also about him. He feared not only that she'd be hurt, but that he wasn't enough to protect her.

It broke her, to see a man as strong as he was so defeated. The grip he had on things, the business success — it all made sense.

He was trying to prove he was worth something in those areas to make up for what he thought he lacked.

And Ashley could think of no other way to prove to him what she thought of him than one.

She let her robe slip from her body and fall to the floor, leaving her naked.

Torrin clenched his fists as he stared at Ashley's nude form.

She was stunning. She made a mockery of the statues from the classics, like a work of art he shouldn't have ever been blessed enough to lay eyes on.

"You don't know what you're doing," he said.

She met his gaze head-on, the sort of certainty there that made him fear he might lose this fight. "You keep warning me off, saying it's for my own good, but I'm still here. Stop trying to make choices for me." She crossed the room with slow steps, as though approaching an animal she feared might bite.

"It's too dangerous," he said when she reached him, when she set a hand on his bare chest, the first skin-to-skin contact he'd felt there in so long. It seared him deeper than the burns had, left a more permanent scar.

She rose to her tiptoes but didn't take a kiss. Instead, she remained close enough that her breath blew across his lips and left the tingle of mint from her toothpaste behind. "That's my choice to accept the risk. You're worth that risk, Torrin."

He gave in.

What man could resist that sweet voice, that declaration? If she'd screamed, if she'd cried, those things he could have stood against. If she'd stripped down and spread her thighs, he could have walked out.

What undid him was the absolute truth in her tone, that she made him feel for the first time like he was worth something.

His first mate had been with him not knowing his life, not knowing the dangers. He'd tried to protect her from them, but she'd never made the choice to take the risk. He had never even disrobed entirely in front of his old mate, always sure she'd leave if she ever truly saw him.

Ashley did, though. She knew this could cost her everything, she'd seen him all and she didn't turn away.

How could he say no to that? To her hand reaching into the darkness and solitude of his life and offering something more?

He hadn't felt as though he were worth a damn, ever, but when he took the kiss she'd teased him with? He felt worthy of her.

Not because of him, but only because she saw him as such.

They moved backward, and he leaned on her, using her for balance as they went toward the bed. The hot shower had eased the muscles of his hip, and any pain that might have been there fled as arousal took its place.

He'd heard before that bonded alphas could ignore injuries of all types for their mates, and it seemed true. His cock was hard, pressed between them and behind the towel, and he had nothing in mind other than satisfying his mate in whatever way she needed, for as long as she wanted.

She was soft against him, impossibly giving. Ashley's breasts pressed to him, and he could finally have her. He didn't have to worry about fluids, about her carrying his scent. Maybe he should have still worried, have done what was right no matter how difficult, but he couldn't turn her down.

He needed this more than he needed food, more than air. He felt as though he could live off nothing but her touches.

She moved onto the bed and he followed, falling into the cradle of her hips, into the space between her thighs, which she parted just for him.

Ashley pulled at the towel until it came free, until she could toss it away and have nothing between them. The water still on his skin spread to hers, making her glisten in the rays of light that crept above the mountain ranges to the east as the sun rose.

He sat back despite her complaints, needing to see her fully spread out for him. Her thighs lay open in invitation, her soft stomach leading up to full breasts that shifted when she panted.

Had he ever seen such a sensual woman? One who craved his touch so badly? Who gave herself so fully to the moment?

Her rosy nipples had pulled into tight points, such teasing little peaks he wanted to lavish attention on, that he wanted to worship and suck for hours.

She was a feast before him, skin flushed and drowning him in the scent of her arousal.

Torrin slid his hands up the insides of her thighs until he reached her pussy. He'd used the vibrator on her to avoid any direct contact before, but this time he'd feel all of her.

He slit was drenched as he dragged his thumbs through her folds, his touch full of reverence. She deserved to be worshipped, and work be damned, he'd spend as long as he wished exploring her body. Her clit was hidden beneath its hood, but it swelled under his touch. He rubbed his thumb against it while he slipped two fingers into her with his other hand.

Fuck. She was drenched, her pussy tight and pulsing around his fingers. He had to keep himself focused because right then, he wanted nothing more than to feel her around his cock, to claim her fully, to make her *his*.

Instead, he took a deep breath and worked her luscious body toward release.

"You are magnificent," he said, his voice rough with his own want. "So much more than I deserve. However, I only have two hands, and given that my cousins aren't here to help, you'll have to do some of the work. Your breasts deserve attention, dove." The nickname rolled from his tongue, a sweet endearment he used as though it would explain to her what she meant to him.

His dove. The fragile creature, too peaceful for his world, but beautiful. The symbol of peace, something he'd never had in his life before, the sign of something to save him.

Ashley followed the command, moaning softly as though the order alone turned her on more than the actions.

Then again, that was yet another way she drew him. So naturally submissive. *Lovely.*

She cupped her breasts, full in her small hands, before brushing her thumbs over her nipples. She gasped, a quick hitch, and her pussy tightened.

So responsive.

He smiled, a real smile, something he rarely did. How could he not, though?

Torrin rocked his palm, sliding those fingers into her deep before pulling them back, making sure to tease the sensitive front wall of her pussy while his thumbs toyed with her clit.

Her breathing was erratic, quick and shallow and broken by moaning cries.

"Don't come yet," he demanded, his voice taking on that commanding tone that did sinful things to her. In fact, she cried out, her pussy tightening so hard he knew she'd nearly come by the order alone.

She opened her eyes, confusion drowning out the blue as she trembled.

Torrin had mercy and stopped touching her clit, though he continued to fuck her with strong, slow thrusts of his long fingers. "You'll come with my cock inside you, and not a moment before. My cousins may spoil you, but I prefer to see you work for your pleasure. So you'll wait."

"I can't," she whined so pitifully.

The sound made his cock jerk with interest, especially as she writhed slightly and tried to follow the command.

"You can, and you will, because it pleases me. You do want to please me, don't you?"

Her mouth opened on a soundless cry, her back arching, and he thought for a moment she'd broken.

Instead, she trembled, a shake in her body when she fought to obey.

He knew he couldn't push her much further, not yet. Later, yes. Later, when they'd done this for longer, when she'd had time to learn control, but not yet.

So he had mercy and withdrew his fingers from her over-sensitive body.

He leaned forward, allowing himself the pleasure of licking across each hard nipple even as her fingers still played there, before he settled over her.

She was small beneath him, full of so much coursing energy that any place he brushed her, she gasped, as though her entire body had turned into one giant erogenous zone.

Sure, making a woman come over and over again was wonderful, but there was a sick sense of pleasure he got from denial as well, from watching a woman walk that line of need, seeing them struggle against themselves for control.

And no woman had ever looked so lovely there as Ashley.

He reached between them and grasped his cock, then stroked her hot, wet slit with it. "Do you want me, dove?"

She wound her arms around him, beneath his, so her nails dug into his back. She touched both good skin on one side and burns on the other, but she didn't flinch, didn't act as if the mangled skin bothered her.

Where the reminder might have taken him out of the moment, her breathless answer chased away his fears. "Yes."

"Then beg." He nipped the fullness of her bottom lip and ground his cock against her greedy clit.

She cried out, giving him the chance to lick into her mouth, to taste more of that mint, more of her.

The begging, it wasn't even sexual. Okay, so the idea of it turned him on, of course, but it went deeper. He needed to know without a doubt that she wanted him.

She made him feel, made him think for those rare moments that there was something worth a damn inside him, and he was starving for more of it.

She dug her nails into him as if she couldn't help it. She probably couldn't. "I need you," she whispered, her body held taut, those denied orgasms, the ones she'd tried so hard to hold off still simmering inside her, threatening to boil over.

She didn't stop pleading, though. Her voice dropped more, something between breathlessness and moans, and she begged so sweetly. She didn't demand — *no, not my dove* — but just asked over and over for him.

Torrin pressed his forehead to hers before sliding into the warm heat of her body. She enveloped him, taking him without resistance, so wet that he had no problem going as deep as possible into her welcoming cunt.

Though, as soon as he bottomed out, when every inch of his hard cock was buried inside her sweet body, she whimpered with desperation.

"Come, dove," he growled against her lips.

She shattered beneath him, so much like the night she'd spent in his bed yet so much better. This time her pussy squeezed down on his shaft, her body writhed and her hips rolled against him. The chaos he'd caused in her was his to enjoy fully, with nothing between them.

And as he intended to do just that, he rocked his hips, fucking her through the orgasm even when she tightened around him impossibly.

Her body was perfect, and she didn't bother trying to hide a speck of her pleasure from him.

With Ashley, there was no deceit. *Well, you are lying to her...* He shoved away the thought. She had seen more of him, *accepted* more of him than any woman before.

That alone had his body ready to tumble over the end with her, wanting nothing more than to lock himself inside her, than to fill her with his seed. His scent would cling to her, a part of her, and that had him groaning and fucking harder into her.

Not that she minded the roughness. She clung to him, lifting her hips to take him deeper, clutching harder and scratching her nails down his back.

An ache in his cock grew, one that wouldn't be denied.

He reached down with one hand and caught her thigh, pulling it up to angle her hips and allow him deeper.

His knot swelled, and he growled at the rightness of that feeling.

She whined, but he bit softly at her bottom lip.

"Take my knot, dove," he demanded as he thrusted harder, growing thick enough that this time, he locked behind her pubic bone.

The sensation felt life-changing, as if he'd always waited for this moment, as if it were more important than anything else.

Her hands went from his sides to his chest, where she shoved, panicked little noises falling from her perfect lips.

Torrin gathered her against his chest as he came, as another orgasm racked her pretty little body, caused by his knot.

Words wouldn't form, not when she pulsed around him, when each wave of her pussy milked his aching knot again and prolonged his release.

He held her tight despite the way she squirmed, whimpered and cried out. The best reassurance he could give right then was the brush of his lips to hers.

The moment he could think again—at least somewhat, since no one could have thought much when trapped inside Ashley's perfect, drenched cunt—

he rolled to his good side, Ashley still trapped by his knot.

Her leg was tossed up and over his hip, her body pressed to his without an inch of space between them, her forehead to his chest as her rapid little breaths spilled across his skin.

He slid his fingers through her soft hair, pushing it from her face.

She took the chance to trace the mangled skin left behind by the injury that had rendered him needed less than.

She didn't touch him with pity, though. She didn't look at those marks as some proof that he'd failed, that he'd been ruined by them.

When she dipped her head to press a short line of kisses to the top of the burns, to the place she could reach on his side, she stole what little resistance he had left. How could he do anything but accept her, crumble before that sweet strength she had?

He caught her chin and lifted her gaze to his, then uttered the words he'd never said before, the ones far too dangerous to ever let escape his lips. "I love you."

Ashley went still, staring at him as though those were the last words she'd ever expected him to say.

Me too.

"Really?" She didn't ask it fishing for compliments—no, not Ashley. She said it with the same sort of deep-down self-doubt he understood, that he lived with, that told him he wasn't worthy of such a gift.

Torrin dragged his thumb against her jawline in a gentle caress. "Yes, really. Now, relax and close your eyes. It's still early."

"But work—"

"Can wait. I don't think there is anywhere I'd rather be right now."

Her smile was slow, hesitant, but she settled down, even as small shudders ran through her, especially when a movement would cause his knot to tug against her body, a reminder that they were still locked together.

She curled against his chest, her breath warm, until she whispered so softly, he wondered if he was meant to hear it at all, "I love you, too."

The words frightened him more than they should have, perhaps, but in that moment, he realized that he couldn't lose her.

And the world had a habit of taking away the things that meant the most to him.

Chapter Seventeen

Ashley wanted to like Kara, but she struggled to.

The omega was funny, snarky and tough. She felt like an older sister that Ashley had never had.

It hadn't taken more than ten minutes before Kara had started to offer Ashley suggestions on how best to outsmart the alphas.

Still, each time Ashley felt like giving in and being nice, she'd remember that Kara and Liam had slept together.

Multiple times.

Suddenly all that sweet forgiveness she generally had drifted away, and Ashley wanted to scratch the woman's eyes out.

Which was not only stupid, because they were both adults and fighting over men was for teenagers, but also because Kara was so far outside of Ashley's weight class when it came to an ability to fight.

None of that stopped the jealousy, though, or her annoyance that a woman who was so obviously a part of their lives—and would no doubt continue to be a part of their lives—had slept with one of the men Ashley loved.

"We won't be long," Erik said for the third time.

"I could have stayed at the apartment," she pointed out, even though she knew exactly why they'd refused that. They had a meeting and didn't trust hired security to watch her without them.

It meant that when a meeting would require all three going, they had decided to 'drop her off' with Kara, as if she were in need of a babysitter.

Again, the other omega's history with them chafed.

Torrin answered her. "I didn't want you to be stuck there and bored. You've had no time with other women since moving in with us."

Yep. Other women, meaning the ones they've slept with.

"Right," Ashley said, because she couldn't bring herself to say the things she thought, especially in from of Kara.

She didn't need anyone else to see her insecurities.

Erik nodded toward the back room. "Kara, could we have a word?"

And isn't that overly obvious? Ashley huffed softly and crossed her arms, refusing to actually state how much she hated feeling excluded.

Liam tilted his head, having caught her reaction. He waved the others off without him and didn't move until only he and Ashley stayed in the room.

She tried to look around the house, at anything other than the alpha still there. It worked at distracting her, at least until he set a hand on her hip and pulled her against him. She looked up to meet his gaze, since ignoring him probably wasn't possible, what with his body against hers.

"What?" Ashley knew she'd snapped the question out, but she couldn't help it.

His eyebrow lifted, as if her reaction proved something was wrong. "What's going on in that head of yours?"

"Nothing."

He leaned in closer. "Haven't I told you that you are horrible at lying?"

Ashley let out a slow sigh. "How about nothing I want to talk to you about, then?"

"Aren't you feisty today?" He stepped back but grasped her arm and tugged.

Ashley pulled, but he wouldn't relent. "Where are we going?"

"To talk."

He led her into a bathroom, then shut the door behind them.

"We don't need to talk in a bathroom."

Liam twisted Ashley, grasped her hips, then lifted her so she sat on the sink counter. He moved forward, between her thighs, then grasped her chin so she had no choice but to look him in the eyes. "Why does Kara bother you so much?"

Just the name on his lips drew a flinch from her, and Ashley hated that. She didn't want to be the jealous woman, but she couldn't shake that feeling.

She opened her mouth, but Liam cut her off first. "Don't tell me it doesn't. I'm not above paddling your ass if you keep lying to me."

Heat spread across her cheeks at the thought of that.

A smile crept across his lips. "Well, good to know you like that idea, though it means it might not be the best threat. Come on now, sweet, just talk to me."

Ashley blew out a breath, then looked down to avoid his gaze. "I know I shouldn't be bothered, but I am, okay?"

"Why? Just because I've slept with her?"

There was no way to get out of there without being honest, so Ashley admitted the truth. "I just keep thinking about it. She's pretty, tough, and you clearly love her."

"I love her like a friend. As far as the rest, yeah, she's basically me with a vagina, and I have no desire to spend any more time with myself. I don't know how to help you understand this." He locked his gaze to hers, and for once, she didn't feel like he was hiding anything.

"You haven't even slept with me yet," she finally said. "So she's had you in a way I haven't."

The curl of his lip into a smirk said Ashley had just either made the best decision or biggest mistake of her life. "Well, lucky for you, that can be remedied right now."

His words didn't even register at first when he found the button to her jeans with his deft hands. He flicked it open and had the zipper down before she realized why she should probably fight him on this.

They were in a bathroom at someone else's house, with other people in the other room.

It was so *not* the right time for this.

She shoved at his chest, but he wouldn't give her an inch of space. "We aren't alone."

"Well, in case you've forgotten, I don't mind an audience." He teased her with kisses along the side of her throat, his warm breath and soft lips helping to convince her more than his words could. "And besides,

I've been thinking about this for a while, anyway. I'm tired of waiting."

He worked her jeans down, then yanked off one boot so he could get her pants and underwear off that foot, leaving them hanging on the other.

It felt debased and wild and crazy, and Ashley moaned at the first touch of his skilled fingers to her clit.

"You are everything I could want," he whispered as he worked a finger into her, his thumb at her clit, his touch demanding. He wasn't going slow, almost like he intended to prove something to her right then, as quickly as he could.

Ashley leaned back when he pushed so her shoulder blades touched the mirror, angling her pussy for better access.

"What happened with Kara was nothing. It wasn't important to either of us, and was more like an uncomfortable physical than sex. I can assure you, I didn't feel like *this* with her." He exchanged the single finger for two, as if making a point, as if proving to her that this was different.

And she believed it. It helped to have him there, touching her and praising her and soothing the fears that had spawned from her inability to trust.

He flicked the fastening of his slacks open, then pulled down his zipper. Ashley let herself stare, enjoyed the sight of his cock, thick and hard and *hers*. He stroked himself with his free hand, the action hypnotizing her.

"You see, sweet, this is how fucking badly I want you. I've never felt like this, never needed someone like I need you. I've gone my whole fucking life not needing anyone, never wanting to need anyone, then you came along. I think it's one reason I did that with Kara, because I knew neither of us wanted the other, so it was safe. With you? With you it's different, and I love it and I hate it and it's more than I've ever had before." He withdrew his fingers, and the hot, blunt head of his dick pressed to her drenched and needy cunt. His voice dropped low, losing that smooth quality he usually had, as if some of that civility had been stripped away. "So you've got no reason to be jealous of anyone, ever, because you've got your claws in me in a way no one else ever has."

Ashley cried out, not caring if anyone heard when he plunged into her. It wasn't how Erik or even Torrin had taken her. They'd eased her into it, where Liam took everything. He seated himself in one hard thrust — not that she wasn't ready — that made her feel every millimeter.

He was thick, stretching her in a wonderfully sinful way. Liam slid his hands beneath her thighs and to her hips, forcing her legs wide as they rested over his forearms. With his grip, he pulled back and slammed into her again.

Her head bounced against the mirror, but she hardly noticed with the sparks of pleasure that sprang up throughout her body. He didn't touch her clit, but she didn't think she even needed it, not with how his shaft hit every single spot inside her that lit her up.

Being so lewdly displayed for him did something for her as well, especially how his gaze heated. The cool air of the room slid across her damp, swollen clit like the most torturous tease, causing her nipples to tighten despite being tucked into her shirt and ignored.

But Liam didn't slow at all. He fucked her with hard thrusts, pulling back then plunging deeper. The sounds of the bathroom were filthy, the slapping of bodies, the moans and gasping, panting breaths.

The point was clear, though. Ashley already knew well that Liam could slow down, that he could tease and play her body like an expert with an instrument. He could keep her along that edge of orgasm or shove her to one with ease.

That wasn't his lesson right then.

He was showing her his passion, showing her how much he wanted — and needed — her. This wasn't calculated, it wasn't him showing off — it was him giving her a glimpse of how deeply he felt.

And that did everything to assuage her fears, to let her release them as she drowned in the passion he shared with her.

He fucked her like a man possessed, and when his knot started to swell, she didn't fight it.

What was there to fight? Liam had taken her over entirely, made her want to give in, to give him everything and take everything in return.

He knotted her, and the moment he locked into place, it pushed her into a breathtaking release without him having to even touch her clit. She squeezed down around him, the sensation of his hot cum filling her better than all the teasing touches or sweet nights. It was instinctual and primal and a bond nothing else could replicate.

He found her lips with his, sweet despite the waves of pleasure that still crashed over her from the way his cock jerked, from how his knot kept her stimulated and trapped.

He told her more with that kiss, which was a funny thing since Liam was the one with a way with words, but while the things he said were suspect, his body told the truth.

He'd claimed her, taken her apart with his passion and his need, and now those gentle touches put her back together.

And it worked. She didn't care about Kara. She didn't care about any female in his past, about anything beyond them.

He's mine, and I won't let him go without a fight.

* * * *

Liam shouldn't have been smiling so widely, having been clearly caught having sex with his mate in a bathroom at a friend's home, but he was shameless enough not to care.

When he'd finally been able to pull free of Ashley's luscious body, when they'd dressed and left the bathroom, Kara, Erik and Torrin had all been waiting in the living room. The alphas had the good sense to not say anything, since Ashley wasn't the sort to want to bring attention to it.

Kara, on the other hand, had the largest grin he'd ever seen and had been quick to point out that she'd purposely made sure that countertop could easily hold the weight of a person for that specific reason.

Leaving Ashley hadn't been easy, and Liam kept trying to bring his mind to the task at hand, yet he couldn't seem to forget how good she smelled, how wonderfully she had wrapped around him.

And all the things he'd said that he'd never uttered before.

Declarations of love were not his thing, yet he'd poured them out to her without a second thought.

And stranger still? He'd meant them.

He had no issue lying when he needed to, feigning interest in a female for information when it would benefit him. His words to her hadn't been fake, though.

He'd meant every one of them.

"Did you work everything out?" Torrin leaned against the table.

Liam nodded, arms crossed. "I think so."

"This is why it isn't smart to shit where you eat," Erik said. "You should have never touched Kara."

"Seemed like a good idea at the time."

"No it didn't," Torrin said. "You just liked the idea of having someone you knew you'd never fall for."

Liam snarled in Torrin's direction, with no real heat behind the action. He hated having others dissect his behavior, even if they were right.

Erik huffed a soft laugh. "It's funny that you fell so hard after how you worked to never do so. It feels like cosmic justice."

"Laugh it up, you two. You're both as deep in as I am."

"True enough," Erik said. "We're all fucked if that girl decides to call it quits."

Torrin didn't speak, but he nodded. A shadow on his face said his fear was not quite the same, and Liam could tell in the expression he was thinking back to Gilly. He didn't fear she'd leave—he feared she'd die.

It seemed they all had their fears, their fuck-ups, but Ashley had managed to get past them all.

Not by tearing down walls, but by turning them to dust out of persistence and sweetness.

That gentle nature was something they'd never had, something that had never been a part of their lives. Even as children, they'd lacked any of that.

She offered something they craved so desperately, something they hadn't realized they needed.

The door opened, drawing Liam from his thoughts. This meeting needed focus.

They weren't playing with people to take lightly.

They'd sent the address for the meeting — an office building in the upper area of a mall. Dangerous meetings had two possibilities. Somewhere out of the way or somewhere busy. They both had their benefits, but when dealing with people who liked to stay in the shadows, busy won out. They were likely to remain on their best behavior, because dealing with bodies in crowded spaces was a hassle.

Three men entered. One was obviously in charge, while the other two had the stance of bodyguards. None had guns, something that the extra security outside the door had checked for.

The man who stood at the center didn't shake hands with Torrin, though after a slight nod, he took a seat at the other side of the table. "Thank you for meeting with me."

"I was interested in what you wanted to discuss," Torrin said. "A good businessman never ignores a potential deal. I would appreciate a name, though."

The man sat up straight in his chair, with the same bearing as Torrin. He appeared used to dealing with meetings and negotiations. "You can call me Mr. Bisson. I would prefer not to spend too much time pretending. Let's be frank."

Torrin waved Bisson on, as if to agree.

"We have the same problem. Gregory has become more unstable as time has gone on. He's become a liability."

"I wouldn't disagree, but that doesn't explain why you wanted to see me. From my understanding, your organization is more than large enough to deal with him on his own."

Bisson nodded, as if conceding that point. "There are still a few who wouldn't dare stand up against him, not because they care about him but because they're afraid of what could happen if they fail. To be fair, so am I. Gregory isn't known for his understanding nature."

"So you want me to do your dirty work?"

"You would be well compensated," Bisson explained. "I wouldn't ask you to do so for nothing. I've had time to look over your business here in this city, and you've done a respectable job. I think, if given the right resources, you could easily expand that range of influence much further."

Liam held in a curse at that. If there was one way to tempt Torrin, that would be it.

Thankfully, Torrin played it close to his chest. "I thought we were going to be frank?"

Bisson smiled, then set his arm on the table and leaned forward. "I want you to remove Gregory from being a problem. His obsession with that omega has gone too far, cost us too much. He isn't trustworthy, and if I can't trust him, I don't want him around. Do this and you'll take over his position."

"Those people you work with will happily take me in after I kill their associate? Because I feel like that would be a difficult sell."

"Like I said, they know it needs to be done. There have been enough whispers, but no one has been willing to act, to put their name on it in case it fails. You, though, you have the thing he wants the most — that female. You'd be able to get close enough to him to get rid of him. Draw him out with an offer to turn her over and deal with him."

"Gregory placed a contract on the female. If he dies, she ends up with a price on her head."

Bisson waved the detail off. "I know the broker he uses. I'll have it removed."

Torrin nodded, folding his hands together, lacing his fingers as if thinking. "I don't usually deal in human trafficking."

"Everyone has their lines. That's fine. This area has proven too troublesome for that anyway. We have one more large auction coming up after scouts procure a few more omegas, then we're moving that out of the area. That isn't the only use, though. You think we don't handle drugs, weapons, blackmail—anything that needs to be done? With the grip you have in this area, you'd be useful to us and we could help you expand past here, further than you could imagine."

Torrin didn't answer right away, using that silence as he did so well.

If it unnerved Bisson, he didn't show it. "Take some time to consider it, but not too much. I don't know how much longer Gregory's patience will last." He rose, his bodyguards flanking him. "It was nice to meet you, Mr. Kansas, and I look forward to doing business with you."

They left, the noise from the mall flooding in when they opened the door.

Once the door shut and they were alone, Erik turned toward Torrin. "Well, that's not what I expected."

Torrin shook his head. "Me either. Though…"

"You can't really be thinking about it," Liam argued. "Even if we aren't involved in the trafficking directly, it's a line we've never crossed."

"We've walked that line enough before, dealt with people who did things we didn't agree with. If we do this, Ashley is safe and we gain a lot of useful resources."

Liam cut a harsh look at his cousin, at the man who had always reached for too much when it came to power. "This isn't about her—it's about you. It's about you extending your reach."

"And with that, I could better keep her safe, keep you all safe. Besides, what other option do you see?"

Liam opened his mouth, then snapped it shut. He didn't know, but he was sure there had to be something else. "We'll figure it out, but it can't be *this*. This is like crawling into bed with snakes. Eventually, you get bit."

Torrin turned his gaze to Erik. "And you? What do you say?"

Erik pressed his lips together, the look of a man who didn't care to answer. Finally, he sighed softly. "I think that there are a lot of things they'd ask me to do when they realized my skills, and very few of them I would like to do. I think we've worked well without masters, and while they call themselves associates, they would be masters."

"For a time, perhaps, but we always come out on top."

Erik shook his head. "Always is a dangerous game to play, because the more you play it, the more the odds turn against you. Eventually, it won't go our way."

Torrin's gaze drew away from them and landed on his cane, the one leaning against the wall, out of reach, which would mean he'd either need to limp there or ask one of them to get it, and didn't that speak volumes?

Liam could see it there, the need for power, the taste of it on his tongue a way to distract himself.

Torrin drew his hand into a fist, his face a mask of certainty. "I'll call Gregory tonight and set up an exchange. By next week, he will be dead, Ashley will be safe, and we'll have enough power to never have to worry about it again."

Liam pressed his lips together and watched as Torrin made a choice he wouldn't be able to take back.

Chapter Eighteen

Funny how even a limo could feel small to Ashley once all three alphas piled in.

Torrin spoke on his phone, his gaze out of the window on a call he'd been on for the past ten minutes.

He always worked, rarely ever taking a break from it. She'd had to almost pull him at times from the work to get him into bed for the evening. Not that she minded, and despite him almost never smiling, she could see the tightened muscles in his cheeks as she did so, as he gave in to her. He'd never admit it, but she knew he enjoyed her fussing over him.

Erik sat to her left, his arm pressed to hers. He didn't often speak, but seemed to like contact, as if that small touch were enough for him to know she was there despite them not talking.

Liam, on the other hand, behaved like a little brother most often, teasing her and forever acting out for her attention.

It had been easy to fall into that routine. The trips to work and back had become a cherished part of her day, and fears of Gregory had faded into the background.

The alphas had assured her they were working on the problem, and the added security remained a welcome constant in her life.

Still, she felt settled and safe in a way she hadn't in so long. She slept through the night, pressed up against one or more of them. Concerns of the man who had plagued her life were so far removed, she went days without a single thought of him.

She would visit with Kara from time to time, and had grown to enjoy the woman's company, as odd as she might be.

It was an honest life, one she'd never thought she'd have.

A sting in her ear drew her attention back to Liam. "You're ignoring me."

"So you flick my ear?"

He shrugged. "I would have preferred fucking you until you paid attention, but there isn't a lot of room in here." That grin of his, the one so full of mischief that she shuddered when it appeared, spread across his lips. "But we could test that out. I mean, I've been wrong before."

He reached for her, but before he could touch her, the limo jerked to the left hard enough that she fell into Erik. A sound caught her attention, and it took a moment for her to realize it was the limo.

The driver spoke up from the intercom once the vehicle came to a stop. "Flat tire."

Erik got out of the car first, with Liam, Ashley and Torrin exiting after. No doubt they'd call for a new car, and Ashley wasn't going to sit in the limo to wait.

They were in a deserted parking lot Ashley didn't recognize. She'd grown used to the surrounding areas, at least the parts they traveled. This didn't seem familiar at all.

"Where are we?" Erik asked.

Liam slid a hand behind him, keeping Ashley pressed to his back.

"There was traffic," the driver said. "We had to go around."

That didn't seem to ease any of the alphas.

Liam's voice came out pleasant, but his grip on Ashley didn't loosen. "Traffic always gets to us. So, should we call for another car? I'd rather get home quicker and not wait for the tire to get changed."

"Already called," the driver said. "New car will be here any moment."

Sure enough, the roar of another engine tore through the silence, and a black town car — so much like the ones they normally used — pulled into the parking lot.

She might not have the senses they did, but her past of running from Gregory had given her a good ability to recognize when something was wrong.

There was something very wrong.

The town car stopped, and from inside, four men poured out. She could only see feet from her spot, hidden behind Liam, but so many people couldn't mean anything good.

Erik turned a vicious look on the driver. "How much were you paid?"

"Enough," the man said.

"I assure you, it wasn't." The coldness of Erik's voice and the simmering violence terrified Ashley.

Liam shifted her more, pressed her further behind him, to shield her more with his body.

"We were set to meet in a few days," Torrin said.

"I don't like leaving things to chance. People tend to be more honest when surprised, so I moved up the schedule of our hand-off." That voice, the one carved into her psyche. *Gregory.*

She couldn't see him, and she wasn't sure if that was better or not. The idea of having him out of sight terrified her, yet she wasn't sure she was ready to face him, not after so many years. There was a safety in being tucked behind Liam.

But what hand-off was he talking about?

"You show up with armed men. Why should we trust you'll keep your word?" Torrin asked.

"Because you lack choices and thus leverage. I'm still willing to keep my word, though. Hand Ashley over to me and you'll have what I promised you. No one needs to die here today."

Ashley's stomach dropped. *Gregory negotiated with the alphas and they didn't tell me?*

Sickness gnawed at her, at the idea they'd kept it from her, that she'd been so out of the loop, and with fear that they really intended to hand her over. How could she be in the same spot again? Why hadn't she learned her lesson?

Violence swirled, thick like smoke, enough to choke on. Liam's hand was strong against her, holding her tightly. Despite how she couldn't breathe when she realized they'd lied, that grip said one thing at least — *they aren't going to hand me over.*

Ashley expected some quip, for the alphas to say something before moving. That was how it always happened in the movies. Violence never just occurred. It was softened with funny words and lessons, and yet none of that happened.

There was nothing to prepare her for the ugliness of it.

Erik moved first, taking the gun from the holster at his hip and firing, impossibly fast and without a moment of hesitation. Liam did the same, just as Torrin yanked her back, trapping her between the limo and his body. Still, she couldn't see anything, and that was worse. Only the grunts of pain and the loud blasts of the guns told her what happened.

The alphas moved backward, Ashley pushed along with them, until they crouched behind the back of the limo.

"You could have made this easy," Gregory shouted above the noise.

Torrin gripped the back of her shirt to keep her down, behind the cover. "You aren't getting her," he called back.

"I heard a rumor you had a meeting with a mutual friend. I knew he'd been looking for someone to take me out for years, but imagine my surprise when I heard it was you. I didn't believe it."

Ashley turned her gaze to Torrin, confusion making it hard to make sense of the words. Why would anyone ask Torrin and his cousins to kill someone? Businessmen didn't do that.

Gregory wouldn't stop his tirade, though. "I mean, from everything you three have done, maybe it shouldn't have surprised me. I just thought of you as more run-of-the-mill criminals, not the sort who would dare take a shot at someone like me. You'll kill other drug dealers and break kneecaps for business, but killing me? That's a whole different league."

Bile crept up Ashley's throat, burning as things fitted into place.

The security, the way the alphas had been so vague about what they did, the respect — no, fear — she'd seen in some of their clients.

They weren't at all what she'd thought, were they? It was like learning about Gregory all over again.

"Until next time," Gregory called before the slam of a door and squealing tires said he'd left.

It wasn't over, though. Rocks crunched beneath running feet, and Liam took off.

Ashley rose, finding bodies of three men she didn't recognize on the pavement, red leaking from them as they didn't move.

Liam overtook the driver, who had tried to run, then hauled him back with a grip on the back of his neck, a grip Liam had used on her before but which had never seemed so sinister.

Torrin took a moment to check Ashley over, but he said nothing to her directly. It was for the best, because she had no idea what to say back.

Erik walked up to the driver, his expression that distant, cold one Ashley hated. It was what she'd seen in him before, but never had it taken up so much of him. "You betrayed us," he said.

The driver trembled, all his bravery from earlier having fled. "I'm sorry," he pleaded. "I didn't have a choice."

"You had a choice," Torrin said. "You could have come to us if they threatened you, but instead you took the money happily, willing to see us all killed."

Erik didn't snarl, and that was even more frightening. If he'd been enraged, she'd have understood, but he spoke coolly, as though none of what happened was any more meaningful than tying his shoes. "If you had only betrayed us, I might have let it go. However, you were trusted with her. You were tasked with driving her on her own before. That I can't let slide."

What little color remained in the man's face drained away when he saw the expression on Erik's face. When Erik moved, it was with a speed that had Ashley stumbling backward. His hand was nothing but a blur, a flash of silver at the end.

Red poured from the driver's throat, and Ashley covered her mouth as his body fell in a heap.

Blood spread from him, a sickening gurgle that caused her to lose the fight with her stomach.

She twisted away and hunched over, one hand on the limo, and vomited. Each time she stopped heaving, the memory of it came back to her. Not just the blood, but Erik's calm face, the way Liam and Torrin had looked on as if it were entirely normal.

It all became clear.

I fell in love with monsters.

* * * *

Erik paced the safehouse, missing the apartment. It wasn't the stuff, but rather the feeling.

He turned his gaze to Ashley before having to admit that it wasn't the apartment he missed — it was the way she'd brought the place to life.

She stared out of the window, her face pale, refusing to talk or look at any of them.

All their secrets were out now. Everything they'd tried to hide was on the table, and she'd not reacted well.

Then again, what had he expected? She was sweet, innocent, naive. She wouldn't have reacted well to finding out the males she'd bonded to were at best criminals, at worst murderers.

They hadn't bothered to try to speak to her on the way to the safehouse. What was there to say?

Once she'd finished throwing up, they'd given her a water as Torrin had called someone they trusted for a car, one that couldn't be traced.

Not that he was certain how to deal with any of it.

"I want to leave," Ashley said, her voice wavering around the words.

Erik turned to face her, Liam and Torrin doing the same.

Liam answered. "It's not safe anywhere else right now."

"I don't care. I don't want to be here, not with you."

Erik took a step toward her, wanting to brush her hair from her face, to remind her that she *knew* them. Even if she hadn't known everything, she still knew them, and if he could only touch her, she'd remember.

Except she jumped back a step as if *he* were the largest danger there.

Pain clawed at his chest, the memories of his old mate walking out on him, of the fear in her face. There it was again, his old friend, that terror on the face of a loved one, the one he'd known he would see eventually on Ashley's.

"You can't leave," Liam said again, voice soft. "It's too dangerous out there."

She shook her head. "I'm not so sure it's safe here, either."

"We'd never let anything happen to you," he tried again.

"And I'm supposed to believe that?"

"Haven't we proven it?" Torrin asked.

She seemed to snap then, all that gentle demeanor that Erik knew draining away until hurt and anger took over. "No, you haven't proven it. I trusted you! I told you how often I'd been betrayed, lied to, used, and now I find out you were doing the same. After I told you how much it mattered to me to not be lied to, you did the exact thing to me everyone else always has."

"We weren't using you," Torrin argued.

"Of course you were! You were using my stupidity to make me fall for you, knowing I never would have if I'd realized what sort of people you really were. And what about the hand-off?"

"We were buying time. I was never going to give you to him," Torrin said.

"You could have talked to me, told me about it."

"You didn't need to know."

Even Erik winced at the stupidity of that answer.

She lifted her chin, anger dancing in her deep blue eyes. "I didn't need to know? It's my life."

"And this is our world. I'll do whatever it takes to keep you safe."

"You'll do whatever you want to keep *you* safe. You didn't lie to me because you were worried about me — you lied because you knew I'd never accept it. You all knew I couldn't live with this, so you decided to keep me in the dark for your own benefit. Don't you dare pretend it was for me. And his friend's offer? You're planning on doing his dirty work? What, so you can become omega slavers, too?"

"It wasn't like that." No matter how much Torrin tried to explain, her harsh look said she refused to hear any of it. "His associates gave us a good deal. If we get rid of him, you'll be safe."

"And you'll have new *associates*? It wasn't about me. It was about you getting what you want, like always."

Sure, Erik and Liam had said the same thing, but hearing it from Ashley made it worse.

Still, Torrin persisted. "More allies would keep you safer."

"You just want power and you don't care what you have to do or who you have to walk over to get it. You didn't need to be this person. You're smart enough to do business without it, but you are so desperate to have people look past your limp that you'll mow down anyone in your way to get there. I knew that—I guess I just didn't realize that included me."

The jab silenced them all, even more so because Erik wasn't sure there was a response it. Was there a way to explain to her that wasn't true? That she mattered to them?

But…did she matter more than their business? Than Torrin's power? Than the life they'd spent so long cultivating? It was easy to make a choice when it seemed to be the same benefit, but if they were truly put head to head?

"Everything I did was for your benefit. I will not watch you get slaughtered like my last mate!"

"And I won't be with males who think so little of me that they lie to me, right to my face. This was never for me. You could have gone to the police instead. I can't believe with your contacts, you don't have someone you could reach who wasn't connected to him."

"That would have labeled us snitches and ruined all the contacts we have. We'd lose everything."

"Exactly," she said. "It's easy to say you did this for me when you think the choice that is best for me is also best for you. When you pit them against one another, though, when you have to pick, you'll always pick yourself. I'm just a possession for you, something for you to own along with everything else you have."

Erik opened his mouth to rebut her statement, but her next words came out so soft, so sad, they stole his breath.

"You're just like Gregory."

He couldn't even argue with her on that point.

* * * *

Ashley hurt. It was a pain so deep, she had no idea how to handle it.

It was as though all that happiness that she'd cultivated in her weeks with the alphas had collapsed in on itself and left a hollow ache instead.

She'd walked out on the alphas after their argument, retreating to one of the rooms. They hadn't bothered her since, and each moment without them grew that clawing, tearing pain inside her.

Everything she'd thought she found was fake. That was the worst part of it, that she'd been happy, that she'd been so damned content, then discovered it was as lie. It made her recognize that it was gone.

She'd never get it back.

That loss broke her, shattering her heart into pieces so small, she thought she could scatter them like glitter.

The night dragged on and sleep wouldn't come. It wasn't fear of Gregory. She wasn't sure she feared him anymore.

The hurt was so deep, and she'd realized that all men weren't honest no matter what, so why fear Gregory?

It was like realizing the game was always rigged, so why worry about playing?

She'd lose in the end. Whether it was by loving men who had betrayed her or living her life under Gregory's thumb, did it really matter?

She got out of the bed, frustration tearing at her, feelings too large to even understand coursing through her.

The alphas had done this to her, had made her want things — need things — they couldn't give to her.

She left her room, dressed in nothing. She knew damned well why she was seeking them out.

The fewer clothes, the better.

She found the alphas in the guest bedroom, with Liam and Torrin asleep on the bed and Erik stretched out in a chair, his feet up on the end of the bed.

They didn't look all that peaceful, even asleep, as if they couldn't settle fully.

I will not feel guilty about that.

Liam's bare chest drew her in. The alphas had made her feel out of control and helpless and stupid. They could damned well help her deal with it.

Liam woke the moment she slid over him, the blanket keeping her from touching him directly. He drew in a surprised breath, but she ignored it and leaned down to kiss his jawline.

She wasn't gentle when she traced his strong jaw. She wanted to bite at his skin, to draw blood, to make him hurt like she was.

But…that wasn't her. So instead, she rolled her hips, his cock hardening so she could feel it even with the blanket between them.

The chair creaked, telling her Erik had woken, and a hand on her back said Torrin was aware, too.

"Dove," Torrin whispered. "What are you doing?"

Ashley didn't want to talk. She didn't want to bare her soul anymore to men she didn't trust. They'd seen more of her than they deserved, so she'd guard anything else.

She tried to keep her focus on where her lips met Liam's throat, but when she reached out to stroke up Torrin's leg, over the sweats he wore, a hand slid into her hair and pulled, tearing her from what she wanted most.

Erik was the one who had done it, she realized as he forced her to meet his dark gaze, to stare into the eyes she'd thought she'd known so well. "You're still angry. You don't want this."

"I do," she argued.

"You think we can't see it? Can't smell the hurt and anger on you?" His grip didn't relent, and even the sting in her scalp was familiar.

It only hurt more, the way she liked it, the way she remembered how sweetly they'd taken her, that they'd used a grip in her hair to control her.

She'd felt safe when they did it before. She felt that safety again, and she hated it.

I know they're liars now. I should know better than to fall for this.

"You made me feel this way," she spat. "You did this to me."

"And you think this will help? You think having sex with us now, feeling the way you do, is a good idea?"

She dug her nails into Torrin's leg and rocked her hips, grinding her cunt against Liam's erection. "I don't care. Are you happy now? I don't care about anything. I don't care if Gregory finds me, I don't care if I have to start over, I don't care if I just disintegrate into nothing here with you. I just don't care. I thought I had something — you made me think I had something — then you took it away. Are you going to take this away, too?"

He dragged his finger below her eye, catching a tear. She hated that she was crying, but she couldn't help it. It was all too much.

He exchanged a look with the others, as if he needed to know what they thought.

The idea of having sex with them was horrible, but the idea of them turning her away was worse.

"We'll give you whatever you need," he said, his voice soft, as if he were trying so hard to not be the man she'd seen take that driver's life. He leaned in for a kiss, but she turned her head. It was too familiar, too painful.

She pulled at the blanket, rewarded by it shifting out of the way, only to find Liam naked.

She shifted up to her knees, her anger and hurt driving her as she grasped his cock and pressed it to her. She didn't toy with him, didn't get off on the sweet exploration that she had before. Instead, it felt mechanical, like a means to an end.

Before she could slide down, Torrin caught her hip. "You're not ready."

"I don't care."

Torrin offered a kiss to her shoulder before he found her clit with his fingers. "I care. We've done enough damage. We won't hurt you like this, not ever."

A little painful sex was nothing compared to having her heart ripped out.

Still, the stroke of Torrin's agile fingers to her clit turned her body against her. No matter what she felt, she knew she'd never be able to resist them. *Why? How can I still want them after I know what they are?*

Liam reached up her body to cup her breast, teasing the nipple. It mixed pleasure with the pain, and that was what she wanted.

She needed to feel something else, to do anything to break the tension inside her.

It didn't take long before she was moaning, before her pussy was drenched and she rode that impossible high they always gave to her.

Ashley grasped his cock, and this time no one stopped her when she fitted Liam against her cunt, when she slid his thick shaft into her.

A thin whine left her lips, but she didn't stop. The stretching of her body was just another sensation warring inside her, and she took it, used it to push away the day, the truth, all of it.

When her body met his, when she'd taken every inch of him, she set her hands on his chest and rode him, going up slowly before coming down hard, letting him plunge in as deep as possible.

Liam caught the back of her neck and pulled her down to his lips, but she turned her face. She didn't want his kiss.

It meant too much.

He pressed his lips to her jaw instead. "You mean everything to me, sweet. You have to know that, to believe that."

She pressed her eyes tightly shut, trying to block them out. She couldn't let his voice creep in.

He cupped her cheeks and pressed her forehead to his. "What do you need? Tell me, and I'll give it to you."

"I need more."

"More what?"

She whimpered and rolled her hips. "I need to not hurt anymore. Just for a little while, give me enough so I won't hurt."

His groan wasn't one of pleasure, but was saturated in regret.

He only regretted getting caught, though, not what had happened, not what he had done to her. If he cared about those things, he'd never have done it in the first place.

Torrin spoke instead. "We'll give you everything, dove, always." A tightness in her hair said he'd gripped it, pulling until she angled to the side. Warmth at her lips had her darting her tongue out. Salty precum was her reward, and she relaxed into the grasp of Torrin's hand. He rubbed his cock against her lips, a teasing touch that said he'd do what he wanted.

Which was exactly what she needed.

After a moment—far too long, really—he pulled softly at her hair until she parted her lips and took his thick, hard cock into her mouth.

Ashley kept her eyes closed while she worshipped his shaft, and she hated herself and him for it. How could she be so angry and yet fall so easily for this? How could he hurt her so much, and yet she melted for him?

The answers mattered less than the questions, and she pushed them aside, trying to lose herself in the feeling, in his taste, in his scent. He controlled the action, never going deep, letting her twist her tongue around the tip of his cock and hollow her cheeks to suck, to lick the precum from the slit at the head.

"Enough?" he asked.

No. She shook her head, or tried the best she could.

Large, warm hands ran over her hips.

Erik. She shuddered as she remembered what those hands had done earlier, how easily they'd taken a life.

His voice rose above the groans in the room, above her own broken whines. "If you want to be overwhelmed, I can do it." His lips pressed back to her in a kiss that was too gentle, too sweet. "Do you trust me?"

No.

She didn't need to respond, or maybe she had and she hadn't realized it. Whatever the truth, they heard her answer loud and clear.

He dragged his tongue up her spine, the wetness left behind from it catching a chill from the air. "I won't hurt you, not like this. Do you want more? Because I'll give you more, but you have to tell me yes."

Torrin tugged at her hair until she released his cock, until she had to answer, had to participate.

"I want everything you can give me," she answered honestly.

"Good girl," Torrin praised but didn't return her to his cock. Instead, he slid his thumb past her lips, allowing her to suck on that, to wrap her tongue along the digit in some parody of what she wanted.

She didn't ask why—the answer clear when Erik grasped her ass cheeks, spread her and slid his finger until he pressed against a spot on her that was untouched.

Ashley tensed, unsure.

"If you don't want to, either tell us or tap twice with your hand. This is still your choice," Torrin told her.

Even without an answer, Erik continued to tease, not trying to press into her but ghosting over her ass with clear intent.

And Ashley knew she wouldn't tell them no.

This was what she'd wanted. She needed them to take away the hurt they'd caused, at least for a little while, and that meant *this*. It meant them pushing her past her boundaries, past what she'd had before, until she couldn't think, couldn't remember, could only catch a glimpse of what she'd thought she had found.

When she didn't tell them no, Erik pressed another kiss to her lower back. Something cold and wet dripped on her. It took her a second to realize it must have been lube, and she knew she was right when Erik set a slick finger against her ass.

He didn't tease anymore, instead pressing hard enough to sink that single finger into her to the first knuckle.

She cried out, shifting her hips, the foreign intrusion feeling strange.

Not bad, not painful, just odd.

"Relax for us, sweet," Liam whispered.

But his sweet words and pet name weren't what she wanted to hear. Those things forced her to think about their connection, about the bond between them. She needed this to be just bodies.

She released Torrin's thumb. "I need…" She couldn't bring herself to say it.

How could she tell him that she needed his commanding voice? That she didn't need them to be gentle, or careful, or sweet. She needed them to hold her down, to rumble out the commands she couldn't resist and to force her so she didn't have to think.

Leave it to Torrin to understand, though. He stroked his fingers over her cheek. "You're sure? I didn't think you'd want that, not with how you're feeling."

"Please," she begged.

He slid his thumb over her bottom lip. "Anything." He paused for a moment, and when he spoke again, it held that edge of demand she needed, the one that never failed to force her body to obey. "Relax. Let him in, omega."

She almost sobbed in relief when she could ease into that order, when she could let everything go. She took a breath and relaxed, loosening her muscles.

Erik took advantage, delving even farther into her. When she wasn't tense, the sensation went from strange to good. It teased nerve endings that had never been toyed with before.

It added to the feeling of fullness caused by Liam's cock, which seemed impossibly larger since she couldn't move.

One finger turned into two, and the stretch had her whimpering.

Torrin's thumb slipped past her lips again. "Suck."

Ashley did as he said, and just as he'd planned, no doubt, it distracted her.

Erik loosened her, working his fingers into her with slow and determined thrusts. He twisted his wrist, stroking all the nerve endings in her untrained ass.

Too soon, he withdrew, and she whined at both the loss and the knowledge of what would come next.

He stroked her ass, grasping a cheek in his strong hand. The blunt head of his cock pushed against her, the cool wetness telling her he'd added more lube.

She shifted, her nerves getting the better of her.

"Be still," Torrin ordered. "You will let him fuck your ass."

The crude words melted her resolve, and Ashley went lax against Liam. She focused on not fighting, on wrapping her tongue around Torrin's thumb.

The burn was exquisite as Erik sank into her. His cock was thick and hot and her body gave for it in a way she'd never experienced.

Between him and Liam's dick, she felt impossibly full, and it only increased with each rock of his hips forward, each inch he took.

She panted hard, Torrin's thumb forgotten, the distraction not nearly enough to keep her from focusing on that full sensation, on how she stretched to accommodate Erik's girth.

"You can do it," Liam coaxed, his words too sweet.

Erik didn't speak, but the grasping of his hands and the rub of his thumbs against her skin were caresses of their own.

She was moaning, sweat on her brow by the time Erik's body met hers, when she'd taken all of him, when she felt trapped and fully fucked.

Torrin rubbed his thumb against her tongue, an odd but surprisingly welcome touch. "Such a good girl. Now, you'll let us fuck you, taking you exactly as we want to. We will own every inch of your body, every hole, and you'll love it, won't you?" He pulled his thumb free of her.

She wasn't sure if he expected an answer, but she gave one anyway, unable to help it. "Yes."

"You'll do that because you know we wouldn't hurt you, because you trust us." He said it like a fact even as he waited for her to respond, for her to agree.

But she couldn't. The words wouldn't come.

He sighed softly before replacing his finger with his cock again, and this time, he didn't hold back. He didn't fuck into her mouth, but rather controlled the depth and speed by using her hair like a leash.

They all did that. Liam teased her sensitive nipples while Erik grasped her hips and used that to control her movements. He would pull her up, causing her to fuck herself on Liam's cock while he thrust into her ass. He set an opposite rhythm, so she was never fully empty — when he retreated, Liam advanced. It kept her on that edge, made her desperate for more.

Yet, as much as she enjoyed it, she fought against her release.

She didn't want to come. She didn't want to fall down that hole with them, to lose the tension. When it was over, she'd feel as hopeless as before, except she'd be knotted and faced with the alphas who had caused it.

So even as they toyed with her body, even as they fucked her so expertly, she gave in to everything except her own orgasm.

Torrin growled softly, as if he knew she was denying them. Even still, when she took him as deep as possible, when a tremble in his thighs proved how close he was, he came. His seed was thick and warm, and she swallowed as quickly as she could, licking him clean afterward for any speck she might have missed.

Still, she resisted the boiling passion inside her, held tight to it so it wouldn't snap.

Erik's silence broke on a snarl, which oddly enough pleased her. His silence frightened her, that feelingless thing he could become, but the snarl? The animalistic side? That she liked. That she understood. He plunged in so his body was flush to hers when he came deep in her ass. Each twitch of his cock from his release again tempted the orgasm she'd held at bay. Her entire body felt electric, as though sparks of energy coursed through it, lighting up each spot inside her.

She curled her fingers into Liam's chest to hold off, to fight against the crashing waves of pleasure.

When Erik pulled out, she felt empty, and an embarrassing moan left her.

Liam moved fast, flipping them once Erik had shifted away. Liam grasped her thigh, hiking it up like a man possessed, like a man who had been pushed too far.

He fucked her with hard, deep thrusts. "I fucking love you," he snarled into her ear. "We all do. You know it even if you don't want to, even if you fight it. We'll prove it to you."

Ashley buried her face in his throat, not wanting to hear it. What was worse was that it was true.

She knew they loved her. She loved them. None of that changed anything, though.

His knot grew, and he jerked her closer as he locked in place.

That was what she couldn't fight, though. No matter how she tried, her body ran on instincts too deep, and she shattered.

Somehow, that hurt the most. It was the fact she'd tried to ignore, to hide from.

Even knowing the truth, even finding out they'd lied to her and who they really were didn't matter.

She loved them and there was no way to fight that.

Chapter Nineteen

Torrin hadn't wanted to shower that morning. He'd liked having Ashley's scent clinging to him, and part of him feared that it never would again.

She'd fallen asleep there, tied to Liam. Her exhaustion had showed in that even when he'd been able to withdraw, she'd still not woken. Erik and Liam had lain in the bed with her, though he doubted either had slept. Instead, they'd stared at her, as though they could somehow understand where it had gone bad or how it could be resolved.

Could it be fixed?

Torrin, for his part, had left.

He'd sat in the living room, alone with his thoughts, with his ability to go over every place he'd gotten things so terribly wrong, and there was no shortage of them.

Ashley wasn't incorrect.

Lying to himself was pointless. Power had always been a driving force behind what he'd done.

But…it had also been for her. Could he ever become what she wanted?

He tried to picture a different life, one where he wasn't so mired in shadows. Could he live without the things that power had afforded him?

He thought back to the times he'd been counted out because of his injury, the times when people had assumed him to be weak. Could he go back to losing the fear and respect he'd cultivated over the years?

He dragged his hands over his face. If he could, it would make her safer. He tried to imagine a life where he didn't have to worry about enemies. Where he never had to fear law enforcement or retribution. They had enough money to go legit, to turn their backs on the darker sides of their business.

In fact, they could easily sell the businesses they had and start something new, something without the baggage, something far away where none of this would follow them.

But then he wouldn't be the alpha others feared. He'd be the cripple, the one to be pitied.

It seemed too great a sacrifice.

Which leaves us where?

Torrin sighed, caught in a trap of his own making, and certain there was no way out where he could keep the things he valued most.

And if I have to choose?

He feared making the wrong choice.

* * * *

Ashley enjoyed the silence. The safehouse was a small, two-bedroom place on the outskirts of town. In any other situation, she might really like the place.

However, it wasn't ideal for living in with three alphas she currently couldn't stand.

Avoiding them had proven impossible. She rarely left her room, choosing to sequester herself there instead of facing them. Not that it worked.

They took turns bringing her meals, water, anything she needed, without her asking. Each time was like another wound to her heart, though, a reminder of what she'd thought they had.

They still had a security detail but had lessened it. The fewer people who knew where they were, the better.

Kara had come over, though she hadn't tried to talk to Ashley. Instead, she'd sat in the living room with the alphas, no doubt planning.

Which was sadly fitting. Of course they were coming up with a way to deal with the issue, all the while leaving Ashley out. No one cared what she wanted, what she thought.

One of the security guards walked into her room, a not uncommon occurrence. They liked to check all the doors, visually confirm she was there and safe. It was better than when the alphas did it themselves.

"I'm fine," Ashley said, waving him off. She couldn't even hear the alphas, and a peek through the open door showed they weren't in the living room.

Probably moved to the bedroom so I wouldn't risk overhearing.

The guard shut the door quietly, and that was the first time Ashley got that same feeling she'd had outside the limo. He set his hand on his pistol, but it wasn't to draw it. Instead, it seemed to be a clear warning to remain silent.

Ashley nodded as she gulped.

The guard pulled a phone from his pocket, then hit a button on the front and handed it off to Ashley.

She knew before lifting it who would be on the other end.

"Gregory," she said.

"It's good to hear your voice. We don't have a lot of time. You're going to follow the man who gave you this phone, get into a car with him and come to me. Before you ask why, you're going to do this to save your precious alphas and that thief. Clearly, I know exactly where you are. I would rather you come willingly, or else I'll have to send men in to get you. There is no way that will happen without death, and while I wouldn't mind killing them, I'd prefer not to risk you."

Ashley gripped the phone tightly in her hand, feeling trapped and outmaneuvered again. How was it that Gregory was *always* a step ahead?

She tried to think about her options, but there weren't any. Gregory was not a liar, and if he said he had men capable of attacking them, it was the truth. Her alphas were tough, but they weren't bulletproof.

"And you promise that you won't hurt them if I come?"

"If you come back to me now, I will not attack the safehouse. You have my word."

Ashley knew her only choice. It didn't matter how angry she was with Torrin, with Liam or Erik. It didn't matter that they'd lied, that they'd hurt her.

She wouldn't let them get killed if she could stop it, so she handed the phone back and stood, ready to go back to hell just to save the men she still loved.

* * * *

The empty room threatened to set off Torrin's temper. Ashley was gone, as was one of the men he'd hired for security. Had it only been her, he might have thought she'd run.

Though, the moment they'd checked the cameras, the truth had become clear. The one in her bedroom had recorded her side of the conversation, had shown the phone call where she'd agreed to go.

The soft-hearted fool. She should have refused, should have called out. They would have easily dealt with one man, and if there were more?

They'd have dealt with them, too.

"I hate when people are noble," Kara complained, though her sullen words hid worry and fear. It wasn't something many would pick up in her voice, but he could. "Now I have to help."

Torrin stared at the computer screen where they watched Ashley disappear into the darkness of the yard, where she'd slid from the window after the security guard had turned that sensor off. *She went for us. She gave up everything to save us.*

That kept repeating in his head like a mantra, like a taunt. She'd wanted freedom. Nothing more, just the chance to live her life, and yet she'd turned around and given it all up for Torrin and his cousins. She hadn't even hesitated.

"What's the plan?" Kara asked.

"We get her back," Liam said.

"We kill anyone who tries to stop us," Erik added.

"I like the simplicity. Anything more specific, though?"

There was only one choice, one way to do things so Torrin could have what he wanted most.

Torrin turned his gaze to Kara. "Call your brother. We're going to need his help."

* * * *

Had Gregory always looked so...frail?

She'd found him intimidating before. She'd stayed up at nights in fear of him. His flat, empty eyes had always inspired terror in her, yet she found none of that anymore.

Instead, he seemed weak. He walked through the penthouse she'd been taken to with the arrogant gait of a man who thought he had power, but she could see the mask of it now.

Ashley wondered why she had feared him so.

Sure, he could destroy her, but anything could. People were killed walking down streets. Gregory reminded her of a rat, the sort that would jump forward, hoping prey much larger would run away, startled.

She'd been so afraid as she'd waited for him to arrive at the penthouse she'd been brought to, but when he'd appeared, when she'd finally seen him, none of it remained.

He no longer looked like the monster she'd been sure he was before.

"My dear," Gregory said as he finally looked her way. "It's so good to finally have you home."

"This isn't home," she said, her voice stronger than she'd expected it to be. She'd always whimpered when speaking to him, always dropped her gaze. This time she stared him straight in the eye.

He slowed his pace, as if her reaction surprised him. "Well, well, you've come into your own, haven't you?

Was it the time away, or I wonder if it was those alphas?" He spat out the word *alphas*, as though it were distasteful. "No worry, though. Things take time. Just as you had to adjust to them, to life on the run, you will adjust to life here, with me."

Like hell.

Ashley rose from the couch. "I don't love you."

"Not yet, perhaps, but you will."

She shook her head. "I won't, not ever. I could *never* love you."

"But you love those alphas?" He tilted his head, reminding her of a dog trying to figure something out. "I can smell them all over you. Don't worry, as I said, I'm not angry, not with you. I don't blame you."

Of course he didn't blame her, because he didn't respect her. He saw her as a thing to be owned, as a toy with no agency of her own. If others used the toy, he blamed the ones who did it, not the object.

He set a hand on her hip, pulling her against him. It was the first time they'd touched in years, since the time he'd tried to kiss her. His other hand grasped her chin and tilted her face toward his. The touch felt like a cheap, filthy replica of what her alphas had done. "You have such fire inside you. A few times I had updates while you were on the run, and it had seemed as though you'd lost that. It's nice to see it back."

He leaned in and brushed his lips to hers, the touch sickening and brief and enough to push Ashley over the edge of good sense. She swung her hand, catching him across the face with a slap. The hit was weak, given her angle, but it was still a victory, no matter how small.

She'd put her foot down. She'd said no to a man who had taken so much from her. Instead of running, instead of cowering, she'd stood up to him.

Gregory pressed his lips together in a thin line, pink blossoming on his pale skin from the strike. He pinched her chin, his fingers rough. "Are you trying to push me, dear? Hoping I will give you a reason to hate me? I won't hurt you, no matter how much you fight me, how much you struggle or lash out. Breaking people is like breaking animals, and it takes time. Lucky for us both, we have all the time in the world."

She tried to strike him again, but he caught her wrist. He pressed his lips to her hand, as if forgiving her, as if her fight meant nothing, before he stepped backward. "I'll give you some time to acquaint yourself with your new life, my dear."

Ashley stood in the room, trying to hold on to the impotent anger swarming her, because if she didn't, if she let it, it would transform into despair as his words mocked her.

All the time in the world.

Chapter Twenty

Liam stared at the penthouse Gregory was in, the one he'd taken Ashley to. Finding it hadn't been difficult once they'd called in help. Funny that they'd had so many contacts of their own, so many they'd gotten beneath their thumbs with blackmail or the threat of violence, but none of them had been able to help. Instead, it had been Kara and her contacts.

Her brother, the other alphas he shared his mate with, their friends. An entire network of people existed together not out of fear or blackmail or requirement, but something more. As thankful as Liam was, it still unnerved him.

Seated beside him on the rooftop across from the penthouse was Kieran, an alpha mated to the same omega as Kara's brother, Kane. He had a sniper rifle already set up but had said little. He was the strong and silent type.

"Why are you here? What's in this for you?" Liam asked when the silence and tension got to him.

Kieran was older, his hair silvered at the temples. He was well known for his technology company that set up network systems, but his ease with the rifle he'd brought said he knew his way around a fight.

The other alpha didn't turn to face Liam, his focus through the scope of the weapon. "My mate wouldn't be happy if anything happened to Kane. I would be less bothered by it, but when she's unhappy, we're all unhappy."

Liam huffed softly. "Nice try, but I can spot a lie too well for that."

Kieran said nothing for a long moment. He seemed the type to rarely speak without thinking. "It wasn't a lie, but it wasn't the entire truth. My mate was targeted by this same group. I think you'll find there aren't many omegas or alphas in this area who haven't had a run in with these slavers. I would have come no matter what when I heard who the target was."

"Dealing with him is second priority," Liam warned, his voice dropping low, full of threat. "My mate's safety is most important."

Kieran nodded, but Liam wasn't sure how honest that was. Dealing with people who had different motivations was always a tricky business. It was why he preferred to work with only his brother and his cousin. Conflicts of interest had buried more people than he cared to count.

Still, for Ashley, for her safety, he'd bite his tongue and accept the help, no matter how much he disliked it.

She mattered more than anything else, and he wasn't ready to lose her just yet.

Erik kept Kane in sight, because despite him being Kara's brother, he didn't trust the other alpha.

Erik had kept an eye on the man, watched as his recklessness mirrored Kara's. The two were so much alike, and so different from him.

Which was shown well when Kane wouldn't stop talking. His tattoos made him look like he'd be the brooding, quiet type, but his mouth refused to quit running.

In a strange way, it felt like being beside Kara again.

"So then this fucker jumped out of the shadows, you know, around the corner. Fucking ugly asshole, the sort that requires a bag and duct tape for anyone to even think about—"

"Would you shut up?"

Kane didn't seem to take offense, and even smirked, a look identical to all the times Kara had done it. Though Kara hadn't done it while Erik was terrified for his mate, so maybe that was why Kane could get beneath his skin and she couldn't.

"Wasn't sure you were even listening, since you didn't say shit about my amazing story with the flying squirrels."

Erik gave him a withering look, but the man didn't look the least bit chastised. "Why don't you keep your mind on the job instead of talking nonstop?"

"Is that how you do it? All businesslike? Not my way, asshole, not my way." He adjusted himself on the balcony, then stared out at the other building, as if he might see where Kieran and Liam had set up. "Besides, you look tense enough to not need the fuckers who have your mate to take you out. A heart attack'll do it first."

Erik pressed his lips together, pulling in a slow breath through his nose to hold together his rapidly disintegrating temper. "You don't understand. *Your* mate isn't in danger."

"Not right now, no, but someone who was under the bastard in there had a knife to my mate's throat not so many months ago. I know how it feels, and even if I don't like you at all — and guess what, asshole, I don't — I ain't about to want you to feel what that's like. So you're gonna relax before you jump the gun and make a mistake, and you can listen to my awesome stories, and as soon as we get word, we'll hop our pretty asses across that balcony divider and we'll fuck some shit up and get your mate back. What do you say?"

Erik forced himself to really look at Kane for a moment, to see beneath his bad-boy exterior, beneath the multitude of tattoos and general shitty attitude, to see a man more capable than he'd have given him credit for.

Erik shook his arms out, realizing his hand had been curled around a blade. Maybe Kane wasn't so wrong.

"Sounds good," Erik admitted, and focused on the most important parts.

Fuck some shit up and get my mate back.

The sun had gone down, and Ashley hadn't seen Gregory again. She'd explored the penthouse, but only the bathroom and master bedroom were unlocked. No guard followed her, though one stood inside the front door and she was sure more were outside. The slider that went to the balcony was unlocked, but when she'd approached it, the guard had warned her off.

Inside the kitchen, she'd gotten a glass of water, amazed when no one followed her. Then again, Gregory didn't see her as a threat, and clearly neither did her guards.

The knives sat in a butcher-block holder on the counter, but taking one would be obvious. Instead, she snuck a steak knife from a drawer. *Easier to hide, harder to miss.* She tucked it into the waist of her pants, ignoring the way the serrated edge caught and aggravated her skin.

Just having the weapon made her feel more in control, more able to handle whatever was thrown at her.

Would the alphas come?

She sighed as he admitted, yeah, they probably would. Or they'd send someone. They needed to take care of Gregory for their *business* anyway.

But just because she knew they'd show eventually didn't mean she had to wait for it. She'd spent her life running, hiding, avoiding conflict. *Enough of that.*

The door opened and Gregory entered. He wore the same suit as before, his face as unreadable as ever. *What made him the way he is?*

She thought about Torrin, about how he shared that unflappable exterior. The difference?

Torrin had something real beneath it. Gregory, try as he might, didn't seem to have anything real inside him. Nothing beyond the need for power, the desire to own.

Ashley's words came back to her, and she flinched at how she'd hurled them at Torrin. If she got out of this, she'd have to apologize. She'd been harsh.

No, she couldn't trust him, and yes, what she'd said was true, but that didn't make it right to say. For all the things Ashley was, she'd never been cruel.

"My darling," Gregory said as he slid off his coat. He moved with the casual motions of a man coming home after a long day at work to his loving mate.

"I'm not your darling," she said.

"You are. And tonight, I think we find ourselves in a good fortune."

Ashley bit her tongue as she considered her circumstances. *Not fortunate for me.*

Gregory continued coming into the room, undoing the buttons at his wrist so he could roll up the sleeves of his white dress shirt. He lacked the appeal Liam had when he did the same thing. "I had time to think about your defiance. While I know I'll win, I realized that I am fighting against something I have never fought against before. Before, you ran from me, but you had nothing to run towards. Now, however, you seem to have created some little fantasy for yourself, something to hold on to and think you could return to."

The words made Ashley swallow. Nothing good could come of such a line of thought. "What do you mean?"

"Animals who are taken from the wild never make such good pets as those who were raised in captivity. Do you know why? Because the ones who were wild remember it, strive to return to it, despite how much better their lives have become. You are no different. The only way to rectify this is to ensure you have nowhere to run to."

Her blood chilled, as if it had thickened and sludged through her veins and threatened to turn to ice. She couldn't even ask what he meant — didn't need to ask.

"I had been making plans to deal with those alphas. I don't care for them sullying my things, and they dared to try to go behind my back, so I thought, if I dealt with them, if you saw you have nowhere to go, then you would accept your fate."

"You can't," Ashley whispered, Gregory inspiring the old fear she'd had. No, not even that, it was beyond that fear. It was new, a living, breathing terror inside her at the thought that he'd go after them. All her claims about not caring, about believing Gregory to no longer be a threat, dissolved. She'd no longer feared what he could do to her, but she'd failed to think about what he could still do to others.

She should have seen it before, but she'd been so sure that once he had her, he wouldn't care about them anymore.

Foolish girl.

Gregory looked at her, his lips curling slightly as though he liked her reaction. "Luckily for me, that won't be necessary."

Her moment of relief was short-lived when the door opened and Torrin walked in, his limp more pronounced than usual, so he leaned heavily on the cane.

Ashley came forward, but a sharp look from Gregory made her stop.

Torrin was unarmed but appeared unhurt.

Gregory rolled up his other sleeve as he continued to talk, as one of the guards who came in with Torrin grabbed a chair from the table and pulled it to the center of the room. "Torrin showed up today, no weapons, no backup. What luck, right?"

Ashley tore her gaze from Gregory to look at Torrin, trying to tell him with a look alone that it had been a stupid choice.

He had to have a plan. Torrin always had a plan. Where she'd been angry over that before, where it had frustrated her, she could only pray that he'd been the same sneaky, deceptive alpha she had come to know him as.

Where are Erik and Liam?

The guard shoved at Torrin's shoulder, making him sit in the chair hard, his leg giving out. He nearly toppled from it, his cane being knocked from his hand and falling to the floor.

Even still, he sat tall, proud.

Gregory nodded at another seat, and the guard pulled it over so he could sit in front of Torrin. He wasn't close enough for Torrin to be able to reach him, but near enough to read his features easily. "Now, I find myself wondering why you would risk this? You, who have been so careful to remain out of my reach, who could have run if you so wanted — why would you come to me knowing the risk? Without so much as your bodyguards?"

Torrin kept his gaze on Gregory, not Ashley, and she missed his dark eyes. She missed the way they softened just for her, the crinkle near the corner when he did that *almost* smile he would give to her alone.

"I want to make a deal."

"You have nothing I want anymore."

"I do. You know people wanted me to kill you, but you don't know who exactly was involved, how deep it goes."

"What do I care, though? Once I make an example of you, no one will dare make such a mistake again."

"You know better than that. Plots to kill people like you don't happen on a whim. If it happened once, it will happen again, unless you can root out all the people involved."

Gregory sat back. "And what is it you want in return? If it's Ashley, I can assure you, that isn't on the table."

Torrin shook his head. "I consider losing her the price of doing business. You'll call off whatever your plans against myself and my cousins, and you'll let me move into the business once we deal with those who went after you. You'll have open positions at that point."

Ashley went lightheaded. She set a hand on the couch and lowered herself onto it, her knees weak and her stomach sick.

Torrin was turning on her. He'd realized he couldn't defeat Gregory and was giving in. He'd rather have the power Gregory offered than her.

He'd run the numbers in his head and realized what everyone seemed to realize — Ashley wasn't worth the cost.

Gregory sat back and set one ankle on the opposite knee. "My problem is, I don't trust you." He nodded toward Torrin.

The guard who had brought over the chair walked up, and the punch he delivered to Torrin made a sickening crunch. Blood poured from Torrin's nose, smearing over his face and making him lose that regal quality he normally had.

Not that he showed any other reaction. He wiped at the blood, despite it still leaking, but made no complaint. "Trust in my record. You've had enough time to see what I've done, what I'm willing to do to get what I want."

"I thought that meant Ashley."

Torrin's jaw popped slightly, the first sign of a reaction. "So did I. Things change, however, and I had to decide what I wanted more, what mattered more to me. Her or power. I made the obvious choice."

Gregory nodded again, and this time the guard caught the chair with his foot and kicked, pulling it from beneath Torrin.

It was almost worse than the punch, to watch Torrin, a man so proud, fall into a heap on the ground. He might have caught himself if not for his hip.

"That sounds good, but what can you really offer me? Sure, I might get a few names, but in the long run?"

"I heard you're having trouble with procuring omegas in the area, that you're planning on pulling out. I own this area. Every street, every bar, every low-life here, I know and have my claws in. I can make sure this area becomes profitable again, keep law enforcement out of our way."

Gregory tapped his finger against his jaw as if thinking. He nodded once more, and the guard placed a foot on Torrin's bad hip. "We've had problems moving livestock here, I'll admit. It used to be a good area, close enough to good paying clients but far enough to keep us quiet. Your offer is tempting. We do away with those who went after me and revamp this area. Hell, I could even offer you up a lovely omega slave to make up for taking Ashley."

Torrin's face was pinched in pain as the guard ground the foot down on his hip. He pushed at the leg, but in his position, there was nothing he could do to stop it.

Ashley held her breath, wanting nothing more than to stop this but having no idea how to do so.

Gregory rose from the seat. "I've wondered, how did you hurt your hip? I've seen you walk around, that limp, that cane, acting as if you're above everyone else. You pretend like it doesn't make you less, but that's why you're as vicious as you are, isn't it?"

The guard let up, and when Torrin spoke, his voice lacked that confidence it normally had. Pain saturated it. "I took a baseball bat to it during a fire because someone stood in my way. It was him or me, and I chose me."

Gregory knelt, getting close to Torrin's face. "You have backbone. Probably comes from being damaged. The thing is, you can't offer me anything that's greater than what your death can give me. With you gone, Ashley won't fight so hard, especially if I promise to leave your cousins alone. I find a good amount of leverage goes a long way."

Ashley threw herself forward at that, at the certainty in Gregory's voice. "You can't," she cried out.

Gregory stood and caught her before she reached Torrin. "I explained this to you," he said, his voice calm, even deceptively sweet, as if explaining something he didn't like but which had to be done. "With him gone, you'll be happier. It might hurt now, but it will help in the long run."

"I'll do anything," she said, looking directly at Gregory. "I'll stay with you. I won't ever run again. I won't fight you. I'll do whatever you say. Just let him go."

Gregory caught her chin so she looked him in the eye. "You've fought long and hard for your freedom. You'd give it up so easily? For males who betrayed you? For this one who's ready to sell you to me for a bit of power?"

Ashley knew the answer without having to think about it. *Yes.* Without a doubt, she'd give up everything for Torrin, for Liam and Erik. She'd sacrifice the freedom she'd fought so hard for because she loved them.

If their safety meant her freedom, she'd make the trade without question. What they might have done, their betrayal—none of that changed how she felt.

She couldn't let them suffer for her, and she couldn't imagine enduring years with Gregory unless she *knew* they were out there somewhere.

"Yes. Whatever you want," she said.

Torrin laughed, a bitter sound that Ashley had never heard before. It was dark, as if those manners he used, that shell he wore to hide who he really was, had been ripped away. "You're right about leverage." He pulled at the buttons of his shirt until wires came into view.

Gregory cursed softly, surprise across his features. Ashley had *never* seen Gregory surprised. "If you think to blackmail me, you're a fool. I own everyone who could hurt me with that."

"Not everyone," Torrin said. "And when this becomes public, do you really think the people you do own will stick around? If you start sinking, once your usefulness dwindles, do you really think anyone will stick around? You will rot in prison if you're lucky. There's FBI agents listening in, and you've said more than enough to bury yourself."

"You're as guilty as I am. Even if they let you off for helping them, you'll have to give everything up. You won't be able to go back to your old life, not with the police staring over your shoulder. Plus, whenever it does get out, do you really think your old friends will be fine with you snitching? That they won't come after you?"

Torrin bared his teeth, red covering the whites. "Maybe. Maybe not. I do know for sure that either way, you'll be out of the picture."

Gregory darted his gaze around the room, looking like an animal caught in a corner, unable to escape. "What keeps me from just killing you?"

"Nothing. Except this."

As soon as he spoke, glass shattered.

Ashley let out a scream as the deafening sound in the room shocked her. Bodies moved, falling, screams, gunfire.

The guards in the room fell, the action so fast they didn't have time to draw their weapons. The one who had struck Torrin went down first, and she tore her gaze from the first splash of red. The main door flew open, but a shot in that direction kept the additional guards at bay.

Gregory hauled Ashley against him, using her in front of him, ducking behind her. He had a gun that went from pointing at Ashley to the chaos, back and forth in a shaking hand.

From the shattered slider, two more came in. One was a man she didn't recognize, with tattoos over his arms and up his throat. Beside him was Erik, the sling gone, a blade in his hand. When two guards rushed in from the hallway, the new man and Erik met them with ease before they could reach Torrin.

The speed at which Erik moved was astounding, but seeing it when pitted against other men, against those who would happily kill Erik, Torrin and her, she didn't find the fear she had before.

Erik was lethal, but for the first time, she understood *why*. He plunged the blade into one of the guards as the other man, the one with the tattoos, used the pistol in his hand to end another. When a third rushed the room, a bullet took him out, but she hadn't seen anyone shoot it.

Torrin rose once Erik came closer and offered a hand to help him to his feet. "You're outnumbered and out of options. My cousin is across the way with a sniper who has you in his crosshairs. In a van on the street are the two FBI agents handling the slavery cases, and Kara, who have recorded everything you've said. You have two choices right now. You can help the FBI take down the slavery ring."

"Or?"

"Or we can kill you for real and take down the ring when we're brought into the fold as payment for your death."

Gregory gripped Ashley tighter, the action making it harder to breathe. "You won't kill me," he said, shaking his head. "You need me. The FBI only agreed to overlook your past if you gave them to me alive, right? You kill me, that's all done for." He pulled her backward, with the others in the room giving them space, not wanting to provoke him. While his gun trembled, indicating he obviously wasn't comfortable with it, even a novice could kill someone.

Ashley looked at the alphas, *her* alphas. Torrin stood, blood down his face, the evidence of what he'd suffered to get what they needed stained into his shirt. His willingness to endure not only pain but humiliation for her said more than he ever could. Erik was beside him, that beast she'd feared before shining brightly through his eyes, yet she didn't fear it anymore. How could she, when she'd seen what it was up against? She'd watched as that side of him had protected her and those she cared about. Even though she couldn't see him, she knew Liam was across the roofline, knew he'd watched over her like the others.

Gregory wasn't just threatening her. She'd accepted his treatment before because it was only her freedom he threatened, and she'd never had much to lose.

Now, though, she had everything to lose. He was threatening to take *them* away from her.

As they passed through the front door, Ashley made her move. She braced her foot on the other side of the doorway and kicked, knocking them both against the frame. Gregory's grip loosened and she took advantage. She grasped the steak knife from her waist and brought it up, digging it into the side of his throat.

She didn't plunge it in, but a stream of blood escaped, trailing down his neck and soaking into the collar of his shirt.

"They might not kill you," she said, "but I will."

"You don't have it in you." Even as he said it, his tone lacked his normal certainty.

Ashley dug the point in deeper. "Look into my eyes, Gregory. You've chased me for years, destroyed everything I had, took everything that mattered to me away. You've given me every reason to kill you, so you get this one chance. Put down the gun or I will stick this knife so far into your neck that no doctor will be able to save you. And before you think I'm bluffing, you know damned well I'm a terrible liar."

They locked gazes for a heartbeat, during which Ashley didn't back down, didn't give him an inch. It *wasn't* a bluff. No matter how it might have terrified her, she was so far past caring, and she'd do exactly as she said if he pressed her.

She understood Erik better at that moment, when the thought of killing Gregory not only didn't bother her, but she relished it. The abstract idea of killing someone seemed so far removed, but when she held a knife, when she looked into the face of someone who was willing to take everything from her, the abstract didn't matter.

Consequences be damned. He'd ruined her life and hurt and threatened her mates. She *wanted* to do what she'd said she would.

Gregory must have read that, because the gun clattered to the floor.

Ashley stumbled backward, the adrenaline from the moment collapsing inside her until she trembled.

She was free.

What now?

Chapter Twenty-One

Erik kept his distance back at the apartment, but he couldn't bring himself to leave the room Ashley was in. This buzzing in his head demanded he stay near her, that he keep her in his sight. He'd bet it was the same instincts that had rebelled at the idea of her being harmed.

A doctor had met them at the apartment to look over Ashley and to patch up Torrin. He had set Torrin's nose and checked his hip, though it didn't appear there was much lasting damage. With him gone, though, leaving Ashley and the alphas alone, no one spoke.

What was there to say?

Ashley looked shaken. She'd nearly collapsed after threatening Gregory, though even Erik would have thought twice about defying her at that moment.

She'd been a beacon of righteous fury, the perfect vision of a female pushed too far. Erik wasn't sure he'd ever seen her so beautiful.

After that, though, she'd said little. She hadn't argued about going back to their place. *Our place? Maybe. Maybe she'll still want to leave.*

With Gregory in custody with the FBI agents Kane knew, the ones who had worked with his mate, the ones they were sure weren't in business with Gregory, they all had a moment to catch their breath.

Not that they'd have long. Gregory had agreed to help the FBI with the slavery ring. They couldn't give him much leeway, because he wasn't trustworthy, but he had good reason to keep the FBI happy.

If he played nicely, then he could live his days out in witness protection in some tiny little corner of nowhere, with no friends, no family, no money and no power. It felt like a fitting end, at least if Erik wasn't allowed to actually kill him.

However, that meant the alphas had to leave. Since they'd been given the task to kill him, there wasn't any choice but for them to disappear. A car explosion was set up for a week from then, something Gregory could take credit for.

It meant leaving and starting over, but that seemed as good a plan as any. When everything came to light, when the agents took down that slavery ring, no doubt they'd get outed as sources. Their lives in that city were over. It was better to pack up and try to create something somewhere else.

"Here." Liam passed a cup of tea to Erik and took another to Ashley.

She accepted it, her legs folded in front of her as she sat on the couch, her gaze down. "Are you sure it's over?"

Erik came closer, but still gave her room, unsure she'd want him anywhere near her.

She'd now seen him kill more than one person, and he doubted she'd be comfortable with him around her. "Yes. Gregory isn't a threat, and he's already called off the contract on you. You're safe. You have your life back."

She stared down at the cup though she hadn't drunk any of it yet. "And you guys? How does working with the police affect you?"

Liam answered that one. "They'll overlook our past. After next week, we'll start over somewhere else. New names, new lives. Even if we could stay, after turning in Gregory, there's no way we wouldn't have people after us. It's better to go along with the whole fake-death thing."

"So I ruined you?"

Erik sat on the coffee table, close enough he could just brush her with his fingers if he reached all the way out. "A fresh start isn't always a bad thing."

Ashley turned to look at Torrin, worry in those expressive blue eyes of hers when she spotted the bandage over his nose, the skin around his eyes already darkening. "You gave up everything you wanted. You could have been killed."

Torrin answered the question she didn't ask. *Why?* "You were worth it."

"What if I can't stay here? What if I want to go home?"

"Then you were still worth it."

Torrin's words mirrored what they'd all already talked about, agreed to. The cost was more than worth Ashley's safety, her freedom, and as much as it killed them all...

That freedom had to include freedom from them.

If they forced her to stay, they were no better than Gregory.

She'd had no choice for so long, that she deserved that, and they'd make sure she had it.

Even if it killed them, they'd let her go.

"I want to go home," she whispered.

Erik nodded, not surprised.

This is going to hurt.

* * * *

Liam walked beside Ashley, carrying her small suitcase. The rest of her things were being shipped to her fathers' house, where she was headed.

Her talk with them had been private, yet he'd overhead parts. Her relief, their tears. So many years of her on the run, and finally she'd be able to settle.

He wished he was happier about it. He wanted her content, but he'd hoped that contentment would happen with him, with her in his bed, where she belonged.

Things didn't work out for people like him, though, and he'd let her go. It was the least he could do, this one, unselfish thing.

"You'll go through security here, and your gate is to the left. F18. There's a map just past that turn." He rambled on about directions, about plane security, about anything other than her leaving.

That was a topic he couldn't even think about, let alone discuss.

"I've been on a plane before," she said, not looking him in the eye.

"I know. I just don't know what else to say," he admitted softly.

Erik held out the ticket they'd bought for her. "You're in first class. If you need anything at all, the flight attendants already know you're..." He paused as if unsure how to finish that statement. After an awkward hesitation, he tried again. "They know you know us. If you have any problems, they'll handle it. Your fathers will be at the airport waiting for you when you land."

She took the ticket and held it tightly.

Torrin came forward, the click of his cane against the floor louder than usual. He'd done that more, relied more heavily on the aid, as if he no longer worried about looking weak as he once had. "Your fathers have agreed to call us when your plane lands. If you need anything, ever —"

"Why haven't you asked me to stay?" She blurted the question out, looking up and into each of their eyes. "You could have. You could have told me not to leave."

Torrin didn't answer, and even Liam looked away.

Erik sighed before speaking up. "Because it has to be your choice. It's your life, and for the first time, you get to decide how you want it to be. You've got to do what you want."

"What do you want?"

Easy answer. "You." Erik held his hand up before she spoke. "But we want you only when it's your choice."

"Gregory stole a lot from you, dove. You've spent years just trying to survive. Even moving in with us, none of that was your choice. It was what you had to do. You told me once I was just like him, and you were right. I put what I wanted above what you needed. That can't happen again. You wanted to go home, so you'll go home." Torrin spoke softly, keeping his distance as they each had. If they got too close, they might grab her and not let go.

She crushed the ticket in her hand, and Liam could see the war in her eyes. She wanted to stay, but there were too many questions, too many fears.

Maybe they'd ruined it. Maybe, by lying to her, they'd created a wound that would never really heal.

Liam set her bag down beside her, then risked saying what he had to. "You need to know you can go, but that doesn't mean it has to be forever. You can come back, someday, when you want to, you know." *Idiot.* The words were clumsy.

They were at a fucking airport. It was supposed to be some sort of romantic movement, yet he tripped over awkward words. Why couldn't he be smooth right then? He'd charmed countless women over the years, but the one time it mattered, he couldn't string together a coherent sentence.

Ashley nodded, wrapping her fingers around her bag and taking a step backward. "Thanks."

Liam rubbed his hand on the back of his neck. "We're going to go."

"You don't want to watch until I get through security?"

Yes. He wanted to watch her forever, to never let her out of his sight.

Torrin answered, instead. "No need. There's no danger to you now, and I don't think it's a good idea."

When her eyebrows drew near one another, Liam explained. "Alphas don't do well watching their mate walk away. It's best if we don't see it. Take care of yourself, Ashley."

With that, they turned, leaving her standing there, ticket in hand.

Liam left not only her, but his heart as he walked out of the airport.

* * * *

Torrin sat in the limo and cursed himself for not taking the pain pills. While he normally hated them, the idea of not being so lucid had merit.

Did we really let her go?

He could tell himself over and over that it was what had to happen, but that didn't change that he hated it, that every part of him wanted to go get her.

He wanted to do whatever it took to get her to stay. He could offer her anything—pretty words, money, promises. He'd do anything to if only she stayed.

But he knew he couldn't. She'd stay because he'd made her, then, and that wasn't fair. Instead, he had to give up the choice, give up that power to her, and it had proven even harder than enduring the pain Gregory's goon had inflicted on him.

So he sat in the limo and let the ache of his hip distract him from the agony in his chest. Even the throbbing of his broken nose was nothing in comparison.

"Maybe we could go visit her," Liam said.

"Right," Erik answered, but his tone said the same thing.

She won't ask us to.

If she left, if she went back home, she was gone. She'd resume her old life and they would be just a bump in the road for her. Nothing more than the alphas who had lied to her.

Time would pass and her memories of them would fade until she found someone new and they became nothing but a story she remembered from time to time.

Meanwhile, Torrin would nurse yet another broken heart. Liam and Erik would go back to sharing random females to pass the lonely years, and none of them would ever really recover.

That was fair, though, wasn't it? They'd been the ones to ruin it, the ones who hadn't deserved her. It seemed fitting that they suffer for it.

She'd suffered enough.

"Fuck you," Liam muttered. At Torrin's look, Liam went on. "I was pretty happy not caring about anyone, and look what you had to go and do."

The words were sullen, and it was just enough for Torrin to let out a small laugh at the sorrow of it.

The ride home was slow, especially since it took an hour before they'd even been willing to leave the airport parking lot. What was the point? To go back to an empty, depressing apartment?

In another few days, they'd be leaving. The thought of leaving the apartment ached, the idea that when he walked into his home it wouldn't have Ashley's scent. He wouldn't see the couch and think of how she'd looked curled up on it, or see the coffee mugs and think about the scent of her favorite tea.

He hadn't done the work needed to find a new place to live because it just seemed like too much effort.

They took the elevator up, each step harder than the last. When they entered the apartment, Ashley's scent was everywhere, just as he'd known it would be, teasing him, taunting him.

Except, just as he was ready to ask for some of the pills the doctor had left for him, he caught sight of a bag by the couch. The same black bag that Erik had handed to Ashley.

Torrin twisted toward the living room to find Ashley there. Not a fantasy, not some phantom memory, but the woman he craved with everything he had, the only person who had ever made him want to be better, to believe he *could* be better.

She nibbled at her bottom lip, arms tucked into the center pocket of her pullover sweater.

"You said if I wanted to come back some time…"

She didn't make it through the statement before Liam crossed the room and yanked her into a kiss that silenced her.

They should have given her room, but fuck it, they'd said their goodbyes, accepted her being gone, had been prepared to deal with the heartache, so her being there was like a gift they wouldn't question.

Ashley's head spun from the passion behind Liam's kiss. He stole her breath, his body hard against hers, acting as though he hadn't seen her in months rather than the hour or so it had been.

"Why are you back?" he asked against her lips when he broke apart enough to speak.

Even as she answered, he didn't move away, still brushed his lips to hers. "I was standing there, ready to go through security, and I realized…I didn't want to leave."

"You said you wanted to go home," Torrin said, his rough voice one she missed already.

"I miss my family, but I think what I wanted was the *ability* to go home, to know I could. To be sure whatever I did was really my choice. When I stood there, and I thought about home, I realized that the only place I saw was with you."

Torrin caught her chin and turned her face to his, taking his own kiss, gentler than Liam. "You're sure?"

She nodded, pushing away from them, needing space to think, to say what she needed to say. "I needed you to let me go, but once you did, once I got to make the choice, I realized I didn't want to be anywhere else."

"What about your fathers?" Erik asked.

"I called them. They'll fly out here to see me. I just..." She shook her head, frustrated as the things she'd thought to say wouldn't come together just right. "When I was standing there, and I got to decide what I wanted, the answer was obvious. I want *you*. I want to be here, with you three. I don't know what that means, how it'll work, but I know that I don't want to leave."

"You're not angry anymore?" Torrin asked.

"I can't say I'm not hurt. You can't ever lie to me again like that. But we all make mistakes, we all get scared and do things we wish we could take back. Besides, you've done everything you could to make it right. You said a fresh start wasn't such a bad thing, so I thought maybe we could all have that."

"I will make it right," Torrin said. "No matter how long it takes, I'll show you I can be more." Ashley cupped his cheeks and pulled him down for a kiss, the sort that she could lose herself in, the kind that erased everything else. She tugged softly until he got onto the couch with her, until he blanketed her body with his.

"You're the first thing that's ever made me want to be better," he whispered against her lips as he slipped his hand beneath her shirt, teasing over her skin in a reverent touch. "I've always lived my life trying to outrun something, feeling like if I worked a little harder, I'd be able to keep everything safe. You made me realized none of that mattered if I don't have anything worth keeping safe."

Ashley moaned softly when his fingers found her bra.

The couch dipped as Liam sat beside them, tugging her attention to him, to that smirk he had that she could see beneath. "You scare the hell out of me, sweet. You see me like no one else does. No matter how much I try to hide, you worm your way under all my defenses." He ran his finger over her cheek, then traced her full lip until she captured it with her tongue and sucked it past her lips. His grin spread. "I've never let someone get this close, never dared to want anything like I want you. I always said that people like me, we never get what we want, but you prove me wrong. There's never been anything I wanted like you, and even if I don't deserve you, I sure as hell will keep you as long as I can."

He pulled his finger free, then pressed a single, sweet kiss to her lips.

Ashley turned as Torrin rose off her, as he worked the buttons of his shirt free.

Erik stood, just out of reach as he'd been since…since he'd killed the driver. He wasn't just out of reach physically, but that weariness in his eyes spoke volumes.

Ashley beckoned him closer with a finger, and he obeyed as if he couldn't help it. He sat on the couch but didn't touch her.

"I don't like the way you looked at me," he admitted. "I've been through losing a mate because she was afraid of me, lived with someone who never trusted me. I know what that's like, and I hate that look on your face."

Ashley reached for him, even when he flinched. Funny, because she doubted that he'd flinch at the worst torture, yet it seemed she could wound him deeper. "I'm not afraid of you," she said. "I was, or I was afraid of the person I thought you were. I thought there was some part of you I hadn't seen before, something scary and dangerous."

"There is," he whispered back.

Ashley moved closer until she could lean against him, until there was no way for him to hide. "There isn't. I get that, now. It's just you. I would have shoved that blade into Gregory if he hadn't dropped the gun. We all have that inside of us, but I know you." She danced gentle kisses across his lips, coaxing him to relax, to return the affection. "I know you, and I'm not afraid of you."

The words seemed as if they broke that leash he had on himself. He wrapped his arms around her and pulled her tighter against him, claiming her mouth as if testing her. Would she back away? Would she turn him down?

Not a chance.

When she met his aggression with her own, he groaned heavily.

She broke the kiss to pull in an unsteady breath, then shifted so she could see the three of them. "You gave up a lot for me," she said, the last of her fears weighing on her. "What if you regret it? What if you resent me for it?"

Torrin shook his head before he slid his fingers into her hair and gripped tightly. "There's no chance of that. I'm still a very good businessman, and I know a great deal when I see one. You are worth more than anything we gave up, and I'd do it all over again in an instant."

Ashley moaned at the feeling of him tugging softly against her scalp, that delicious sting she'd missed.

He released her in time for Liam to pulled her to her feet.

"Where are we going?"

"We are taking you to bed," Liam said, his grip and tone giving no room for arguments.

"You were gone far too long," Erik agreed, following them. "And I plan to make up for it."

"I was gone for like, an hour," Ashley pointed out, laughing at the way the alphas acted as though it had been months.

"Too long," Liam said, repeating Erik.

When they pulled her into the bedroom, Torrin caught her chin, pinning her with his dark gaze. "You came back to us, dove. It's time to reward you for being such a good girl."

The praise and the ghost of a smile on his lips melted her, and she gave up arguing.

After everything, after so much heartbreak, Ashley had what she hadn't had in so long.

A home. A place to belong. People who loved her and who she loved in return.

As she looked at the three alphas who were larger than life, who were so much more than she'd ever expected to have, she smiled at her luck.

The path to get here had been hard, had almost killed her, but it was worth every tear and heartache to finally have this.

There was no better place than here, claimed by her alphas.

Want to see more from this author?
Here's a taster for you to enjoy!

Ready or Not: Third Time Lucky
Jayce Carter

Excerpt

Jasmine stared at the inside of the small casita, her boxes filling the space, and wondered how the hell she'd ended up here.

Moving back to their hometown was the sort of thing that happened when people failed.

And boy did I fail.

She blew a strand of her red hair from her face as she tried to figure out how long this mess would take to sort out. Unpacking had always been her least favorite part of the moving process. She loved *actually* moving. The adventure, the chance to breathe in the air of a new city, to meet new people…it all rejuvenated her, spoke to her wandering soul.

Unpacking felt like putting down roots, and that was something she loathed.

But she also refused to live out of boxes, which meant that renting this place was perfect. It was fully furnished, the rent was cheap and the agency she'd gone through assured her the landlord was a breeze to deal with. She wouldn't have to worry about upkeep, about maintaining anything, and she'd have access to a beautiful pool.

The twelve-month lease had made her hesitate — she never cared to sign her name to any commitment that long — but she'd done it the moment the rental agency had sent her pictures. The casita had two bedrooms, which was perfect for her. She could sleep in one and the other would serve as an office.

Still, a year?

She thought about the last long-term commitment she'd signed, when she'd put her name on that damned marriage license.

That didn't work out so well, did it?

And here I am, starting over again.

Her nice house, the beachfront place in Texas she'd worked so hard to buy, now had her ex living in it. He'd managed to get more than his fair share of their assets — meaning damn near everything — because he'd been the son of the local judge in that little paradise town. Connections went a long way, and he was the town's golden child while she was the unruly outsider girl who had broken his heart.

It hadn't taken long for her to lose everything, and when she couldn't decide where to go next, she'd figured home to lick her wounds made as much sense as anything else. Not that it was over. Her ex still refused to sign the final papers.

Jasmine opened a box labeled *office shit* and went to set up her computer on the desk. She worked as a software engineer, and telecommuting meant she could pick up and move whenever. Given another year — especially with the low rent — she could save enough money to go anywhere she wanted.

Staying in this town wouldn't be an option long-term. Sure, the small mountain community had its charm. It was a vacation spot, close enough to the deserts and large cities of southern California that people flocked to it in the summer to escape the heat and in the winter to enjoy the snow. In theory, it was the perfect place to grow up.

Theory never meant much in reality, though, and her childhood there had been dreadful. The picturesque settings hadn't changed the darkness in her home, the fear, the ugliness that had lived there.

Still, no matter how bad things had gotten, the trees had always made her feel free. She'd been able to walk out of that small shack of a house she'd lived in and stare up at the tallest trees that stretched toward the sky, and everything else would fade away.

She'd been beaten down during her divorce with Aaron, no doubt about that, but she wasn't done for. Just like she'd picked herself up after her shitty childhood, she'd do so again now.

The office came together quickly, and she broke down the cardboard boxes and put them in the recycling bin by the side gate. She made the bed with her sheets, wanting to get the most important things done first. A place to sleep and one to work were all she really needed.

Being back in her hometown kept forcing her mind to the past, to the good times and the not so great. It had been five years since she'd returned for the funeral of her stepdad.

That had been a joyous occasion — to be sure he was really gone, to watch him lowered into the ground and know it was over. It had lifted some of the darkness of the town for her.

She might have even stuck around for a week or two if it hadn't been for *him*.

Jasmine tried to stop that train of thought before she got a picture of the one who was always there in the back of her head.

What is it about first loves that does that? They tattoo themselves onto a person's soul, and no matter how much time passes, no matter what happens, they never really go away. The memory of being tangled up together with her first—and only—love after the funeral, of his lips, of his dark hair and darker eyes, of the way he smelled of oil and cinnamon…it all swept over her.

He wasn't the one who got away, because she had left him. Was he still there, living in the town?

It wouldn't feel like the same place if he wasn't, but then again, she didn't want to see him, either.

She sighed as she collapsed on the couch, ready to put all the nonsense of her past behind her and start over.

If only things were so easy.

Finn loved his home. He'd bought it when he'd turned twenty-two, and he hadn't ever been so proud of another thing. It had started off as a rundown fixer-upper that wasn't too far from being condemned. His parents had co-signed the loan for him, but he'd come up with all the money himself. Now, ten years later, no one would recognize the place.

He'd worked tirelessly on it, doing all the work himself. By trade he was a mechanic, but his father had been a contractor and that had given Finn the ability to do the work himself.

Finn didn't enjoy travel, being a homebody at heart, but sometimes he couldn't avoid it. He set his suitcase by the front door, thankful to be back after three weeks away. His parents had upped and moved to Florida, claiming that was what all people did once they reached seventy, and he'd gone for his regular visit.

In the time he'd been gone, the new tenant had moved in. While he liked doing things himself, he preferred using an agency for renters. Dealing with running background checks and collecting rent wasn't his thing, and when he'd tried it at first, he'd been a pushover and accepted every excuse in the book.

Having professionals handle it had been well worth the percentage of the rent they took.

His new tenant, the one for the casita in his back yard, was a woman, according to the email he hadn't bothered to really read. He didn't care much for details. She had credit issues after an ugly divorce, was from out of town, but made more than enough to cover the rent and had been at her job for eight years.

That was good enough for him. He wasn't a fussy man, and he hadn't had problems with tenants before. Mostly they all minded their own business.

Still, it was best to go introduce himself. The last thing he needed was to get the cops called on him at his own house if she spotted him in the dark and didn't know who he was.

Finn ran his fingers through his hair, trying to look presentable. His life as a mechanic had left him not caring much about that, since he rarely dressed up without a streak of grease he'd missed somewhere on him. He figured it was just one of the hazards of his job.

He didn't need to impress her, but he didn't want to look like some no-good asshole she'd have to worry about sharing space with, either.

He crossed the back yard, making his way around the large pool, its water that crystal blue that always made him want to take a dip.

"Son of a bitch," came a feminine voice from inside the casita.

It drew a smile from him. He'd prefer a tough woman who cursed rather than some delicate flower. They'd get along just fine.

He knocked on the door, hard enough so she'd hear it above the country music that was blaring.

"Just a minute!"

Finn tucked his thumbs into the belt loops of his jeans, waiting for her to open, for him to get the little meet-and-greet out of the way.

He wanted to cook a steak for dinner. Hell, maybe he'd cook an extra for his new tenant, just a little 'welcome to the house' thing. The weather was hot, but cooking outside meant the house wouldn't swelter.

Except then he saw his new tenant, the woman who had agreed to rent the casita for the next year.

Jasmine.

He'd never forget that red hair, or those bright green eyes, or the freckles that covered her cheeks and ran across the bridge of her pert little nose.

The woman who had run away from him. The woman who had broken his heart — *twice* — was his tenant.

Well, shit.

Home of Erotic Romance

Sign up for our newsletter and find out about all our
romance book releases, eBook sales and promotions,
sneak peeks and FREE romance books!

About the Author

Jayce Carter lives in Southern California with her husband and two spawns. She originally wanted to take over the world but realized that would require wearing pants. This led her to choosing writing, a completely pants-free occupation. She has a fear of heights yet rock climbs for fun and enjoys making up excuses for not going out and socializing.

Jayce loves to hear from readers. You can find her contact information, website details and author profile page at https://www.totallybound.com

www.ingramcontent.com/pod-product-compliance
Lightning Source LLC
Chambersburg PA
CBHW022027260626
47156CB00017B/403